DIMEBAG BANDITS

DIMEBAG BANDITS

A Novel

BY Craig Furchtenicht

This is a work of fiction. Names, characters, places and organizations are either a product of the author's deluded imagination or are used fictitiously. Any similarities to actual people, living or deceased, events, locations or organized groups are merely coincidental.

For my loving wife, Henrietta.
Thanks for being my constant inspiration
and my harshest critic.
You were right about all those pages in life
that it takes to make a book.
It took me a while, but
I think I finally got it.

Also, for Todd W. and Wes V.
The original Dimebag Bandits
You are truly missed

CHAPTER 1

Stacey cursed the darkness as he repeatedly stabbed the key at the lock on the overhead door. The damn security light was out again. That made the second time in less than a year. It made him wonder just where the hell the money that he forked out to the power company went every month. He was definitely going to be making a call in the morning, just as soon as he sobered up.

The headlamp from his idling Harley Panhead did little good. If he had been a bit more in control of his faculties when he pulled up to the bar, he probably would have noticed the light. As it stood, the only illumination from the bike was directed to the left of the door, completely useless to him now.

He cursed his old lady as well. Sheila was nowhere to be found when he got home after a twelve hour shift at the bar. His guess was that she was probably out banging that scumbag from Cedar Ridge, a goddamn cop of all people. Not that it should make any difference who she was screwing around with, but it did. So, as drunk as he was, he turned his bike around to go looking for her. After an hour of riding around and no Sheila, he headed back to the bar to sleep it off in his office.

To hell with her. To hell with all women for that matter. They were as useless as the headlamp shining on the dumpster while the lock in front of him was impossible to see. And that little bitch Marlene, calling in sick on the busiest night of the week. That made the third time in a month. If she didn't have such a sweet rack on her he would have fired her a long time ago. He might just do that anyway.

If it wasn't for Marlene he would have been home hours ago, probably in time to catch Sheila before she got bored and decided to step out on him again. Then he wouldn't be standing there aimlessly poking around at the lock like an old blind man in a whorehouse.

Finally he got the key to slam home and the lock popped opened. The heavy overhead door rattled as he heaved it upward. He was home free, or so he thought. The engine of his Harley abruptly cut off, leaving his head buzzing from the sudden absence of noise. The thought to turn around and investigate barely registered when his head lit up like the grand finale on the fourth of July.

He never went completely out after whatever it was that hit him across the back of the head. His brain shrieked in agony from the base of his neck to the top of his skull. He lay on his back and looked up as his vision went from black to blurry. With the overhead open there was just enough ambient light to make out the four masked men standing over him.

“We've come for the good stuff, barkeep,” the tallest one said.

Two of the others grabbed him by the arms and dragged him inside. Stacey was a big man but he was too drunk and disoriented to even consider resisting. By the time the notion of defending himself had crossed his mind, the tall one snatched him by the ponytail and twisted. The fourth intruder walked the bike in behind them and slammed the door shut.

“The good stuff, Stacey. Don't make this hard,” the tall one demanded. He pried up on the ponytail, stretching the hair on the back of his neck to the point of uprooting it from the skin. Stacey screamed and began to fight back. His right arm broke free and he pounded his fist against the guy on his left. The one who pushed the bike in ran around to face him. He flashed a set of glistening white teeth through the mouth hole of his mask and kicked him in the solar plexus.

His lungs seized up as he struggled for breath. Blackness seeped back into his peripheral vision as he dropped to the concrete floor. A sobering thought occurred to him as he lay there, chest heaving for air that would not come. I’m gonna die right here in this bar, while the bitch I named the place after is off giving it up to some fucking cop.

When he finally regained consciousness he found that his hands were crudely bound behind his back. He didn't know what they had used, but whatever it was tore deeply into the flesh on his wrists. The lights were on in the storeroom and he could see three of them sitting on empty cases of beer, watching him. Behind him the engine of his bike revved over and over. His head throbbed as he turned to look.

It was the bastard that kicked him, straddling across the seat with a grin on his face. It made Stacey ill to hear the sonofabitch wind the motor to the point of blowing it up. He watched helplessly through the blue fog of exhaust that filled the room. He would just as soon see some dude riding his old lady than to mess with his bike. Of course, he thought to himself, maybe that's why I'm in this mess now.

“See, boys. I told you I didn't kill him.” The guy hopped off the bike and sauntered over to him. He knelt down and lifted Stacey's head by the ponytail. “You're not dead are you, buddy?” He leaned his face even closer and whispered, “But you're gonna be if you don't show us where it is.”

“Fuck you,” Stacey growled and looked him straight into the eyes as much as his throbbing head would allow. He knew he was in trouble, but there was no way he was going to show this punk any fear. He had not backed down to anyone in fifty years. He damn sure wasn't going to start with this guy.

He found himself being dragged by the hair toward his bike. It was not until he felt the heat radiating from the exhaust that he realized what was about to happen. He thrashed his legs as two of them struggled to hold him still. He fought with everything in him as his head was forced closer to the hot pipe. He tried not to scream when the skin on his cheek began to smoke, but it was no use. The pain was exquisite. The hand holding the back of his head released the pressure. With the eye that was not already swelling shut he could see remnants of his flesh burnt onto the exhaust pipe. It hissed and popped like meat scraps on a griddle. Stacey became an instant vegetarian.

"You were saying something, Stacey?"

"Yeah, I said fuck you, you pile of... aghh!" His reply was interrupted with another firm push to the back of his head. This time two hands pushed from behind, rubbing his face into the hot chrome like someone would rub a dog's face into a soiled carpet. His entire left eyebrow was permanently erased from existence in roughly three seconds. The smell lingered in the air and lodged in his throat as he sobbed.

"We can do this all night, man."

He craned his neck away from the heat and cried out, "Okay, okay!" It was the sound of his own pained cries that did it, along with the tears that streamed down the ruined flesh of his cheek. Within minutes they had broken him and at that point he was willing to give them anything to make it stop.

"Atta boy," A gloved hand patted him on the back. The engine on the Harley stopped. "Now where is it?"

He hesitated for a moment. Not because he was having second thoughts, but because he was suddenly finding it very hard to keep from passing out. He felt himself being lifted to his feet. Someone slapped him hard on the back of the head. The pain from the burns intensified and brought him back around. He could feel his pulse through every tortured nerve ending.

"You want to me to start on the other side?"

"The office," he said, nodding his head to a door just beyond the storeroom. "In there, behind the couch. Take it all."

They did just that. The wall safe behind the couch was there just like Stacey had promised. In it was exactly what they were looking for, though not nearly as much as they had anticipated. Certainly it was not enough to justify permanent disfigurement to protect it. Some people were just stubborn that way. They knew that it was more of a matter of principle than a money thing. Nobody liked to get robbed. Not even bad people who gladly would have done the same thing if given the opportunity.

They left Stacey with his hands and feet bound, laying on the storeroom floor of Sheila's Tap. He spent the rest of the night and most of the next morning there. He cursed the bastards who did this. He cursed himself for breaking down so easily. He even cursed the motorcycle that he would take months to bring himself to ride again. Most of all he cursed women, especially when he came to the realization that Marlene was probably going to be a no show again.

CHAPTER 2

It seemed to Kori like he had been sitting alone in the cramped interrogation room for days. In reality, the clock on the otherwise bare wall showed that he had only been in there for about forty minutes. That was not counting the two hours that the detectives spent hammering him with pointed questions. When they realized that he was either not going to give them anything useful or had nothing of use to tell, they left him by himself to think things over.

They were probably hoping that if he spent enough time by himself, he would crack and give them something more to go on. He was not sure what else they wanted from him. He already admitted that the vials, the ones the muscle head's girlfriend had given them, came from him. He told them how he had stolen them from the medicine locker at work and sold them to the guy. That was all that they had on him and he was damned sure not going to tell them anything they didn't know about.

Besides, the police were the last of his problems at that point. He was facing jail time for sure, but that was nothing compared to the wrath that he would face when his stepfather got wind of this. He was already on Clayton's shit list and this would definitely put him over the top. He also had to worry about how to deal with Dr. Ross. After all, the drugs in question had belonged to his clinic. He did not even want to think about how much missing inventory an actual audit could reveal.

Outside of the room, the police station was business as usual. The two uniformed officers that had arrested him were long gone. They had stuck around just long enough to meet with the detectives after they filed their paperwork. Through the opened blinds Kori watched them huddle in the hallway outside the door. The younger uniformed cop kept looking through the window as he listened to his more seasoned colleagues exchange notes. He looked at Kori with an expression that was a mixture of both pity and disgust.

When they finished their conversation the cops bid the detectives farewell with customary handshakes and went their separate ways. The younger cop hung back for a moment as if he wanted to enter the room and talk to him alone, but his partner barked an order from somewhere out of view. Their eyes met briefly and then the he was gone. The exchange peaked Kori's curiosity, but he was still relieved to see him go. The last thing he wanted at that moment was to talk to another cop.

He looked around the room and its sparse furnishings. Save for a clock that taunted him with its slow mechanical second hand, it was little more than four bare walls. The numbers on the face displayed both regular and military time. A small camera was mounted in the corner near the door. It was pointed in the general direction of the heavy metal table in the center of the room. The two plastic chairs that the detectives had used now sat empty. The only other thing in the room was a thin manila folder with his name handwritten across the front.

Several pieces of paper stuck out of the corner of the folder and he was tempted to reach across and pull them out. They obviously contained any information that the detectives had on him and more importantly what charges were being filed against him. The only thing stopping him from looking inside was the camera watching his every move. Maybe it was some sort of trick that the detectives were playing. Did they leave the folder behind just to see how long it would take him to look inside? But why would they do that? Was it some sort of test?

It was not as if he were compounding the degree of guilt against him by looking inside. Besides, the file was his. It was his name was that was printed right there on the front of it. In his mind he had justified every reason to open the folder. Regardless, he felt some deep sense of guilt and had to steel himself before he could act. The hallway was clear but that could change at any time. He had to move quickly before the detectives came back.

The table was wider than it looked. He had to extend himself with one foot off the floor to reach the other side. He guessed that this was to keep people from reaching across and assaulting their inquisitors during the questioning. The thought had crossed his mind at least once during the past few hours. With his fingertips on the corner, he started to drag the folder toward him. Suddenly a commotion erupted in the hallway outside. He quickly sat back in his seat and folded his arms.

Through the window he saw two officers dragging a woman in handcuffs down the hall. She appeared to be in her late fifties, but it was hard for Kori to tell with all of the makeup she had pancaked onto her face. Her hair was long and frizzy from years of over-bleaching. Most of it was matted to her face by either sweat or tears. She twisted back and forth in an attempt to break free from the large officer holding tightly to the restraints behind her back. The other officer, a stocky woman with a classic mullet hairdo, gripped an arm with both hands and repeatedly shouted at her to calm down.

Kori stood up and watched through the glass as they

finally managed to force the woman into a sitting position on a bench and secured her there. As the officers stepped back the woman kicked her bare feet and strung together a steady flow of profanity. The officers did not seem to notice.

She was dressed in a skin tight skirt that was two sizes too small for her and a tank top. The shirt was smeared with blood and what appeared to be mud. Mascara dripped down her flush cheeks and neck, mingling with the sweat that pooled between her breasts.

Her handcuffs were attached to a heavy eye bolt that protruded from the edge of the bench. She turned her body slightly inward to lean against the wall and collapsed in defeat. For a moment she sat perfectly still except for the steady rise and fall of her chest. Satisfied that she was no longer a problem, the officers left her there. Kori stood up and walked around the table. He pressed his face to the glass and watched her. He had never seen a prostitute in real life before, at least not one that close up. He could not help but to feel sorry for her.

He started to wonder what kind of circumstances or life choices she made had brought her to this place. He was reminded of his own situation and felt guilty for even thinking about making the comparison. Although his problems were not entirely his fault, there was no way that he had it anywhere near as rough as this woman. He was not normally an affectionate person but he wanted to go out into the hallway and comfort her. He did not know why he felt compelled to do so. Maybe he just wanted to feel human again for a change.

Suddenly the woman sensed him watching her. She stiffened and looked up at him through her swollen eyes. He smiled at her and she smiled back through a mouthful of hair and missing teeth. She sat up slowly, obviously tired and sore from her ordeal. In one swift move she propped both feet up on the wooden bench and spread her legs to him. Then she reared her head back and spit at the glass between them.

"There, asshole. Now you got somethin' to stare at," She yelled. She cackled loudly while maintaining the pose, squatting and staring down between her own bruised thighs. Her bony hips pumped up and down a few times until she nearly lost her balance and fell from her seat. She was not wearing any underpants.

Stunned, Kori took a step back and nearly tripped over one of the empty chairs. He watched the spittle slowly ooze down the glass in front of him. There were tiny bits of chewing tobacco mixed with it. For some reason this repulsed him even more than the unsolicited flashing. He had not seen many naked women either, but to him her womanhood looked less like a vagina and more like a yawning gorilla that he had once seen at the Blank Park Zoo. He quickly returned to his chair.

"Hey, knock it off!" Someone yelled at her from somewhere down the hall. She put her feet down and assumed her previous position. She eyed Kori with a sour look for a moment before turning her attention in the direction of whoever yelled at her. She smacked her lips and blew a kiss.

The mullet cop escorted a middle-aged man dressed in black to the bench. Kori watched through the window, trying to ignore the streak of hooker spit drying on the glass. Upon closer examination he realized that the man was a priest. He found it odd that it took two officers to restrain a one hundred pound woman, but it only took one female to bring in a six foot man. She latched the priest to the bench next to the hooker, who made it a point to express that she was none too pleased with the idea.

Part of one of the priest's ears was missing. To Kori it looked like someone had taken a bite out of it. He also observed that along with blood, his clothing was caked in the same mud that was on the hooker. When the female officer left them, the priest leaned over and whispered something in her ear. She shook her head back and forth and turned away from him. The priest leaned over and tried to kiss her on the mouth. She responded by head butting him square on the bridge of the nose.

Blood poured from his nose and onto his chin. It collected in his beard before dripping all over the front of his shirt, staining his cleric's collar a bright red. With his hands cuffed behind him, the priest could only lean his head back to slow the bleeding. He licked away the blood as it collected around his mouth. Dread filled Kori's heart. Were these the kind of people that he was going to be locked up with?

Within minutes the hallway was full of policemen, milling about and trying to sort out what had happened. Kori put his head on the table and pretended to sleep. The last thing he wanted was to be questioned as a witness to a clergyman-hooker fight. He had had enough questioning for one day already.

It had occurred to him that it might be as good of an opportunity as any to sneak a peek at the folder, while all hell was breaking loose in the hallway. He kept his head on the table and listened as the hooker unleashed another barrage of insults at the staff. He was about to reach across the table once again when the door swung open.

"They say that a guilty man sleeps well when he is finally caught and locked away."

Kori's heart skipped a beat at the sound of the voice and he looked up to see his stepfather glaring down at him. Behind him stood Dr. Ross, whose face was so red that he looked as if he were on the verge of a massive coronary. The good doctor was shaking like a leaf and sweating profusely. Not Clayton. His eyes blazed with fury, but his outward appearance was calm and stoic. The only time Clayton ever broke a sweat was behind the pulpit.

"Clayton, just let me..." Kori started to explain, his voice cracking nervously.

"I don't want to hear it," Clayton cut him off with an outstretched palm. He had ended many an argument at home with that same gesture and it always achieved the same result. "Save it for your mother. She is at home right this moment, cleaning up the house after half of the West Des Moines police force tore it apart. Searching for God knows what."

Kori sunk down into his seat at the thought of this. There had only been the two officers at his home when they came to arrest him. He had not imagined that they would search the entire place after he was hauled away in the back of the police cruiser. He tried to do a quick rundown in his mind of what else they could have possibly found. Most of his stash was in the garage in a pretty good hiding place, at least in his estimation. He guessed that was yet to be determined.

"In my house!" Clayton slammed the palm of his hand on the metal table, causing both Kori and Dr. Ross to jump. For a brief moment everyone in the hallway quieted down and looked in the direction of the interrogation room. Even the hooker stopped her tirade for a second or two.

Dr. Ross placed a hand on the back of Clayton's shoulder, slowly as if he expected it to be hot to the touch. "Reverend, why don't we continue the conversation with the boy after we get him home."

Talk of going home instead of spending the night in jail surprised Kori. The prospect of it also terrified him. He was not sure which would be worse. It must have been written all over his face because the fire in Clayton's eyes burned even brighter.

He leaned as closely into Kori as the table would allow.

"That's right. Lucky for you, the good doctor decided not to press charges. In the best interest of the church, of course." As if on cue, Dr. Ross nodded in agreement. "Also lucky for you, the chief of police is also a member of the Trinity Counsel." Clayton looked around and lowered his voice. "He promised to sweep most of the nastier charges under the rug. Also in the interest of the church."

"Amen." Dr. Ross chirped from the doorway. He straightened his posture a bit like a school child preparing to recite the pledge of allegiance. Clayton gave him a hearty amen back and stood away from the table. His eyes never broke away from Kori.

"Now get up, before someone changes their mind." Clayton lifted the folder from the table and thumbed through it for a moment. He shook his head in disgust as he pored over the contents. After he was finished he closed the file and looked up. "By the way, you can forget about joining the congregation on the trip. I won't have a thief and a dope peddler polluting the souls of my flock. You may not be going to jail, but I guarantee you will be going somewhere far worse."

Clayton and the doctor left the room without waiting for him. He wondered whether they were ashamed to be seen with him or if they half expected him not to follow. Probably both, he guessed. He could not say that he was actually disappointed that he was not going on his stepfather's quest to "save the world from itself". He could think of much better things to do than to hang out in the backwoods states with a bunch of bible beaters.

In the hall Clayton stopped to "put hands" on the hooker whose attachment to the bench now included leg restraints. He always felt compelled to do things like that in front of a crowd. It never hurt to try and drum up more business for the church. However, the hooker was having none of it. She tried to pull away when Clayton touched her and rattled off a few lines of scripture. When she reached the limit of her restraints and could not get away she kicked at him with shackled feet.

"Get the hell away from me, you cocksucker!" she screamed.

"That's exactly what I'm trying to do, my child." Clayton replied. "I'm getting Hell away from your tortured soul."

The priest was still bleeding from his newly broken nose, even though the staff nurse had taped a heavy pad of absorbent gauze across his face. He leaned his head close to Clayton's hands and smiled up at him, expecting some unspoken camaraderie to be shared between men of the faith. "What about me?"

Clayton studied the priest's blood soaked garb and snarled his nose in disgust. "There's no hope for you, asshole." He pulled a small bottle of hand sanitizer from his pocket and scrubbed his hands as he walked away.

Kori caught up to him at the exit door. Clayton was standing in the doorway with his back to him, blocking the way outside. He stood there, leaving Kori hanging in awkward silence. It was a technique that he often utilized behind the pulpit. He was confident that the same effect would be achieved on the boy.

“Do you know what I meant when I said that you would be going to a place worse than jail, son?” he asked as he slowly turned around. The fire was back in his eyes once again.

Kori hated it when he called him son, although he would never dare tell Clayton that. He looked down at his feet to avoid his stepfather's burning stare. At that moment he hated Clayton more than he had ever hated anyone or anything. He sighed and spoke in a barely audible voice, “I guess, Hell.”

“You guess, Hell?” This seemed to amuse Clayton. He let out a dry laugh and smiled. “Well, ultimately you are going to hell. That's a given. But in the meantime your thieving butt is going back to Cedar Ridge, where I should have left you in the first place.”

CHAPTER 3

Brenden watched the junkie emerge from the trunk of the car, entangled in a mess of speaker wires. The display of persistence filled him with both admiration and disgust. He had to fight back the urge to slam down the lid of the trunk on his head and shove him back in. If he didn't need the guy so badly, he probably would have done just that.

It was not as if Soup Campbell was a close friend. Nobody was really friends with Soup. Not even his immediate family trusted the guy any further than they could throw him. His given name was Gary Campbell, but everyone called him Soup. Even his own mother had called him that since he was a young boy. His father probably would have called him that, too. If anyone could figure out who that was.

"Maybe you should have swiped the owner's manual while you were at it," Brenden said as he watched Soup struggle to his feet. He knew there was no sense in trying to discourage him from finishing now. There was no reasoning with Soup when he was speeding out. He just wished that he would quit jacking around and get it done. Who decides to install a set of speakers a few hours before committing a robbery, anyway? A junkie, that's who.

"Yeah, you're a funny guy." Sweat dripped from Soup's forehead as he bent over the mess of wires. It made Brenden's teeth hurt to watch him chew on one of the ends with his teeth. His teeth were in remarkably good shape for a speed freak. Soup ignored the wire cutters that Brenden held in front of him and stripped the coating from the end. He spat out the peeled off casing and asked, "So when's your brother supposed to get here?"

"Dunno. Soon I guess."

"So he's down for working with us tonight?" Soup found another loose end and gripped it between his front teeth.

"I haven't exactly asked him yet," Brenden confessed. He squeezed in next to Soup and started rummaging through the trunk. Plumes of road dust rose up as he picked through the contents. He opened a grocery sack and looked inside. "Mom called the old man this morning and said she was bringing him back. I don't know the whole story, but it sounds like he got himself in some deep shit. She said something about him needing a job to pay some fines or something. I told the old man I could get him one."

Soup did not have to ask what exactly Brenden's idea of a job meant. The upper half of his body disappeared inside the trunk and he went to work with the soldering gun. "So it's gonna be a five way split now?"

"We'll work that out later." He opened the bag and pulled out an assortment of gloves and knitted masks. He shook one of the masks and dust filled the air. "Why is that going to be a problem?"

"Not with me. I've been saying that we've needed more help for years, you know that. But I ain't so sure how the wonder twins are gonna take it." Satisfied with his handiwork, Soup eased back out and looked around the yard. "I'll deal with Chris. You can talk to Todd, but I don't think he cares either way. Where the hell are those two assholes, anyways?"

"Where do you think? Back behind the shed, either smoking it up or pissing again. That's all they've done all day." Brenden waved away the dust cloud that floated in front of his face and held up the mask. "Damn, dude. If that crap you guys smoke don't kill you, these will."

"We all gotta die someday," Soup said with a shrug. He

yelled in the direction of the shed. “When you two finish your sword fight, you wanna come over here and help us get this shit ready?” He shook his head in disgust. “Fucking assholes wanna play all day and then expect us to do all the dirty work. Yeah we need some new blood, 'cause these two are testing my goddamn patience.”

As if on cue, an angry scream rose up from behind the shed. Todd emerged from behind the building first, in a full sprint. He was laughing wildly, barely able to keep his balance as he ran across the yard. Little Chris followed closely behind, swinging a broken tree branch and cursing at the top of his lungs. Each swing came closer to connecting with the back of Todd's head as he slowly gained on him. His face was crimson red and the front of his pants were soaked with what appeared to be urine.

Soup reached out and snagged him with one arm as he ran past. He grabbed the stick with the other hand and wrenched it from his bony hands. Chris did not struggle to maintain control of the branch, but fought desperately to break away from Soup's grasp. He continued to scream and spit at Todd, who stood a few feet out of his reach.

“Whoa. Slow down there, killer.” Soup said. He tossed the tree branch aside.

“Motherfucker kicked me in the ass while I was taking a piss!” Chris yelled. Tears ran down his face as he hopped up and down, the only direction his efforts would take him against the strength of his cousin's grip. “Let me go, Soup! Goddammit!”

“I swear, I didn't mean to kick you that hard.” Todd claimed, still laughing uncontrollably. He stepped closer and stuck his hand out as an offering of a truce. He was laughing so hard that his outstretched hand would not hold still.

“It went in my fucking mouth!” Chris screamed and kicked both feet in the air.

Todd pulled his hand away, but not soon enough to match his wiry friend's speed. The left toe caught him above the wrist, sending a bolt of pain up his entire arm. The smile vanished from Todd's face as he shook off the sting. His hand balled into a fist and he cocked it back, ready to deliver a punch to Chris's face.

“Enough!” Brenden stepped in between. He grabbed Todd by the shirt and walked him backwards. The grocery sack dangled from his wrist sent up a cloud of dust with every step. “You two want to kill each other, then do it tomorrow. We've got work to do tonight. I don't need the both of you all busted up before we even get started.”

He handed the sack to Todd. “Go in the house and throw these in the dryer for about twenty minutes.” Then he turned to Chris, who was busy rubbing the places on his arms where Soup had held him. “And you, go wash that spot out of your pants. I don't want to spend the rest of the night smelling your piss.”

As the two went to the house Brenden turned his attention back to the Impala's trunk. Something had caught his eye before the melee had begun. Soup was about to shut the lid when he stopped him. “Hang on a second.” He reached in behind the spare tire and pulled out a small black plastic case. It caught his eye only because it was not nearly as dusty as the rest of the clutter inside the trunk. Obviously it had not been in there long. “What the hell is this?”

Soup gave him a defiant look and quickly snatched the case from his hands. He fumbled with the two clasps for a moment and then opened it up. He pulled out a large handgun. Thanks to the protective case, the gun was virtually free of dust. It shined in the afternoon sunlight. He grinned and posed in his best two-handed stance. “It's my little equalizer. You like?”

“No guns. We've had this discussion before, Soup.” He held out his hand. “Leave it here.”

“I'm not gonna take it out with us,” Soup protested. “It's just that... you know. It would be nice to know if we needed it, we'd have it.”

“Leave it.” Brenden's hand remained stretched out, palms up. “Or I'm out.”

Soup hesitated momentarily and then reluctantly placed the gun back into its case. He handed it to Brenden and without a word turned his back. He slammed the trunk shut and stalked off behind the shed. It was time to play catch up with the others before the night's festivities began.

CHAPTER 4

It was exactly not the warmest of sendoffs.

Within hours after waking up in the morning they were on the road. Kori sat in the backseat of Clayton's SUV with every article of clothing that he owned crammed into the storage compartment behind him. Most of his belongings were already packed for him by the time he had gotten home from the police station, the night before. His mother had not spoken two words to him since then.

The SUV was the big shiny kind with a 'Save the Earth for Our Children's Future' sticker pasted on the back bumper, right under the Jesus fish. It only got sixteen miles to the gallon and could seat something like twelve people or some ridiculous number like that. Clayton and his mother were usually the only two that ever rode in it, which was probably a good thing. Between his belongings and their luggage, Kori barely had enough room to breathe. Not that they would have noticed.

The longer he sat back there in silence, the angrier he became at the sheer coldness in the way they were acting toward him. Sure, he screwed up big time. He had made some foolish decisions that could have caused some serious problems for them all. But for them to sit there and pretend like it was entirely his fault was preposterous.

As far as sendoffs were concerned, they were all bullshit in his opinion. Just a string of lies scripted to bid someone else fond farewell, knowing fully well that as soon as they are gone you planned to look through their dresser drawers and under their mattress, just to see if they may have left anything interesting behind. Something that they might not miss, if and when they return.

There are hundreds of little white lies that everyone lets slip when someone temporarily exits stage left out of one's life. Why not? It makes everyone feel better to be lied to than to hear the plain boring truth.

Kori tried to roll down his window, but Clayton had the controls locked from his front seat panel. He must have known how nauseating his overly applied cologne was to him. Kori kept his breathing to a minimum to prevent tasting it in his mouth.

He stared through the glass at the blur of the endless cornfields. Just then, he desperately needed to hear a few well intended lies. Come on, Mom. Tell me a sweet lie or two. Tell me that you will miss me, even after I'm out of cell phone range. Nothing. Silence. Now that was tough love.

Kori was just the last piece of luggage to drop off and then it was off to the airport for an enlightening autumn seminar in Wyoming or some other backwoods state. He was just part of a last errand to run. The house keys turned over to a service, the dogs dropped off at the kennel and the son who disappoints goes back to the old man in Cedar Ridge for the fall.

The only break from the silence was the steady hum of Clayton's oversized tires on the pavement. They were the kind that could tear through a grassy field like hot butter to get to the other side, where the more pristine side of nature awaited. It was all about access with Clayton. It sure beat the shit out of hiking after a three drink lunch.

His mother turned around and stared at him for a while, drumming her fingertips on the headrest. Her nails were all but chewed down to the quick and void of any polish. Faye Cole just looked at her son, trying to script out her thoughts before articulating them. It was a habit that she had developed over the years. A result of being married to a theology professor turned preacher.

From his pulpit, Clayton had once claimed that hundreds of thousands of animals died a cruel death every year as a result of animal testing. That evening, while entertaining dinner guests, Clayton made the mistake of asking Kori for his opinion on the matter. He often made it a sport to call Kori out in front of a group, especially when that group consisted of his circle of friends. Kori told him that at least the animals died pretty. Clayton did not speak to him for a week.

Kori watched the reflection of his stepfather's eyes in the rear view mirror, shifting between him and the road. Vehicles blew past them from the left lane like they were standing still. Clayton kept the SUV at a cool sixty miles per hour. They couldn't have the newly appointed Midwest regional chairman of the Trinity Enlightenment for Life (TEFL) council getting a blemish on an otherwise perfect driving record. It was a good thing that they were not planning to drive all the way to the seminar, Kori thought to himself.

"Kori, honey..." she started. "You know that we both love you very much." Kori tried to lock in on his stepfather's gaze, but Clayton's eyes jumped evasively back to the road. She let out an exasperated sigh. "I know that this is hard for you, but we can't just leave you roaming around Des Moines for the rest of the year by yourself, considering your..." She paused, once again weighing her words carefully.

Kori rolled his eyes. He was twenty-one years old for god

sake! He wanted to shake her by the shoulders and scream. Come on Mom, just say it! You don't want your favorite son running around the big city, peddling high grade pharmaceuticals while you and the hubby are off praying for world salvation. What would the neighbors think?

"Well, you understand. Don't you?" She talked to him like he was still five years old.

He barely nodded and stared out the window as more cars raced past them. There was no point in arguing with her. It would only get Clayton going about how he had no job and brought nothing to the table. Therefore, he had no right to expect to stay alone while they did "God's work". Whatever the hell that meant.

Faye grabbed him by the chin and turned him to face her. Her eyes looked tired and distant. "When we get back this winter, Clayton and Dr. Ross will try to sort this whole mess out with the Dean of Students. Won't you, Clayton?"

She settled back into her seat and took a hold of Clayton's free hand, which was surprisingly not clutching the wheel in the textbook ten o'clock two o'clock position. He stiffened slightly at her touch. She did not seem to notice.

"All I have to say is that you should feel pretty darned grateful that Dr. Ross decided not to press charges. Suspension from the University is bad enough, but it could have been..." Clayton cleared his throat and shook his balding head. "Should have been much worse."

"Walter Ross is a good man," His mother said. Clayton shook his head in agreement.

"We expected a lot more from you, son." There he went with the son thing, again. "I don't know what you were thinking, pulling a stunt like that."

What was I thinking? Kori thought to himself. Well for starters, he was thinking of how he was going to finish paying his tuition after his so-called loving parents went and handed his entire life savings over to some raving heretic. How selfish of me to regard my education over some idiot's fruitless campaign for senate or mayor or whatever.

The anger built up in Kori's mind as he played out the events leading up to this fateful trip. It had started with Clayton giving away his savings without his knowledge. One day his tuition was covered and the next day he was broke. But the final straw came when the paychecks that he earned from his internship with Dr. Ross started coming up short. Clayton had apparently taken it upon himself to instruct the doctor to deduct half of his pay as charity. That charity being the TEFL, of course.

So he took it upon himself to start skimming from the meds locker at the Trinity Ross veterinary clinic. The drugs were there for the taking. It seemed like such a shame that some of the finest pharmaceutical substances were being wasted on a few rich people's dogs and horses.

Drugs that were so easily obtained, given the right set of keys at a reputable veterinary clinic; especially one that catered to the upper crust of the social food chain. Everyone claiming at least six figures a year lined up with their four-legged substitutes for human interaction at Dr. Ross' door. Even the local racetracks and zoos called on Walter Ross when the situation arose.

For an exaggerated fee, all major credit cards accepted, no luxury was spared at Trinity. A facility that boasted dozens of fully equipped kennels, immaculate stables with fifty acres of sweet pasture, a state of the art surgical center and of course a well-stocked pharmacy that would leave any junkie in awe. Whether it shit in the yard or plowed the field, Walter Ross was the man.

Many of the drugs that had legitimate uses in the field of animal science were also handy alternatives to their more mainstream counterparts. It was shockingly easy to find an eager housewife or club patron, who was willing to swap out their husband's or parent's hard earned cash for a good buzz.

Ketamine and Telazol for the clubbers, all in liquid form, straight from the vial they came. Of course nobody wanted to inject the stuff directly into their skin. Vanity dictates that track marks are unsightly and do not accessorize well with short sleeves. Not to mention the stigma associated with the needle itself. It was so much more convenient to stuff something up one's nose than to go through the tedious ritual of loading up a shot.

Through trial and error, Kori found ways to compensate for this. A thin layer of dope on a cookie sheet in the oven at the lowest temperature possible turned the liquid into a nice marketable powder in less than an hour.

He soon discovered it was best to leave the room with a few windows cracked during this process. In an early experiment, he foolishly tried to hasten the drying time with his mother's microwave on defrost. He left the house and had forgotten about the batch for a few hours. He returned home to find the old Guatemalan lady, who cleaned the house on Tuesdays and Thursdays, passed out on the kitchen floor in a puddle of her own piss. The microwave was open and the dope had burnt to a smoking leathery crisp.

He supposed that some people had no tolerance for quality chemicals.

The housewives went crazy for Diazepam, the same stuff that Dr. Ross prescribed in combination with corticosteroids to treat the "little white shakers" syndrome in Maltese and West Highland white terriers. They were a favorite reality break for the ladies after all of the good talk shows went off the air. Most of the women on his parent's block could not see straight until they had downed a fistful of those babies. It was also a powerful appetite stimulant in cats, which explained why half of the neighbors were pushing two hundred plus.

Equipoise was definitely the bread and butter of his short lived enterprise. For every person in Polk county looking to get high, there were five more looking to get big. It was the magic potion that muscle heads swore by, the Cadillac of all anabolic steroids. They asked for it by name and he delivered. Kori had never lifted so much as a weight in his life, yet everybody in the gym knew him by name when he walked in.

Rehabbing racehorses for the local tracks was a lucrative venture for the Ross Trinity clinic, therefore a very profitable one for Kori as well. That was until some meaty freak showed up in the ER with a boil the size of a golf ball on his ass.

As with most injectable steroids, Equipoise is oil based. That explains why so many bodybuilders develop acne on their backs and legs. The best way to inject it is into the tissue of a large muscle. The ass seems to be a popular one for some reason. The problem is that the drug absorbs into the body fairly easily, but the oil base does not. Repeated injections in the same area can lead to a buildup of oily deposits faster that the body handles them. Having nowhere to go, those deposits eventually develop into boils or cysts.

The worst part is that most of those guys ignore the problem at first. They simply use the bump as a reference point for their next dose. A half inch to the left of that ugly sore, then to the right. Never minding that it was getting bigger by the day until their girlfriend begs them to let her drive them to the emergency room.

This particular girlfriend left the hospital in hysterics as her beau's ass boil was getting lanced and drained. She came back in later with two half empty vials in her hand, vials that had been purchased from Kori. This may not have been a problem if the nurse had not handed them to the staff physician, who in turn called the police.

On the back of each vial were a set of numbers, known as lot codes. These numbers can be used to track down customer shipments in case of a recall. The drugs were traced to a Dr. Walter H. Ross at the Trinity clinic. Of course being the keeper of the keys, Kori was outed immediately after Ross talked his own skinny butt out of going to jail.

Within a matter of hours, Kori was out of a job and a source of income. From what his mother was eluding to, he was also indefinitely suspended from Iowa State as well. He had spent the greater part of the summer stealing drugs to pay for classes that he was now barred from attending. Now he was banished from home and condemned to the purgatory of Cedar Ridge.

His only real regret was neglecting to scratch off those damned lot codes. In hindsight, he probably should have warned the meat head to alternate ass cheeks as well.

Kori bit his tongue and swallowed his anger. There was no use in arguing with Clayton or his mother. Their minds were made up. He was going to spend the next three months swatting flies and dodging rednecks in a place that he and his mother had spent so many years trying to forget. He may have grown up in Cedar Ridge, but it was by no means home to him. Clayton knew that all too well. Surely that was the reasoning behind his decision to leave him there.

He slumped down in his seat and watched his part of the world sailed past him, one mile at a time. At a conservatively safe rate of speed of course.

CHAPTER 5

Cedar Ridge looked exactly how he had remembered it. All of the houses on the short road leading to his father's property looked abandoned. The only indication that there were actually people living inside of them was the wood smoke billowing from the chimneys. Many of the yards were populated with dogs, cats and an assortment of poultry. The former ran down the lanes toward them as they passed. The latter scattered for safety under the abundant cover of junk vehicles that each place seemed to have.

Occasionally, one of the locals standing in the yard stared at their unfamiliar vehicle as it passed by. It struck Kori as odd that each one of them mustered a polite wave of acknowledgment. Of course Clayton stared straight ahead and ignored them. Kori waved back and smiled. Eventually he grew tired of the exchange and resigned to just staring again.

The next house they encountered had an old man standing over a small grass fire in the ditch. His gaunt frame leaned over some sort of garden tool that he used to keep the flames under control. When he saw Clayton's vehicle approaching he stood as upright as he could and smiled. At close proximity Kori realized that the old man had to be at least ninety, if not more. His face resembled that of an Appalachian apple doll, sun stained and full of wrinkles. The old man shifted the tool from one hand to the other and waved.

Kori was too mesmerized by the man's ancient appearance to wave back. He shifted around in his seat as they passed by, watching him through the back glass. He turned just in time to see the smile fade from the man's wrinkly face and the kind wave transforming into a fist with the middle finger prominently sticking upward. The old guy continued to flip them off and started groping the crotch of his loose trousers with the other hand. Stunned, Kori turned back in his seat and decided that it was best to avoid making eye contact with anyone else they encountered.

It did not matter, though. A few minutes later they were pulling into the driveway of his father's place. It took him a moment to merge the faded memory of the place with the idea of seeing it in real life. What he had spent so long trying to forget, he now had to strain to remember.

His mother stepped out of the SUV first. She snarled her tiny nose at the unkempt yard. A few chickens that were pecking aimlessly in the tall grass started to work their way closer to where she stood. A look of panic washed over her and she stepped back to the door of the car. She shooed them loudly and they scattered in four different directions.

Clayton stayed in the vehicle and continued bitching about the higher gas prices in the eastern half of the state, as he had done since they passed the last gas station ten minutes earlier. He looked around nervously as if expecting Joe Woodson to come out of the house at any minute and beat him senseless in a fit of drunken rage. He pushed a button and the trunk door popped open.

Kori unloaded his bags into the lawn and stared at the house. Brenden walked out to greet them, or at least him. He barely acknowledged that their mother was there. The only words that he spoke to her were when she inquired about his father's whereabouts. He told her that Joe had an appointment at the VA and would not be home until later. She did not attempt to hide her relief. As soon as Brenden saw it on her face, he was done with her. He collected Kori's belongings and carried them to the house.

Her eyes welled up a bit and she started back for the SUV, staring back at Brenden and then to Kori. She never told him that she would miss him as she climbed back inside. No sweet lies today. She only offered one last piece of advice through the window. “Don't let your brother get you into any more trouble than you are already in.”

Before he could respond the screen door on the house banged shut behind him. It startled them both and they turned to look. Standing on the front porch was a scrawny little guy dressed in nothing but a pair of underwear that looked as if they had not seen their original state of whiteness for many years. They were several sizes too large and as many shades darker than the pale skin of his body.

He grinned and waved. “Hey, Mrs. Woodson. Nice to see you again.” He giggled and nervously shifted his weight from one bare foot to the other.

“Oh, Lord,” his mother muttered softly.

Someone yelled from inside the house and he quickly hurried back inside.

His mother looked him over once more and brushed away the tears from her eyes. Clayton rolled up the window between them from his control panel, cutting the moment short. The SUV pulled away with his mother staring hopelessly back at the house. A house that she had walked away from seven years earlier with her then “just a friend” Clayton Cole behind the wheel of a different shiny gas guzzling car. The only difference was that Kori was in the backseat that time. This time they rode alone, with his mother crying and Clayton still bitching about four dollar a gallon gas.

CHAPTER 6

Kori had never considered himself to be claustrophobic. He always felt that he was pretty cool and level headed under pressure. So when the car made that last turn onto the dark side street known as Gilbert Court, he was surprised to find an uncomfortable sense of fear wash over him. He could not quite put his finger on the source of his new found trepidation. It could have had a lot to do with the fact that he was stuck in the back of the filthiest vehicle that he had ever been in. Maybe it was because he was sandwiched between two guys that were obviously tweaked out of their minds, or at least well on their way.

The street itself played a good part in his apprehension. For starters, the absence of streetlights became quite apparent when they rounded the last corner. In contrast to the highly visible and well maintained environment of Kirkwood Avenue, this street was little more than a glorified alley. It ran parallel to the train tracks for a couple of blocks and then ended as abruptly and rudely as it started. It was a cancer plagued appendage of more viable streets; possibly once alive and thriving, but now quickly decaying.

Kori suddenly became aware that all conversation in the vehicle had ceased as the Impala slowly chugged down the street. He looked around from person to person and noticed that everyone except Soup, who was driving, had their attention fixed on the end of the dark street. Soup fumbled with the visor above his head, searching for something.

A small bar sat haphazardly to the right. Its exterior was grossly decorated in an unusually large amount of mismatched Christmas lights. A purple and pink sign flickered above the doorway, displaying words that he could not yet make out. The whole place had sort of an oasis feel to it in a cartoon like way.

Aside from a handful of empty storefronts the only sign of life that the street had to offer was the bar. It reminded Kori of the small redneck dives that were found in nearly every backwoods river town in Iowa. Soup let the Impala roll to a stop just short of the entrance to the parking lot. Like the street, there were no overhead lamps in the lot. The only illumination was from the bar's exterior décor.

As his eyes adjusted, Kori was surprised to find the parking lot was nearly full. The cars that occupied the lot were mostly newer sporty models. They seemed out of place among the dumpsters and railroad junk. The neon sign was easy to read now and it became all too clear that this place was no redneck joint.

His earlier anxieties were now justified.

It was beginning to feel as if he were part of an untold sophomoric joke. Five straight guys pull into the crowded parking lot of a local gay bar. He laughed to himself. It was not funny but he could not think of how else to react. What the hell was his brother thinking, taking him to a place like this?

He wondered what his mother would think of him now, sitting in the parking lot of that very proverbial place that her dumb ass husband had so often pounded his fist into the pulpit over. The place that he had warned his faithful flock as they nodded their empty heads and mumbled in agreement. How would his mother feel, knowing that within four hours after she had dropped him at his Dad's doorstep, he was riding in the back of Soup Campbell's Impala along with his hell bound brother and two of his closest junkie friends? Heading to a bar that went by the name "The Glory Hole" of all things.

He shook his head and wished that he had opted to stay

back with his father and watch reruns on TV Land. Better yet, he wished that he could have successfully managed to convince his mother and Clayton to let him stay home in Des Moines, while they roamed the country saving people from their own godless selves.

Soup carefully backed the Impala into a stall close to the street. He deliberately chose one of the few stalls with an empty space flanking either side. It seemed like an unnecessary precaution for a car that looked as if it would be more at home parked in front of a government subsidized housing project. God forbid if someone were to come staggering out and get some of their brand new Lexus paint on his rusty door panel. Brenden leaned his head out of the passenger side window in mock concern for Soup's vintage ride.

Kori quickly assessed the layout of the establishment and developed an appreciation for the chosen location. The proprietors had apparently intended to provide their clientele with a sense of privacy as they climbed back into their vehicles after a busy night of depravity. One could discreetly drive away under the cover of the unlit street, making their way back to the more populated ones and blending back in with the rest of society. A world where their friends, their bosses and their families were none the wiser to the fact that they had spent the better part of the evening in a place so aptly named the Glory Hole.

Todd nudged him from the left and pointed excitedly to the sign. He said something that Kori could not hear. His ears were still numb from the long ride into town, thanks to Soup's insistence on playing his stereo system at a deafening level. The poorly installed speaker's had mercifully cut out a dozen blocks back when the Impala's tires found a deep pothole in the street, but the residual ringing in everyone's ears lingered. Kori bent his head to take another look at the sign. It was partially blocked from his vision by the rear view mirror. He leaned toward Todd and asked, “What'd you say?”

Little Chris, who was in some unwholesome way related to Soup, apparently thought the question was directed at him. He was a perplexed looking little guy with greasy hair and bad teeth. The rotten tooth smell assaulted Kori's nose. It made him want to gag, but he did not want to seem impolite.

“I said”, Chris started out in a tone much higher than necessary. He is as deaf as I am, Kori thought to himself as he held his breath. The tooth smell even burned his eyes. “What the hell kind of name is Glory Hole, anyways?”

He was not just asking Todd, but anyone in the car who was listening. For a few seconds no one said a thing. They all just stared at him and tried to let the question register in their minds. It was easy for them to forget just how dense Chris was at times. It was a reaction that he was used to and did not seem to notice. Todd leaned across to meet him face to face.

“You really don't know what that means, man?” Todd cocked his head and gave Kori a wink. Suddenly more uncomfortable than ever, Kori returned a blank expression and tried to shrink away. It was impossible to do so while stuck between the two of them. There was only one thing more humiliating than sitting in a car full of dudes, parked in front of a gay bar. That was somehow knowing exactly what the bar's lewd name was referring to.

“I wouldn't have asked if I knew, asshole.” Chris bristled up and shot a nervous glance at Soup for support. Soup fumbled for something in his front shirt pocket, ignoring them both. Chris saw that he was going to get no help from the front row and slumped down in his seat. Kori, who had been holding his breath for record time, let his lungs loose and tried to take in cleaner air. An exercise in futility, that was. The rotten tooth smell lingered like an invisible cloud. Chris stared at his hands and began to wring them uncontrollably. He solemnly looked at Todd. “Do you know?”

In the front seat Brenden and Soup chuckled to themselves. They could only guess how this was going to go. Knowing Todd, it was definitely going to be entertaining. Despite his rough exterior, Todd was one of the funniest guys that they knew. He looked around to the others in the car with a serious look on his face. Then he focused his attention on Chris and proceeded to give an encyclopedia worthy description of a glory hole.

"You know the rooms in the back of the adult bookstore, where the perverts pay to watch dirty movies by the minute for tokens?" Todd began to explain. Chris nodded in agreement but his blank expression left Kori wondering just how much he really comprehended. He also wondered how in the hell Todd managed to keep a straight face during all of this.

Kori still had no idea why they were even there. Todd's graphic description made him more uncomfortable by the minute. He self-consciously looked down at his lap just to avoid making eye contact with anyone. The neon sign and lights turned the interior of the car into something that resembled the innards of an Easter basket. His khakis looked grossly psychedelic. He thought of a Gap ad parody that he had once seen. Even Hitler would not be caught dead in these pants.

The lecture continued: "The movies are void of any fillers or plot lines." Todd stopped to make sure that his captive audience was keeping up. When he was satisfied that his slow minded pupil was still breathing he proceeded with the demeanor of a college professor. "The lesser known fact about these beat off booths is that there is..."

In the front seat Soup produced a small folded bit of paper from his pocket. He pulled a piece of tin foil from under the visor and folded it down the middle. In the center crease he poured a bit of white powder from the paper and then deftly folded the bundle back into its original shape with one hand. Kori watched all of this with a fascination usually reserved for car wrecks and fist fights. Soup waved a flame under the foil until a thick smoke rose up. Most of the smoke was immediately sucked in through a short straw between Soup's lips. The rest floated throughout the inside of the car.

Kori held his breath again as the second hand smoke drifted to the backseat. When he could not hold it any more he breathed in deeply. The air tasted sour and laden with chemicals. 'I'm going to die before I even get out of this car', he thought to himself. His heart began to beat unusually fast. 'Oh God, I think I'm high!'

Soup passed the still smoking fold of tinfoil over the front seat headrest. Todd stopped talking long enough to retrieve it. He held his left palm beneath the rig and carefully drew it to himself. Soup held out the straw and Todd took this with much less care but with equal enthusiasm. Kori saw that the straw was actually a shortened down section of a disposable ink pen. He watched as Todd moved the flame back and forth, never letting the flame come into direct contact with the aluminum. The residue began to bubble and smoke. Todd killed the flame and sucked the vapors deeply into his lungs until most of the smoke was gone. His face became slightly flushed and beads of sweat formed on his upper lip as he held it in.

Kori felt Chris tense up beside him. His narrow eyes were

fully focused not on Todd but on the foil. He licked his lips and began to breathe heavily. It made Kori think of a man stranded in a desert, watching his buddy drink the last swallow from the canteen. Todd exhaled and passed the foil to Chris, who snatched it up greedily.

"There even any left?" he whined. He flicked a lighter to answer his own question.

"Fuck if I know." Todd replied, staring out the window at nothing. His voice was slightly shaky now. He turned back to Chris, who was practically setting himself on fire to get a decent hit from the meager leftovers. "So, where was I? Oh yeah."

"What most people don't know about these places is that the owners cut the holes in the partitions that separate one booth from another." His voice dropped to a whisper as if he were telling some long forgotten secret. Chris leaned across Kori's body once again, straining to hear him. "It's from these holes that the pervs are able to blow or be blown by the guy in the next booth. It gives the pervs a way of getting off while remaining anonymous. All of the glory without the hassle." He sat up and grinned at everyone in the car. "Hence, the name glory hole."

To drive this bit of useless trivia home, Todd reached out and roughly shoved Chris' head down into Kori's lap. This sent Chris into a fit of blind rage and he lunged across the seat at Todd. He planted a bony knee into the fleshy part of Kori's thigh as he swung wildly at Todd's face. Kori yelped in pain and drove an elbow into Chris, sweeping him back to his own side of the backseat. Chris slammed his head hard against the door.

Brenden spun around and screamed, "Knock it off!" These were the first words that he had spoken since they had left Cedar Ridge. His voice was harsh and full of anger. Everyone collected themselves in a hurry, knowing full well that it was not a good idea to piss him off any further. He always got uptight right before they went to work. Brenden was all about the business.

He did not mind that the three tweakers insisted on smoking their dope right before the night's work was about to begin. In fact, he expected it. They had been speeding it up all day and the last thing that he needed was for them to start coming down right in the middle of a job. What he did insist on was a complete respect for the seriousness of the task at hand. He was not about to get locked up or worse killed, because the jackasses he was working with could not keep their shit together.

He rarely indulged in the act of chemical enlightenment, aside from the occasional beer or joint. However, he was familiar enough with his colleagues' addictions to know how to manage them. They could get a high as they wanted as long as they respected the work. If it took cracking a few of their skulls to get the end result, so be it. Even Soup, who was built like a brick shit house and as crazy as the rat who lived inside of it, cowered down to Brenden when he was angry.

St. Brenden, the patron saint of junkies and sneak thieves. Kori sat back with his head spinning from the contact buzz. He stared at the brother he barely knew with fear and wonderment. He was not sure what he was letting himself get dragged into, but for some odd reason he was steadily beginning to care less about the consequences.

"All right", Brenden snapped. "Do you dope heads think that you can put that crap down for a minute? Or should we just sit here with our thumbs in our asses and watch while the fucking bar closes? Do you guys want to smoke up all night or do you want to make some money? 'Cause we can just head right back to the Ridge right now if you all want." He looked around the vehicle at no one in particular, getting no response and not expecting one.

Chris stared at the burnt foil for a minute and then reluctantly crumbled it up. He stuffed it in his pants pocket along with the section of pen. He rubbed the place on his head that had connected with the car door then studied his fingers for signs of bleeding.

"Okay, everyone knows the drill?" No response from the cheap seats, just a lot of lip smacking and throats clearing. Kori had no clue what the drill was but did not dare to mention this. He was still trying to figure out why he was even asked to ride along. "We make sure that the Queen is here. We'll text you before you even get close to his place and you check back when you get there. If anything goes hinky send a text, otherwise pick us up in an hour."

Brenden had gone over the plan at least a dozen times before, but no one dared to complain. They accepted his obsessive micro-managing, just as he overlooked their chronic drug use. Although they hunted the same prey, their bounty was very different. Brenden's was a monetary gain and theirs was a chance to score copious amounts of free dope.

"Cool?" Brenden looked around the car.

"Too cool for school, dude," Soup chimed in. He may have been wired to the gills, but he knew his part well. He was a necessary factor in pulling this off and both he and Brenden knew this. He turned to look at Chris, who was still rubbing the bump on his scalp. "You ready, Cuz?"

"He better be," Brenden interjected harshly. The colorful lights of the neon sign made his blonde hair glow like an eerie sort of halo as he turned his body around to face Chris. The little guy tried to shrink as far back into the seat as he could get. Not wanting to meet Brenden's cold stare, he nervously glanced at Soup for support once again. This time Soup had his back.

"Give him a break, man. You've been on his ass all night. He knows what he's gotta do." Soup gave Chris a reassuring wink. He cautiously slapped the back of his hand against Brenden's shoulder. "Chill out, dude."

"I'll chill when this is done," Brenden muttered. The tone

of his voice softened but his eyes never left Chris. "And there better be as much shit as you say there is, too." Chris opened his mouth to respond but Brenden did not give him a chance. He turned to Kori and grinned. "You ready for your first day on the job, little brother? Our first date together and I'm taking you to the gay bar."

Everyone had a good laugh at this as Brenden exited the car. Todd quickly jumped out and ran around to claim the newly vacated seat, calling "shotgun!" as he went. Chris fumbled unsuccessfully for the door handle, cursing under his breath in defeat. Kori drove the ball of his fist into Chris's thigh, hoping to leave it as sore as Chris had made his following his earlier tantrum.

"Keep my seat warm, dickhead!" He jumped through the open door and slammed it shut before Chris could retaliate. The door came within inches of making contact with the top of Chris's head as he lunged after him.

Soup Campbell shifted the Impala into gear, leaving the Woodson brothers to bask in the alternating layers of darkness and flashing neon lights. The sign above the door pulsed almost in time with the dull thud of the bass beat that seeped from the club's walls. From the open parking lot they could faintly hear the constant chattering and laughter of what seemed like a hundred voices.

"Don't start any fights here," Brenden joked as they

walked to the doorway. “I don't want to get my ass beat at no gay bar.”

Kori laughed nervously. “I wasn't planning on it.”

The doorman was easily over six and a half feet tall, dressed only in leather shorts and a neck tie. He smiled at Kori and motioned them in. For the first time that night, Kori really began to realize the gravity of the situation. What had started out as a bad feeling as they turned down that dark street had fully evolved into full on terror as they began the descent down the even darker stairwell.

CHAPTER 7

"What did you say?" Deputy Dale Scheck mumbled. The residual fog of half sleep was slow to lift. It coated his mind and his vocal chords, making him sound as if he were speaking from the inside of a barrel. He hated the evening shift almost as much as he hated his partner.

He had been caught outright, daydreaming again. It was beginning to turn into a bad habit with him and that was not good. In most professions nodding off on the job would land a guy in the office for a well-deserved ass chewing. In his line of work it could get him killed. He hoped that Butch had not yet noticed the pattern developing. Knowing Butch, that was not likely.

Butch did not answer him. He just gave him a disgusted look and kept driving down the road. That was how the dynamic of their partnership worked. Butch did all of the driving and most of the talking. Dale sat back and took it all in. It was not as if he had a choice anyhow. Butch took the liberty of doing all of the navigating as well. He tended to stick to the rural roads for some reason.

The daydreaming seemed to occur more frequently as they patrolled this particular stretch of Quarry Road. It was a peaceful ride with the rumble of gravel under the tires. The seemingly endless blur of timber and cornfields were hypnotizing. The occasional turkey or whitetail deer would break up the monotony from time to time. Quarry road ran parallel with the river for a while, mirroring nearly every bend in the water's current. They rounded the last S-curve and headed up the hill toward the tiny burg of Cedar Ridge.

The serenity vanished as they crossed a bridge that spanned a wide creek. There were no signs posted but it was known to the locals as Widow's Creek. Many bad happenings went down near that bridge over the years. Some of them were by accident, many others not so much. Dale always remembered it as the place where Stu Fisher took his beating.

It was at the hands of the Collins brothers and it was one hell of an ass whooping. One that would leave poor Stu with two surgically fused vertebrae and a permanent limp. A routine traffic stop near the end of his shift panned out to be Stuart Fisher's last day as a Catalpa County sheriff's deputy. It was a bitter sweet time for Dale and he could not help but to feel some sense of guilt every time he dressed for work each day. After all, it was the untimely end to Stu's career that landed him the position. Otherwise, he would still be biding his time at dead end jobs while he impatiently waited for an opening on the department's roster.

When he did get the call Dale was reluctant to accept it. How could he possibly replace the man who had selflessly mentored him throughout his young adulthood? The man who had always been there to watch him wrestle after his own father had passed away during his freshman year. In fact, it was Stu who had come to his house the night Harold Scheck had been forced into a bridge embankment on Interstate 80 by a drunk driver. Stu insisted on personally delivering the horrible news so that his mother did not have to hear it over the phone.

It did not seem right to take over a man's job that way. Not on merit but simply by default. The stitches from the last surgery were not even out yet and they wanted Dale to try and fill his shoes? He had dreamed of getting on the force for years, but not like that.

He had gone to the Stu's house with the job offer in hand, more for peace of mind than advice. He wanted to hear it from the man himself. That it was okay to sign on to a job that had unfairly been taken from him. What he got was more than he had bargained for.

"Christ, kid. What the hell are you wasting your time asking me for?" Stu bellowed, wincing a little as he braced himself in the wicker patio chair. He reached for the glass of iced tea that Margaret had brought out. "You've been waiting for this for a long time."

"Well," Dale replied, pretending to mull over the question. He was ashamed to admit that he could actually calculate the time that he had waited down to the exact day. "I guess it's been about couple of years now, Stu... but."

"But, hell! What's stopping you, boy? Guilt? Pity?" He placed the glass back down on the cork coaster and wiped the wet off on his pant leg. The expression on his face grew very stern. "Don't feel sorry for me, kiddo. I'm the one that should be feeling sorry for you. That job ain't so easy. Prob'ly get stuck riding with that prick Tassler. They do that now since... well you know."

Dale nodded his head. *Yeah, Stu. We all know.*

"You'll see a lot of things that'll stick in your head long after you hang it up for the night. I'll tell you right now that no soap and water can wash away some kinds of dirt." He unconsciously rubbed his palm across the leg of his pants once again. "I remember a few times wanting to hang it up and walk away. Get myself an honest job that didn't make the wife sick with worry every time I stepped out the front door. But then I'd think about Gabby. The day she... the day she didn't make it home. It made the job bearable. Made it worth doing is what I guess I'm getting at."

It shocked Dale to hear Stu mention his daughter's name. He could only recall hearing him speak of her a few times in the years that he had known him. How old had she been, twelve maybe thirteen when she disappeared? Got off the bus from school one day and never made the hundred yards walk to the house. Vanished in thin air. Stu and Margaret never had any more children. Dale guessed that the chance of losing another one was not a risk their broken hearts dared to take.

"I'll tell you something else, too. If you let this get away without at least giving it a shot, you'll spend a good part of the rest of your life hating yourself for it. And rightly so."

Dale had been staring at his untouched glass of tea during the entire lecture. When he finally looked up he found himself locked in the gaze of a prematurely aging man. The tender welcoming eyes of his lifelong mentor grew severe as they studied him. He no longer felt bad for taking the job, but he felt terrible for burdening the old man with the task of convincing him to do so.

"Make the call, boy."

Dale exhaled a sigh of relief and stood up fast enough to

knock the dust from the wicker chair as it slid out from under him. He downed the tea in three gulps and tipped the melting ice cubes over the railing into the flowerbed below. “Alright. You talked me into it.”

Stu raised his graying eyebrows slightly.

“I take that back. You made me talk myself into it. I'll make the call as soon as I get home. Tell Margaret, thanks for the tea. He sat his glass down and started down the steps when Stu called after him.

“We have phone service here in the boonies, too, ya know. Why don't you make the call right now?” He produced a cordless phone from the seat cushion beside him and held it out. Dale grinned sheepishly and took it from him.

Butch snapped his fingers in the air just inches from his face, pulling him out of his trance. Dale looked at his partner and sighed. It seemed that Stu's prophecy had indeed come true. He was partnered with Butch Tassler. He was also right about him being a prick.

All Catalpa county officers were required to patrol in pairs after Stu's run in with the Collin's brothers. A lawsuit filed on behalf of Delbert Collins had hastened Sheriff Baylor's decision to create the new policy. Some slick lawyer from Des Moines claimed that if the deputy in question, namely one Stuart Lloyd Fisher, had not been patrolling alone that evening he might not have been so inclined to blindly empty the clip of his sidearm as Delbert Collins attempted to choke him unconscious from behind. Consequently, four of the fifteen rounds would not have connected with flesh and bone. Three in Delbert's thigh and one into Stu's own leg.

After a drawn out legal battle, Delbert Collins now received a check every month for permanent disability. It was the same check that Stu received in addition to his pension benefits. Not bad for a guy who never worked an honest day in his entire pathetic life.

"You say something, Butch?" He really did not care what Butch had to say. Most of what came out of his partner's mouth was either negative or laden with a tone of sarcasm that he found quite exasperating. When Butch did initiate a conversation, if it could be called that, he typically did so to get a rise out of him.

"I said early bow season starts this weekend, but I forgot you don't hunt." Butch glanced over to see what kind of reaction he was going to get. He enjoyed a challenging debate every now and again, but this kid was like ice. Nothing got under his skin.

"You *know* I don't hunt, Butch."

"Yes, Dale. I am very aware of that," Butch answered. Finally a hint of life in the boy. Maybe the rookie finally grew a pair. "I've been meaning to talk to you about that. How is it that a guy who makes his living carrying a firearm, doesn't have it in him to hunt? I see you snapping pictures with that camera of yours all the time. I just thought you might consider upgrading to something with a little more kick. I mean, don't get me wrong here, but you don't strike me as the tree hugger type... and you grew up here, right?" He waited momentarily for a response, but got nothing. He snapped his fingers inches from Dales face once again. "Right?"

Dale leaned across the seat and got right into his partner's face. He had no regard for the fact that he was blocking Butch's view as they sped down the road. He had had enough bullying for one day. If Butch wanted to see how many of his buttons it took to set him off, he was going to show him.

"Look, we've been over this before. I have nothing against you or anyone else who hunts. I eat meat three times a day and drive a fucking pickup to work. I'm no tree hugger. And yes, I grew up here. A few miles from this very spot as a matter of fact. What do you want me to say...? I'm sorry that I'm one of the five or so guys in the county that doesn't waste my weekends sitting in a tree stand once or twice every fall? Well I'm not. So before you start..."

Butch brought the cruiser to a jarring stop that nearly put Dale into the dashboard. His right shoulder bumped smartly into the shotgun rack mounted between the two seats. Butch's eyes darted from the weapon to his partner, intentionally making sure that the younger man noticed. He was well schooled in the art of subtle intimidation.

"Whoa, whoa! Take it easy, tiger. First of all, don't you

ever get in my face like that again. I don't care how many fucking state medals you won in high school or how many friends you think you have back in the office. Out here, all we got is each other. For good or bad." He forced his own face closer to Dale's with each word until they were nose to nose. "Got it?"

The last words seeped through his clenched teeth, seemingly from the back of his throat rather than his mouth. He feigned attack with a slight jerk that sent Dale retreating back to his own side of the car. A self-betrayal that left Dale regretting even waking up in the morning. Butch eased his foot from the brake and the cruiser began to roll down Quarry Road once again.

Dale stared solemnly out the window as they made their way down the winding road. The wildlife along this stretch was phenomenal. He spotted a few good photo opportunities along the way, but refrained from pulling his camera from its case. Butch seemed to have settled back into a comfortable cloud of smugness after their confrontation. There was no use in getting him going again.

They turned left onto what the locals had dubbed River Road, a dead end that ran parallel with the Cedar River for about a mile. Dale realized that Butch had something more than a simple pass through Cedar Ridge in mind. The rarely used road was a waste of time to patrol this time of year, but Butch had his own agenda.

To the right was a small picnic area and boat ramp utilized mainly by fisherman and teenagers during the warmer months. Dale had partaken in a few underage drinking parties there as a teenager and busted up a great many more during his two years on the job. To the left was a small campground that had been closed since Labor Day. Now it stood deserted except for a single camper, which for reasons Dale did not understand, was allowed to remain in place all year round by the conservation board.

Aside from the small tavern on the corner, there was only one other permanent structure that the road accessed. Virgil Semler, otherwise known as Virge the perv, lived at the end of the road. Dale did not bother to ask why they would be going to see some old hermit who had probably not left his property in more than a decade. He did not want to know, although he did have his suspicions. Whatever business Butch had with Virgil was undoubtedly not about the law, let alone within the parameters of it.

"Just going to check on some mounts he's working on," Butch explained as he pulled into the long lane. Dale considered asking him what kind of taxidermy work was necessary in the week before hunting season even took place, but thought better of it. He stared out the window and said nothing as his partner exited the vehicle.

Butch knocked on the front door and stood back with his arms crossed. He anxiously tapped his foot on the wooden porch boards as he waited. He continued to shift his attention from the heavily curtained window and then back to the cruiser. Dale watched the strange display with increasing curiosity until the door finally opened.

Just a crack at first, then the door opened just wide enough to produce the bald head and a pair of bespectacled eyes. Virgil peered out and then opened the door just long enough to allow Butch to be swallowed up by the darkness within. He shot a cold glance toward the patrol car before slamming it shut.

As soon as the door shut Dale fumbled for the Nikon between his feet. In addition to his passion for photographing wildlife, he had a knack for finding and capturing bits of local oddities that would probably never be appreciated by anyone besides himself. Maybe one day he would get them all published into a coffee table book. Until then they were just more files for his growing scrapbook.

He snapped shots of the house and the yard. Both were overloaded with various tools and contraptions that bordered on antique status. Junk cars were stitched in place by an overgrowth of weeds. A white van that looked like it had not moved in years, but still much newer than the other vehicles sat in the forefront. Several four wheelers and snowmobiles skirted the house's foundation. Dale captured every one of them on film, taking special care to get a shot of the license plate numbers. At least the ones that still had them.

He noticed a sign advertising canoe rentals and inner tubes, none of which could be seen anywhere on the property. In smaller letters, sloppily written in black paint was the word HIDERUGS. Not two words, just one. Dale muttered this word over and over like a mantra. "Hiderugs, hiderugs, highdrugs... high drugs." Interesting. He laughed to himself and snapped a shot of the sign.

The smell inside the house was thick and overpowering, invading Butch's nostrils as he stepped inside. The pungent odor of marijuana smoke hung in the air and mixed with other smells that he did not even want to identify. He did not care about the pot smoke. He entered Virgil's domain not on professional terms but of personal ones. If he were to have entered a home like this in a normal police situation he probably would have been laying some dope head's ass on the floor by now.

"Officer Tassler, to what do I owe the pleasure?" Virgil inquired with a slightly high pitched lisp as he quickly bolted the latch. His small rodent eyes peered through the window curtain. "Do you think that bringing your shadow along for show and tell was such a good idea?" He gestured his hand toward the vague shape of the cruiser that lay beyond the smoky glass.

His eyes carried a desperate air of nervousness that Butch found rather detestable. If the old bastard was not so resourceful he would have split his head open a long time ago, but he truly did need Virgil. So he had no choice but to at least overlook his shortcomings.

"Oh, don't you worry about him. He's not much for conversation, let alone questions. Besides, I told him that I was coming to check on some deer mounts. I honestly don't think he gives two shits about what I do." Butch playfully punched at Virgil's shoulder with a sideways grin. "Don't ask, don't tell. That's our motto."

Virgil relaxed a bit, completely unaware that his yard was currently the subject of an amateur photo shoot. He lowered himself into his recliner. Absently, he fingered the collar of his bathrobe with one hand and lit a cigarette with the other. He considered quitting for the umpteenth time earlier that day. Nervousness was his usual excuse to smoke again and Butch Tassler made him more than nervous. He was downright terrified of the man. He could think of nothing better than getting him out of his house as quickly as possible.

"What can I do for you, Butch?"

"The usual," Butch replied. "No, actually double that. First season starts soon and I need a little extra staying power, if you know what I mean." Butch flashed that vicious grin once again.

"Yeah, sure." Virgil had no idea what he meant and he was sure that he never wanted to find out. He could not imagine hunting with the crazy sonofabitch. Probably just uses his bare hands to get the job done.

"I'm sure there'll be no problem putting a bit more on my tab, right?" The grin instantly vanished and was replaced by a serious 'don't fuck with me' look.

"No, no problem whatsoever," Virgil agreed. Anything to get the bastard out in a hurry. He produced two gram bindles of white powder from his front robe pocket. He found himself wishing that he had both the guts and the foresight to have a couple of grams of D-con loaded up for the deputy when he made his random unannounced house calls. That would be nice, but it would only complicate thing further up the food chain. He shook the thought away and handed over the meth.

Butch was stuffing the packages inside the folds of his wallet and heading for the door before Virgil could get out of his chair. He waved his hand coldly, told him not to bother and let himself out. Virgil sunk back into the fabric of the recliner, lighting another cigarette off the end of the last one. His hands did not stop shaking for hours and the rest of his afternoon was shot.

CHAPTER 8

"What the hell are we doing here?" Kori asked, as he adjusted the green wristband. It never failed, the adhesive strip on the back of the band always managed to expose itself just enough to grab a few hairs and rip them out by the roots. The doorman raised an eyebrow and looked back and forth at them while he banded Brenden's wrist. Brenden put up his other hand in a 'hold that thought' gesture. After paying the cover charge he threw his arm on his brother's shoulder and led him through the door.

"This will take less than an hour if everything goes right." Brenden made a visual sweep of the room and chewed at his lower lip. Then he abruptly grasped the back of Kori's neck and pulled him close. “I'm gonna tell you this once. If you have any more stupid fucking questions, get them out now. Don't ever open your mouth like that in front of anyone in here. Dig?”

Kori pulled away from the grip and rubbed the back of his neck. His face became flush with anger. He was not as mad at his brother as he was with himself. He knew that he had made a mistake. The less attention that they drew to themselves, the better. After all, Iowa City was not that big of a place. Chances of running into any of the patrons of this bar on the street were pretty high.

“Okay. Sorry.” Kori mumbled, looking at the floor.

“Don't worry about it. Let's just have a couple of beers and wait this out.” Brenden nudged him in the side and smiled apologetically. He had a way of charming his way out of most situations. Kori found himself deeply admiring his brother and bitterly envying him at the same time. He smiled back and followed him to the bar.

The plan sounded simple enough. Their job was to hang out at the bar and make sure the Queen was there. When that was established Kori would text Todd with the news. Then they just had to stay put and make sure the Queen did the same. Unless anyone's status changed, all they had to do was wait for the call to go back outside and catch their ride.

It seemed so simple that Kori was having trouble

understanding why they would actually pay him to do this. He understood why he was delegated to the gay bar position. That was obvious. Chris was the only one who actually knew the Queen, so he was out. Soup and Todd looked more like a couple of rock band roadies than gay clubbers, no matter how well they cleaned up. This left only the Woodson brothers up to the task. He still had no idea what everyone else's jobs were.

Brenden ordered two beers and scanned the room again while he waited for the bartender to bring them. Kori wanted to ask him if he saw the Queen yet, but knew better. In the adjoining room a crowd had gathered around a small stage. Gloria Gainer was singing about how she would survive through a sound system somewhere in the darkness of that room. On the stage a tall blonde dressed in drag lip-synced the words and danced around to the delight of the audience. Occasionally someone would tuck a bill into her/his dress and extend their face forward for a kiss on the cheek. Kori looked at Brenden who in turn shrugged and handed him a beer.

A few minutes later the song ended and a raspy voice of another drag queen poured out of the speakers. “One more hand for the Glory Hole's very own Queen Alana! I want to thank you all for coming... ahem, being here tonight.” The crowd laughed and whistled at this. “Be sure to stick around for the next show at midnight.” The lights in the adjoining room brightened and the crowd started filing back into the bar area. Club music erupted from the sound system and some of the crowd began to dance.

Brenden nudged him and nodded toward the doorway. Kori turned to see the tall blonde strutting to the bar with a small entourage in tow. Brenden nudged him again but the meaning was lost to him. He mouthed the word "what?" and stared back dumbly. Brenden rolled his eyes impatiently. He put up his thumb and pinky to the side of his face in the universal sign for telephone. Kori nodded and sent the text: the queen is here.

For the most part, people left the alone as they finished their beers and ordered another round. It was not until these were half gone that the bartender placed a pair of full shot glasses in front of them. The bartender leaned across to Brenden and nodded in the direction of the Queen's group.

"From the gentleman in the corner."

A skinny older guy with a beak nose and a neck too long for his body stiffened up when Brenden looked his way. Slightly mascara lined eyes widened and then swam in a way that only old gay guys can do. His upper lip twitched and his hands unconsciously smoothed out the sides of his skin tight shirt as he looked the brothers up and down.

Brenden told the bartender that he could afford his own drinks and pushed the glasses away. He turned his back to the group and pretended to spark up a deep conversation with Kori. Everyone except the old guy burst into laughter. The Queen threw back her/his head, clapped and let out a deep bellowing laugh. For some strange reason this made Kori think of his old gym coach. The skinny old queer whipped around and stormed off. The overhead lighting reflected off the back of his thinning hair as he bounced back into the other room.

"Well played, straight boy," the Queen called out, tipping the edge of his glass in their direction. Brenden reciprocated in the gesture and left it at that. No one else bothered them after that. The brothers made small talk that amounted to nothing and waited for the call.

CHAPTER 9

Soup stopped the Impala short of the busier part of the street, where they still had plenty of cover from the approaching lights. He loaded up another round of foil and passed it around the car after taking the initial hit for himself. They were pretty well amped by the time they had made most of the thirty block trek to the west end of town. Under Chris's sketchy navigation they had only been forced to turn around and backtrack twice. Soup cursed under his breath, but even he accepted that it was just par for the course.

They were just entering the more affluent neighborhood of University Heights when Todd received Kori's text. The three rode in silence for a few minutes, a preparatory ritual that they knew all too well. Time to reflect on the reality of the situation and the severity of the potential outcomes that it held. Also time to let the last round of crank work its magic on their systems.

Todd finally broke the silence as Soup pulled the car to the curb, half a block from their destination. He craned his head out of the passenger window and studied the scene. "This is a goddamn nice neighborhood, boys. Sure you got that address right, Chris?"

"What do you think, I'm an idiot? Of course this is the right place. What'd you expect? A gingerbread house?" he snapped.

"I thought everybody who lived in the Heights were all doctors and professors and shit. Your girlfriend, the Queen. Is he some kind of professor or something?" Todd settled back into his seat and rummaged through a bag on the floorboard. He doled out masks and gloves to Chris and Soup, keeping the cleanest looking set for himself.

Chris sat there grinning smugly as if he were the sole keeper of the world's best kept secret. His eyebrows danced up and down on his pimply forehead. He shrugged his shoulders and smiled at his companions in the front seat.

"No shit?" Soup said. "A dope dealing professor. Ain't that some shit. What's he teach, Home EC 101?" He laughed and slapped the back of his hand firmly on Todd's chest. The slap stung as loudly as it sounded, leaving Todd gasping for breath. “Get it? Home EC, 'cause he's a...” Todd pointed at Soup and then to his head in a gesture that said, yeah I got it.

Notorious for giving stupid answers to rhetorical questions, Chris shook his head and replied. “No, I think he told me he taught ethics or some shit like that.” This got Todd laughing, despite his inability to breath. He pointed to Soup again, then to Chris and finally to his own head.

“Now that's funny,” he wheezed.

They left the Impala parked in the darkness and headed down the block on foot, allowing Chris to walk twenty yards ahead. Chris led them to a newer looking ranch style house and rang the bell. Todd and Soup strategically positioned themselves on either side of the door, several feet out of view from the wide stain glass sidelights.

Soup did a visual of the front yard and street from his vantage point. Nothing. He surveyed the two late model vehicles parked in the driveway. A Camry and a Lexus convertible were parked neatly in front of the garage. He thought to himself, one thing about these fags. They sure do drive nice cars. Adrenaline thumped inside his skull as he stretched the skin tight pair of leather racing gloves over his hands. He licked his lips and adjusted his feet for optimum traction.

Chris was about to ring the bell again when the front light came on. Todd and Soup held steady, like two prize fighters anticipating the start of the first round. The masks covering their faces could not conceal the fire of excitement in their eyes. I feel a hate crime coming on, Todd thought to himself. Chris hit the doorbell one more time and quickly turned away. He walked down the front steps toward the street, not looking back as the sound of the deadbolt snapped on the other side of the door.

The door opened inward and a voice called out to him. "Can I help you?"

Chris did not reply. He kept walking until he reached the sidewalk. Without turning he casually reached up with both hands and pulled the ski mask over his face. The voice in the doorway materialized into a young man with a build even more slight than his own. The young man stepped out on the landing and threw his hands up impatiently. "Hello! What the fuck is your problem?"

Before he had time to finish the question, they were on him. It was Todd who struck the first blow, stepping out of the darkness and delivering a hay-maker to the side of the head. In a panicked confusion the man turned toward the doorway, but Soup quickly snatched him by the hair with one hand and pulled him back. In a matter of seconds he had him in a choke hold that quashed any chance of screaming for help. Momentum carried them through the open door and they fell into the foyer. Soup never loosened his grip as his full body weight landed on top of his prey. Todd followed them inside, narrowly avoiding stepping on the two as they struggled. Chris was close behind, slamming the door shut behind him.

Soup stayed on him, easing his hold only when the man went limp beneath him. The other two made a quick sweep of the house to make sure that no one else was there. Vaguely familiar with the layout from previous visits, Chris led the way. He was not the brightest bulb in the box, but Chris held his own during working hours and Todd trusted him fully. They found no signs of anyone else and returned to the foyer.

Soup was standing over his barely conscious victim, who sat slumped over with his back to the wall. He was slowly gaining his faculties with the help of several well placed slaps. Each time the open gloved hand connected with flesh the sound echoed throughout the small entry way. Not a word was spoken until the man regained enough composure to look up at them. When he did they realized that he was hardly a man at all, but rather a boy no older than thirteen.

The look of terror on his young face stopped Soup in mid swing. Winded from the struggle, Soup fought to catch his breath. The opened hand of the undelivered slap closed into a fist. He cocked it back and smiled through the mask. "Where is it?"

He only had to ask two more times.

The boy was hesitant at first, denying that there were any drugs in the house. They always did at first. He tried to placate the intruders by suggesting that they just settle for some of the expensive looking knickknacks that adorned virtually every available space in the house. He swore that they were “old and really fucking valuable, you guys.” He motioned to a low glass top table in the living room. His hand trembled as he pointed, swollen and bleeding from fending off punches. “There's some money and my cell phone on the table. Just take it, please.”

“Do we look like a bunch of goddamned antique dealers, asshole?” Todd snarled as he swiped the stack of bills from the table. As an afterthought he pocketed the phone as well. He stared down at the table for a moment and ran his gloved finger across the glass surface. He held it up and the tip was coated in white powder. “Check it out.”

Infuriated, Soup grabbed the boy by the hair and punched him squarely in the back of the head. Dragging him by the hair and shirt, he shoved the boy's face against the glass hard enough for it to crack. “No dope, huh?” He leaned down and pressed his lips closely against the ear that was not mashed into the glass. “I'm gonna ask you this one more time. Where is it?”

“The bedroom,” the boy whimpered. Tears and snot mixed with the coke residue left a Rorschach-esque splotch on the glass. On his face was the matching other half. “It's in the Queen's room.”

Soup held tightly to the patch of hair and let him lead them down the hallway. They entered the master bedroom and the boy immediately pointed to a nightstand on the left side of the bed. Todd pushed his way past them and looked in the drawer. He shot the boy a disgusted look and pulled the drawer completely out. He dumped the contents onto the bed. A few pill bottles and a gallon sized freezer bag full of marijuana, among other unmentionable things spilled across the satin comforter.

"This cannot be all of it," Todd said through clenched teeth. The statement was directed more to Chris than the boy. After all, he had been to this house several times buying dope and scoping the place out. He had promised them the mother lode. Chris stood in the doorway in silence. Not wanting his voice to be recognized, he had not spoken a word since they had entered the house.

Soup let his fist do the talking for the last time. A brutal shot to the kidney dropped the boy to his knees. Unable to catch his breath, he pointed a trembling hand to the nightstand. Before anyone could stop him he pulled the heavy piece of furniture nearly on top of himself to reveal a wall safe hidden neatly behind it. Without being prompted he began to punch out a series of codes on the number pad. He failed on the first attempt and began jamming the numbers hard with his thumb. The lock clicked open and he collapsed with his chest on the back of the upturned nightstand and began to sob.

Soup dragged him by the feet and pulled him out of the way. Todd rolled the nightstand clear of the door. When he opened it they were all stunned. “Holy Christ. Would you look at that.”

The haul nearly filled two of the pillow cases that they had stripped from the bed. They only took the drugs and cash. What they left behind was a sizable collection of sex pictures. The one on the top of the stack appeared to be of the boy and some old fat guy in drag.

There was a brief debate on what to do with the boy. After seeing the picture, Soup wanted to beat him within an inch of his life and leave him where they had found him. Chris was neutral. He just wanted to get the hell out of there. Todd grabbed the photo from the top of the stack and stuffed it into the boy's front shirt pocket, making sure it was partially visible. He had a more logical idea. One that would benefit them all.

They tied the boy to the bed using some nylons from the emptied drawer. The boy did not struggle or protest. He was either beaten too far into a state of shock to care or else he was disturbingly accustomed to this scenario. As they exited the house they flipped on every light switch within reach. Not bothering to close the front door behind them, the trio made sure the coast was clear and started for the Impala. Todd pulled the boy's cell phone from his pocket and dialed 911. He hit the send button placed the phone at the end of the driveway.

The Queen now had bigger problems than losing his dope.

CHAPTER 10

The Woodson brothers were waiting at the end of the parking lot when Soup's boat of a car pulled up. They stepped out of the darkness and climbed into the back seat. Once again Kori found himself crammed in the middle. Chris was sweating heavily and fidgeting with the door lock, too distracted to even look up as they got in. He just shifted more to his side of the seat and stared out the window.

"Well?" Brenden asked. "How was the Queen's castle?"

"It smelled like incense and ass. Other than that, it was great," Todd replied. "Nothing a long hot shower and a twelve pack won't fix."

“That's not what I'm asking.” Brenden said, impatiently. “Was it a good haul, or not?”

“More than good. I don't think even sleeping beauty here knew how much was in that place.” Todd jerked his thumb at Chris, who was sitting behind him. He twisted around to face Kori. “Don't mind him by the way. He always gets his sleep on after we roll. That and he's been up for about a week.”

Soup backed the Impala into the parking lot entrance to turn around. He shifted into drive and slowly inched back onto the street. Suddenly he mashed down on the brakes, startling everyone in the vehicle. Even Chris sat up long enough to looked around and ask what was going on. Soup threw his arm over the back of the seat and let out a deep sigh.

“You know. One thing about these fags, they sure do have nice cars.”

With that, he threw the transmission back into reverse and punched the gas. The Impala launched backwards as everything and everyone in the vehicle was thrust forward. The squealing tires spun on the loose gravel, sending the car diagonally through the lot until the bumper collided with the broad side of a black Volvo. The newer model car in turn slammed into a minivan that was parked next to it. Soup once again shifted into drive and accelerated toward the street. Kori managed to turn around just in time to see the Volvo settle back on all four tires. The driver's side was completely caved in.

Chris snapped out of his catatonic state and started to cheer. He began slapping his hand on the outside of the roof and laughing hysterically. Soup looked back at him and smiled. "You like that, little man?"

"Oh, yeah!" Chris reached forward to high five his cousin and nearly elbowed Kori in the head. Not that Kori would have even noticed if he had. He was too mortified to move at that point.

As they made their way back to the more illuminated streets, Soup caught the reflection of Brenden in the rear view. His laughter was immediately stifled by the look of pure rage on Brenden's face. He self-consciously gripped the wheel with both hands and steered the vehicle in the direction of home. Even Chris had enough wits about him to sense the tension in the car. He sat back in his seat and rested his head on the door.

They took the long way home. Once out of the city limits, a vast series of dirt and gravel country roads kept them off the beaten path. This enabled them to avoid all but a few other vehicles and only cross a handful of bisecting paved roads. The ride was spent in silence with Soup feeling the lasers of hate beaming from Brenden's ice blue eyes.

Everyone bailed out of the car the instant that Soup parked behind Joe Woodson's pickup truck and turned off the engine. Everyone except Brenden, who remained in the back seat. Thankful to be liberated from the tense atmosphere, they went to work unloading the gear from the trunk. Soup handed the pillow cases to Todd and slammed the trunk shut. He bent down and accessed the damage from his impromptu smash and dash. Satisfied that it didn't have too many more dents or scratches than before, he stood up and dusted his hands off.

He never heard Brenden close the car door and approach him from behind. He barely had a chance to turn around before the solid punch caught him high on the cheekbone, buckling his knees and sending him reeling back against the trunk. He considered getting back to his feet but thought better of it when he saw the look on Brenden's face.

“Don't ever do something that fucking stupid around me again!” Brenden stalked across the yard, leaving Soup to nurse his damaged face and pride alone. As crazy as he was, he knew enough to take the lesson and let it go. Give the boss man a few minutes to cool down. Then go inside and help count the nightly take. Then maybe get high.

Kori watched in awe as Todd emptied the pillow cases onto his father's kitchen table. Thin bundles of cash, various Ziploc bags and bottles of pills were strewn across the table cloth. They contrasted with the normal table settings. A bulging bag of yellow pills lay on top of an overturned salt shaker. A stream of salt granules spilled out on some loose twenty dollar bills. Todd pinched a few grains, threw them over his shoulder and proceeded to gather the stray bills into neat piles. Brenden and Chris sorted through the drugs while Soup sat quietly in a chair, rubbing his reddened cheek.

Unsure of the politics involved, Kori left the others to their business and wandered into the living room. It was the first time that he had set foot in the room in over six years.

It was in that very room that his mother had simply walked in one day and announced that she was leaving, moving to Des Moines and taking Kori with her. Reverend Cole had accepted a position at a new church in Ames and had asked her to join him. She had adjusted her posture, as if anticipating the backlash and said, “And I accepted.”

Kori had been fifteen at the time and Brenden his elder by three years.

“What about Brenden?” Kori had asked. He was in total shock. He never saw it coming.

“What do you think, dipshit?” Brenden had stood up quickly and grimaced. He was in a knee brace at the time from a wrestling injury. The injury that kept him from getting a full ride to Iowa. “I'm not exactly flock material am I, Mom? What, Clayton don't want the black sheep telling the others that the shepherd's been banging the church secretary right under their noses?”

Their mother had gasped and then defiantly choked back the look of surprise with a mask of anger. It was a look that she seldom practiced, let alone mastered. She had avoided looking at her half drunken husband or her younger son, both of whom sat in stunned silence. Her pale blue eyes locked on to Brenden's, eyes that matched hers so much that she may have well have been staring into a mirror. Her face had been flush with embarrassment and her unsteady legs threatened to betray her at any moment. She had expected this reaction from Brenden. She probably even deserved it, but to have Kori hear all of this broke her heart.

"Did you really think I didn't know?" He had asked as he pushed past her, shrinking away as she absently reached to touch him. He had walked out the front door and did not return until she made good on her promise to leave. Those were the last words spoken between them until she had brought Kori back, earlier that afternoon.

The scene played out in Kori's mind as he sank deeper into the couch, the same one that he had sat on during that fateful afternoon. The décor of the room had not changed at all. Material objects that his mother had once lovingly arranged to beautify her home were still right where she had left them. They were not dirty, just unkempt. Like artifacts in a forgotten tomb, abandoned and lonely.

He wondered why his father never tried to stop her. He just let Brenden do all of the talking, which inevitably drove her out for good. Maybe it was because he knew all of the things that Brenden said were true. Or that he was just too deep into the bottle to care. Maybe he knew all along that she was already gone, long before she actually left.

Kori fell asleep with the memories in his head mixing with the maddening events of the day. Sounds of kitchen table narcotics negotiations drifted from the other room. That supplemented with a slight contact buzz from the car ride to Iowa City made for some lucid dreams.

CHAPTER 11

The morning came like a slap to the face in the dark. Kori was disoriented from waking in a strange place. His neck and back ached from a night on the broken down sofa, but most of all he was famished. It occurred to him that he had not eaten since early the morning before. He rolled off of the couch and rubbed at the knots in the side of his neck. He made a mental note to see if his old room was as trapped in time as the rest of the house, just as soon as he found something to eat.

The unmistakable sound of groaning springs being stretched to their limit and the smack of wood kissing wood came from the kitchen. Memories from his childhood revolved around the sound of that very kitchen door. Good or bad, that door was an integral part of the Woodson house. Accompanied by glorious arrivals, furious departures and everything in between; that door had seen it all. He strained to listen but heard only soft rustling coming from the kitchen.

"Hungry, fella?" Brenden snapped him out of his brief bout of nostalgia.

Startled, he took a step back and almost tripped over the coffee table. He looked up to see his brother leaning in the doorway, twirling a spatula like a drumstick. He smiled and waved him into the kitchen. Kori did not have to be asked twice.

Not a word was spoken until Kori downed his third grilled cheese and second bowl of tomato soup. Their father sat in silence with a copy of the Press Citizen spread out before him. He slowly spooned cherry nut ice cream straight from the carton into his mouth. Brenden rinsed his plate in the sink and lifted the remaining soup from the stove top. He waved it over the newspaper and asked their father if he wanted it. Joe Woodson only grunted and shook his head, his eyes never leaving the sports section. Brenden shrugged and poured the leftovers down the drain.

Kori leaned back in his chair and muffled a burp with the back of his hand. He watched his father intently. The old man looked different somehow. He was of course older than the last time he had seen him, but it was more than that. He looked healthier, despite the fact that he was literally eating an entire half gallon of ice cream and washing it down with a diet Mountain Dew. Seeing him in such a way conflicted with Kori's past recollections. This was not the same man who he rarely remembered being sober.

"Kid sure was hungry. I guess they don't make grilled cheese much in Cyclone country, huh?" Brenden pulled up a chair and sat down. He nudged the old man playfully with his elbow as he worked the cap from his bottle of Dew.

Joe flipped the paper to the back page and neatly folded it down the middle. He mumbled a barely audible "Mhmm" and took a long drink from the bottle. Kori nearly choked when he noticed the small yellow pill that was stuck to the bottom. It clung there, trapped between the nubs of green plastic and half dissolved by condensation. He shot a nervous glance to his brother, who had apparently noticed as well. They watched as the remainder of the errant pill rode down the sweat on the plastic bottle and hung up between the crevices. The rest of it was little more than an opaque yellow blob on the table.

Brenden just shrugged. "Easy come, easy go. At least it's on the bottle and not in it. Right, Dad?"

Joe muttered another "Mhmm."

Brenden fished a set of keys from his pocket and looked at his brother. Kori sighed and stood up. He was not in the mood for another car ride, especially after the two that he had endured the day before. However, he was also not up for spending any alone time with his father. In his own way he had missed the old man greatly during their separation. He was just not sure how to act around him yet. From the way they had interacted at the table it did not seem like anyone else in the house knew how to act around each other either.

"Come on. There's someone that I want you to meet." Brenden slapped his father playfully on the back as he exited the kitchen. "Later, Dad."

Kori stood up to follow his brother out. Joe unexpectedly grabbed him by the arm as he passed by. He looked up from his nearly empty ice cream carton and met Kori's eyes with his own. Eyes as bright as the sky that contrasted with his sun weathered complexion. Tears welled up but he never broke his gaze. "Glad to have you home, son." He held on to Kori's arm for a moment longer and then went back to spooning ice cream into his mouth.

"Thanks." It was all that he could think to say before he hurried outside. The screen door sounded off, bidding him farewell. He ran to catch up with his brother who waited impatiently in the cab of a large pickup truck. The back of the truck was loaded down with rolls of wire fencing.

"Who's truck, yours?"

"Nah." Brenden fiddled with the radio. "My boss's."

"So, where are we going?"

"Not far." Brenden smiled, backing out of the driveway and onto the road that led them out of Cedar Ridge.

On the way Kori asked a question that had been weighing on him all morning. "He doesn't drink any more, does he?"

"Nope. Hasn't touched a drop since she left," Brenden replied. "He is up to about two gallons of ice cream a day though."

In less than five minutes they pulled into a long gravel lane, leading up to an old farmhouse. Beyond the house several barns and outbuildings were scattered across a wide rocky lot. In the background was a picturesque spread of rolling pastures. Tractors and farm implements were lined up neatly in and around the large metal building closest to the house. Brenden parked the truck beside a yellow end loader and killed the engine. Without a word he got out and started toward the opened door of the building. Kori got out and assessed the place while his brother disappeared inside.

It had the usual attributes of a farmstead. The sweet smell of fresh cut hay and the faint tinge of cattle manure hung in the breeze. More abrasive odors of old motor oil, diesel fuel and the harsh chemical smell of fertilizer came from the building. Cows mulled complacently around a feed bunk, swatting their tails in a futile effort to ward off flies. Somewhere in the distance a dog was barking.

Then it hit him.

“This is Clayton's place, isn't it?” he yelled toward the building's open door.

“Not any more it isn't,” a softly accented voice came from behind the truck. He jumped and turned to face a frail looking wisp of a man. He was dressed in a pair of blue coveralls that hung loosely on his tiny frame. On his feet he wore a pair of knee length rubber boots that were covered in dry cow dung. He seemed to float as he approached, swimming in his oversized clothes. “Jens Aarons.” He quickly unsheathed a gloved hand and offered it out. “You must be Kori.”

“Yeah.” Kori shook the man's hand and nodded. The thick German accent did not match the smiling face. Although his hands were small and soft, his handshake was quite firm. The old man returned the glove to his hand and walked around to the side of the truck. He reached in the bed and grabbed a roll of fencing. Without so much as a grunt he lifted the roll and carried it to the end loader, gently placing it in the bucket.

Kori followed suit and tried to pull out a roll. Damn, he thought to himself. These things weigh as much as he does. It was all he could do to lift out the roll and carry it the short distance to the bucket. The old man continued to smile. He opened the truck door and reached behind the seat. He produced a worn pair of gloves and handed them to Kori.

“Your brother says that you are in need of a job.”

“I am... er, he did?” Kori took the gloves and stared at

them.

"I see you've met Jens," Brenden said as he stepped out of the shed. He reached into the truck and grabbed the two remaining rolls at once. When he got within five feet of the end loader he flung them shot put style one at a time. They landed in the bucket with a loud crash. He walked back to the truck and started pulling out the rest of the gear. "You want to help me with this or are you two gonna stand there all day and make eyes at each other?"

By the end of the afternoon Kori learned several things. One, he was now employed for the second time in his life. He was not sure how he felt about that. His first attempt at legitimate work had ended in the disaster, which ultimately landed him back in Cedar Ridge. He also learned more than he ever wanted to know about fence construction.

That first day was a killer. He had never done any sort of manual labor in his life. He had been brought up to believe that this was something to be proud of. Despite the dull pain that had set up shop in his weary muscles, he felt a sense of accomplishment. Something that, until that day, was completely foreign to him. It was hard work, but he sincerely enjoyed it.

He was beginning to develop a deep admiration for the brother that he barely knew. Brenden was a trooper. He pulled and lifted things twice his body weight with ease. He had no fear and possessed an amazing tolerance for pain. Everything

Brenden did was flawlessly executed with precision and grace. Years of hearing his mother speak so negatively about his older brother started to make less and less sense.

From a hydrant near the corner of the barn, Kori washed away as much of the day's dirt and sweat as he could. The water was ice cold and left goose bumps as it ran down his arms. He watched his brother and Jens chatting near the truck. They seemed to share a bond that went beyond a working relationship. Even their body language exuded a feeling of closeness as they leaned against the tailgate and laughed. Seeing this just compounded the way he felt about his brother.

His interest was piqued when he saw Brenden pull a large stack of cash from his pocket and hand it to the old man. Jens simply nodded, not bothering to count the bills, and walked toward the house. He waved goodbye to Kori and disappeared through his front door.

Brenden took the hose and directed the flow over the back of his down turned head. He quickly snapped upright, sending a rooster tail spray of water against the side of the barn. The water stained the sun baked wood in dark trailing fingers.

“What's the deal? You have to pay Jens to work for him?” Kori asked, jokingly. He wiped droplets of water from his face with the front of his soiled shirt. The sweat soaked fabric made the corners of his eyes sting.

“Huh?” Brenden looked up. He held the hose between his

knees and scrubbed his hands together beneath the flowing water. "Oh, that. No, I was just paying the mortgage. My half anyway."

"Your half? You own Clayton's old farm?"

"No. I own half of it. At least half of the part the bank still don't own," Brenden replied.

"How did that come about, you and Jens getting Clayton's place?"

Brenden gave him an agitated look. "How do you think it came about, dumb ass? We bought it." He snapped the handle of the hydrant shut and frowned. "And quit calling it Clayton's place. There ain't anything here that belongs to that sonofabitch now."

Brenden gave him the Reader's Digest condensed version. He started by surprising Kori with the fact that Clayton had been over four months behind on the mortgage when he skipped town with him and their mother in tow. It was as if he already knew the end was near. Then again, most self-proclaimed prophets do.

Jens, a retired obstetrician at the U of I, had spent his entire career delivering human babies. It was a fulfilling occupation, but all he had ever dreamed of was to be working his own farm. It was a dream that he shared with few people. John Norton, his good friend and manager of the First National Bank in town, was one of those privileged few. When John had mentioned that the Cole farm coming up for possible foreclosure over coffee one morning, Jens was intrigued. He made an offer that included covering Clayton's back payments in exchange for the farm, the equipment and the livestock.

Clayton jumped at the offer. Not only did it save him the burden of a property that could potentially sit on the market for months, but the deal also got him out of hock with the bank. His only vacillation came when Jens inquired about his hired hand. He scoffed at the notion that anyone would want to keep Brenden on as an employee. Jens countered by asking him why he had kept him for so long. At this Clayton left John Norton's office in a huff and muttered, “Do what you want, old man. I'm done here.”

Well Jens did just that. He offered Brenden a job, which he gladly accepted. Months after the family had split up, Brenden was still searching for the best way of giving Clayton the big 'fuck you'. He presented Jens with the idea of an even partnership. Split the costs and the profits right down the middle. No one had to know that he was anything more than a hired hand. No one except them, John at the bank and of course Uncle Sam.

“Long story short, I needed him and he needed me. We'll have the bank note paid off in by the end of the year. Then I'm done rolling dope heads for profit. I'm gonna settle my ass down and live the good life, just me and my boy Jens. When the farm is free and clear I'm gonna mail a copy of the deed to that cocksucker, Clayton. He'll shit when he sees my name on it." A dark smile spread across Brenden's lips. "What? Let me guess. That's not the way Clayton's version of the story plays out."

Kori stared down at his grungy tennis shoes. If this keeps up I'm gonna have to get me a pair of boots, he thought to himself. He knew there was bad blood between his brother and Clayton. No need to bring it to a boil again. It was true that Clayton's version was a lot different than the one he had just heard. He had to admit that this one made much more sense.

"I don't know. He never talked about that stuff," he lied. He looked up at his brother, hoping that he would leave it at that. "The past is the past, right? Nothing we can do about that now."

"Alright little brother," Brenden nudged his shoulder gently, letting him off the hook. "You look whipped. Let's get you home."

CHAPTER 12

Deputy Scheck parked in front of his trailer just before sunset. He sat in his truck and watched in amusement as his neighbors scurried into their tin can homes. The ones who were either on parole or probation got up from their lawn chairs, palmed their beers or intoxicants of choice and headed indoors. The rest kept their heads down and tried to become invisible. Even in his personal vehicle, the mere sight of his uniform made the residents of Creekside Mobile Home Village a little edgy.

It would be hours after he settled in before the most brazen of them dared to show their faces outside again. Even on his days off, when he was wearing civilian clothing, he could feel the cold stares burning into his back as he walked around the park. He was forever dubbed “the cop next door”.

Most of the trailer park children did not share the same disdain for him as the adults did. They chased after his truck on bike and on foot, gathering into a small mob in his postage stamp sized yard. The older kids shoved the smaller ones to the background, jockeying for position to greet him. The scrappier little ones pushed and clawed their way back to the forefront. All commotion ceased when he stepped out of his truck, as if their aggressive behavior might be a violation of some unknown law.

“Hey, Dale!” one of the younger ones yelled, a little girl about nine years old with stringy blond hair. She was perched on a beat up bicycle that was too small for her. She wore a pair of pink cut off sweats that revealed knees covered in scabs, presumably from spills on the undersized bike. She sported a Hawkeye jersey that hung down almost to the bottom of her shorts.

“Hey, Clara,” Dale replied. He was on a first name basis with most of the Creekside youth. In fact, he knew all of their parents by their first names as well. Just for different reasons.

“Hey, Dale!” the rest of the mob cried out in unison, not to be outdone by Clara.

“How many bad guys did you catch today?” Clara's little brother asked. He stuffed his dirty little hands into the pockets of his jeans and leaned forward. All the while his eyes were fixed on the holstered sidearm in Dale's service belt.

Dale leaned forward, mimicking the boy. "All of 'em, Jamie."

He caught movement out of the corner of his eye, a curtain parting from a nearby trailer. Between the gaps in the fabric a pair of eyes watched his welcoming party with great interest. It was Kyle Collins, who happened to be a cousin to the cop-beating Collins brothers. He stood upright and turned to the direction of the spying eyes. The curtains closed instantly and the light behind them shut off. Dale felt the hair on the back of his neck raise up. He forced a smile and turned his attention back to the kids.

"Well almost all of them, pal." He pulled his duffel bag from the passenger seat and locked the door before closing it.

"Cool," Jamie said, approvingly.

"I'm ready for some downtime now, guys." This was met with groans of disappointment from the mob. "Come on now. Even deputies need their sleep. Can't expect me to catch all those bad guys without it." He rubbed the scruff of hair on Jamie's head. It was like petting the fur of a wet dog. "Besides, I think your daddy is looking for you."

The siblings looked in the direction of their trailer at the same time. It pained Dale's heart to see the look of dread on their faces. Those faces spoke a thousand words. It took everything that Dale had not to march across the driveway, pull Kyle Collins from his rat nest of a home and beat him senseless.

As if on cue, Collins opened his door and stuck his head out. It was hard to tell in the fading light, but he looked to be well on his way to a good drunk. He was shirtless and his bare torso glistened with sweat, although it was only in the upper sixties.

"There a problem, officer?" His speech was slurred.

"Not unless you want there to be, Kyle."

Collins was a fairly large man with a reputation for having an equally large temper. He stepped out of his doorway and onto the rickety metal steps. He puffed his chest and stared down Dale with a pair of swollen eyes. Those vacant soulless eyes gave Dale the creeps. His hand instinctively rested on the butt of his service Glock. He suddenly regretted his popularity with the children. There was no way he was going to draw on the big man in front of his own kids or anyone else's, even if it would have been the best thing for all of them.

The staring match only lasted a few seconds. Collins ended it with a smirk and a dismissive grunt. He pointed a pair of thick fingers at his children. "You two, get your asses in the house now." He shifted his eyes back to Dale. "Stay away from my kids, boy. Got no business talkin' to them." He held the door open with an outstretched arm. Clara and Jamie scurried up the steps, ducking under it and disappearing inside the trailer. "You want to talk to somebody, you talk to me."

Before Dale could respond the door slammed shut and

the porch light went dark. Most of the other children made themselves scarce during the confrontation. A few stayed to say their goodbyes before running off to seek out the next diversion. He watched them go with a sad mixture of both pity and envy. The world always looked better through the eyes of the young, when they are totally unaware of the monsters that lay just outside the gate.

His duffel was lying on the ground at his feet. He didn't even remember putting it down. It had been a long twelve hours and he still had one more shift to go before getting two days off. He grabbed the bag with one hand and shook his door key from the ring with the other. He gave the Collins trailer one last glance before stepping into his own.

For a forty year old trailer, his was in very good condition. Much to the delight of the park's owner, he had spent a great amount of his own time and money to make it so. It baffled Teddy Vance as much as anyone why Dale chose to live in what was possibly the worst neighborhood in the small town of Cameron. Locals in town often referred to Creekside as the "Ghetto". His salary could have easily afforded him half the homes on the market in town, yet he chose to live there. It was a logic based purely on nostalgia, something that few could begin to understand. Oh well, he thought to himself, let them wonder.

After showering off the day's road dirt and Tassler's aftershave, he fixed a quick meal. A Salisbury steak TV dinner was on the menu for the evening. He was a decent cook by bachelor standards, but rarely took the time to do so. When he was not riding around the county, ignoring his partner's increasingly aggressive mentality, he spent what little his free time he had pursuing his one and only passion.

He had converted the spare bedroom of his old Skyline trailer into darkroom that any amateur photographer would envy. It took a bit of effort to get the room up to snuff. The drafty windows were replaced with Plexiglas in custom made frames, compliments of Stuart Fisher. Stu had become quite the craftsman following his early retirement. The windows were retrofitted with lightproof shutters and, along with the interior door, sealed with foam rubber weather stripping. This prevented the smell of the acetic acid stop bath from permeating the rest of the trailer. Although he did most of his developing at night, he chose to paint the walls and ceiling with a flat black to prevent any reflections from ruining his projects.

It was after midnight by the time he pulled his daily shots from the final rinse and hung them to dry. As he studied the dozens of photos he became increasingly aware of the banging and grunting from the trailer next door. The twenty something couple in the neighboring lot were up to their nightly bump and grind session. Their bedroom, which was less than fifteen feet away, was directly in line with his darkroom. He wondered if they ever considered soundproofing, but doubted that they had the time or energy after their current activity.

He blocked out the distraction and pored over his handiwork, a great shot of a whitetail leaping a rusty woven wire fence and some not so great shots of a hawk in flight. It was hard to get the right angle from the inside of a moving vehicle. The remainder of the photographs were taken during Tassler's unscheduled stop at Virgil Emerson's place. The hiderug sign, random vehicles and a partial shot of Virgil himself.

Dale had managed to capture the shot just as Virgil had let Tassler into his house. At first he had feared that the old hermit had seen him. He just knew that Tassler would come back to the cruiser fuming. He had wracked his brain for a response to the verbal firestorm that would surely follow, but when his partner returned to the car he said nothing. In fact, he seemed to be in better spirits than he had all day.

His cell phone buzzed in his pocket. He pulled it out and looked at the number displayed on the screen. He frowned and stepped out of the darkroom to answer it.

CHAPTER 13

Kori barely had enough time to shower and get in a much needed nap before Brenden pounded on his bedroom door. He sat up stiffly and rubbed his neck. Every fiber in his body ached from the work that he had done earlier. Getting out of bed was a slow and agonizing process. He staggered to the door and opened it.

Brenden poked his head inside. He had a large blue backpack slung over his shoulder. From the look of it, it was stuffed full. "Man, who decorated this place? The boy scouts?"

Kori yawned and sat back down on the bed, his old bed. He looked around the room at the artifacts of his previous life, all sitting neatly in place where he had left them years ago. "Yeah it's a little outdated. Dusty, too."

"Get dressed. We've got somewhere to go."

"Seriously?" He threw himself down on the pillow and groaned. "Don't you ever sleep?"

"There'll be plenty of time to sleep when we're dead." Brenden replied. "Besides, it won't be like last night. Just down the road."

"Just down the road?" Kori asked, suspiciously.

"Yes. And I'll make it worth your while. Trust me." A car honked outside the house. "That's us. Now hurry up and get dressed."

Kori pulled a change of clothes from a suitcase. He had not even had a chance to unpack his belongings yet. Brenden did not tell him where they were going so he had no idea how to dress. It didn't matter anyway. All of his clothes were styled basically the same. He was going to stick out like a sore thumb regardless of what he wore.

Brenden was waiting for him in the yard. Together they climbed into the back of a newer model Corolla with Todd behind the wheel. It was a tight fit for the five of them, but Kori was happy just to be riding in a vehicle that did not reek of dope smoke and piss. It was probably not the kind of car that one would use to cave in the doors of parked cars at a gay bar. That was moderately comforting.

"Damn, looking sharp, buddy." Todd looked back as they

settled in. “The Perv's gonna love you.”

“Who?” Kori looked around nervously.

“Don't worry about it. He's just messing with you,” Brenden assured him. He smacked Todd in the back of the head. “Just drive, smart ass.”

Virgil was standing in the doorway when they pulled up, craning his head out as far as he could without actually stepping outside. He looked past them and scanned the area with a pair of bespectacled eyes too small for his face. He flashed a greasy smile as they piled out of the car. When he saw Kori his smile fell away and he took a few steps backwards. He opened his mouth to say something but Brenden cut him off.

“It's okay, Virgil. He's cool.”

Kori crowded closer to his brother at the base of the porch. The others paid them no mind as they walked past and entered the house. Virgil continued to stare at the interloper with suspicion. It was obvious that the guy had not been informed that he would be coming and he did not like it. The feeling was mutual.

“Look, man. I can go wait in the car if this is going to be a problem,” he whispered to Brenden. He hoped like hell that his brother would agree. Something about Virgil's place made him uneasy. If the inside looked anything like the outside did, he wanted no part of it.

“No. Oh, hell no!” Brenden turned around so fast that he

nearly knocked Kori down with the heavy backpack. Chest muscles that ached before now awoke into a firestorm of pain. Kori doubled over, gasping and trying not to pass out. Brenden roughly pounded on his back, making the pain worse. "Virgil, this is my brother. The one I was telling you about. Kori, this is Virgil."

Kori looked up with tear filled eyes and nodded. Virgil looked down over the top of his glasses and frowned. He was wearing a ratty green terry cloth bathrobe and sandals. From Kori's vantage point he could clearly see that he wore nothing underneath.

For some reason the sight of him reminded Kori of a series of educational videos that Clayton had once commissioned to promote the Trinity church. The videos were written by a committee of whacked out TEFL leaders and produced by low rent ISU film students. They featured lousy acting and even worse costumes. Members of the congregation were left with the unsavory task of irritating their friends and neighbors by subjecting them to scenes filled with overweight hippies in bathrobes portraying biblical characters. The Jews were all played by their Mexican housekeepers.

Virgil was sporting the green John the Baptist look. At the thought of this, Kori began to giggle uncontrollably between gasps for air.

"Is he having some kind of fit or something?" Virgil

stepped out to take a closer look. He peered around Brenden as if he would catch whatever Kori had if he got too close.

"No, he's fine."

"He don't look fine. Is he epileptic or something?"

"I don't think so." Brenden laughed and pulled Kori by the arm. They walked up the steps and entered the house. Virgil anxiously surveyed the perimeter one last time before following them in and locking the door behind him.

The others had already made themselves at home. Chris and Todd were practically melting into the couch while Soup sprawled out on the loveseat with his feet hanging over the end. His elbows pointed up in the air as he rested his head on interlaced fingers. He stared up at the slowly turning ceiling fan and suddenly broke into a set of abdominal crunches. With each retraction his heavy work boots extended beyond the arm of the loveseat, narrowly missing the surface.

"You scuff my leather and I'll replace it with your hide!" Virgil snapped.

Soup stopped in mid-stretch and shot him a cold stare. He stayed frozen in position and pumped his biceps up and down a few times before continuing his workout. After a dozen more reps he sat up, out of breath. He mockingly dusted the arm of the loveseat with the side of his hand. "Chill out, Virgil. How's a guy supposed to stay in shape around here without you getting your panties all up in a bunch?"

Kori thought about telling him that there were no panties to be bunched up, but decided it best to keep quiet. He held his breath to suppress another bout of the giggles.

"In shape?" Virgil scoffed. His voice jumped an octave. "Laying off that crap you stuff up your nose would help."

"Don't start, old man." Soup involuntarily sniffed deeply. Todd and Chris fidgeted nervously and struggled in vain not to do the same. Within a matter of minutes the three of them were sniffling uncontrollably like welfare children in the waiting room of a free clinic.

"Don't any of you start. Let's just get this counted so we can get out of here," Brenden snapped. He unhooked the straps of the backpack and dumped the contents on the living room table. Kori sat speechless as the same bags of pills, white powder and weed that he had seen the night before spilled out. There were also several handguns and vials of drugs that he did not remember seeing. Virgil and Todd sorted the motley array into neatly arranged rows.

"Wow." Virgil said, holding one of the bags of powder up to the light. "Good week."

"Yeah, the Queen was a good score. Otherwise we would have only done half as good." Brenden studied the look on Virgil's face, trying to gauge the values by his reaction. He was a hard one to read. "So, what do you think?"

Virgil stayed silent as he fingered the merchandise. He

picked up the firearms and gave them a quick look over. He stacked the powder and weed aside and focused his attention to the rest. He read the labels on the vials and made a rough count of the pills through the plastic bags. Staring at the ceiling, he did the math while his lips silently mouthed his calculations.

"I can give you five for the powder, three for the blow and two for the tweak. Another two for the grass." He looked at Brenden to make sure he was following along and to judge his reaction to the low-ball figure. "These pills are a mixed bag, you know that. Say fifteen hundred for the lot. And a bill a piece for the revolvers. How's that grab you?"

"Mixed bag?" Brenden picked up one of the larger bags of pills. They were white, crudely rounded tablets with pictures of blue smurfs stamped on one side. He shook the bag in Virgil's face. "There are at least two thousand tabs of X in this bag alone. Gotta be worth at least a buck, maybe two apiece."

Virgil did not appear to be impressed by this. He waved the bag from his face and picked up another one. It was slightly smaller than the first and filled with yellow pills, the same as the pill that was stuck to the bottom of Joe Woodson's pop earlier that morning. He gave the bag a toss to Brenden, who made no effort to catch it. The bag bounced off his thigh and landed at Kori's feet.

"I'm a business man, not a fucking pharmacist. I don't even know what the hell these things are supposed to be." He lit a cigarette with shaking hands. “How do you suggest that I find out? Go to the drug store and pass out samples?”

Brenden sighed and stared at the bag in silence. He had no clue what the pills were either, but he did know one thing. Virgil was getting nervous. This was either going to work in their favor or the old hermit was going to tighten his purse strings and not pay out shit. He bent pick up the bag but Kori snatched it up and studied the contents.

“Diazepam.”

“Excuse me?” Virgil asked, slightly agitated.

“That's what these are, Diazepam.” Kori shook the bag and bounced it in the palm of his hand. “Same thing as Valium, only a different manufacturer. You know, generic.” He became uncomfortably aware that everyone was staring at him. Brenden had warned him on the way over to keep his mouth shut at Virgil's. He sat the bag back on the table and suddenly wished that he had listened.

Chris spoke up. “Dude, do you mind? We're trying to do some business here.”

“No. Let him talk.” Virgil dismissed the interruption with a wave of his hand. He was now looking at Kori with a new found interest. He still didn't trust him. He was too clean cut to be running with this bunch. He did not fit in and that always presented problems with crews like this. He had seen it happen before. However, the kid had smarts and that could be a useful thing. Useful made money. "Tell me more."

"What do you want to know?" Kori tried to ignore the cold stare that Chris was giving him, a looked that could only be construed as jealous loathing. The rest of the group was listening intently.

"Do they get you high?"

"Sure they will. Like I said, they're exactly like Valium. They're just generic."

"How do you know this?" Virgil asked warily. "You a doctor?" He pointed his thumb at Kori and looked at Brenden. "You didn't tell me your brother was Doogie Howser, M.D." He laughed at his own joke and slapped Kori on the knee, letting his hand linger for a few uncomfortable seconds. "Seriously, how do you know this?"

"Um... I used to work for a veterinarian. They wrote scripts for that stuff all the time for dogs."

"Dogs?" Virgil hollered and threw his hands in the air. "You're trying to sell me dog pills?"

Chris smirked and rolled his eyes in disgust.

"They're a crossover drug," Kori explained. He read the look of uncertainty on everyone's faces and tried to lay it out in terms that they could relate to. "They use a lot of the same drugs for humans and animals. Where do you think PCP came from? Or special K? Trust me, I know. People will buy that stuff and ask for more."

"Alright!" Virgil conceded, knowing that any home field advantage in the negotiation had fallen apart as soon as the new kid opened his mouth. "I'll give you nine for everything."

"Twelve," Brenden countered.

"Ten?"

"Twelve. No less," Brenden picked up the backpack as if he meant to load the drugs back into it and walk out if Virgil dared to make another counteroffer. He had no intentions of leaving with anything other than cash. Holding the dope was almost as risky as getting it in the first place and having it in the house always put him on edge. The last thing he wanted was to wind up a paranoid recluse like Virgil, but he was not about to let the fat bald bastard just take it for pennies on the dollar either. He would easily resell it for five times the asking price and they both knew it.

"Deal," Virgil said as if it pained him to do so. "I'll go get the Jacksons."

It had been long ago agreed upon that twenties were the only acceptable form of payment. Too many eyebrows were raised at banks and local businesses when one of them made a deposit or paid for a pack of Marlboros with a hundred dollar bill. It also made it easier to split the money on payday.

With the transaction completed, everyone seemed anxious to forgo the small talk and get out of there. Kori came to the realization that he was not the only one who Virgil gave the creeps. Virgil reluctantly handed over the dozen banded stacks of bills and everyone jumped to their feet.

Chris intentionally clipped Kori with his shoulder as he passed by, sending another flurry of pain through his body. "Sorry about that," he said, sneering. He began to undo the locks on the front door when Virgil spoke up.

"Aren't you forgetting something, little man?" Virgil tapped him on the shoulder with a thin envelope before he could get the last lock undone. Chris took it and started to put it in his pocket. Suddenly his smile widened and he handed the envelope to Kori, who reflexively took it without thinking.

"New guy is the grocery getter now." He defiantly looked to Brenden. "Only seems right."

Brenden shouldered the backpack and nodded. "Seems about right. Sorry Bro, looks like you're on grocery detail now." He pointed to the stacks of pills on the table. "Besides, you and Virge have a few things to talk about later."

Virgil perked up at the suggestion and winked at Kori. "Yes, we do." Kori felt hot bile creeping up in the back of his throat and shivered. Virgil did not seem to notice. He just smiled and bounced his hairy eyebrows up and down over the frame of his glasses.

"Later, Virgil." Brenden called out. On his way past Chris he shoulder-checked him in the back, nearly knocking him down. "Sorry about that." He turned back and winked at his little brother, who was too creeped out by Virgil to appreciate the gesture.

"Oh, Brenden, one more thing." Virgil followed him outside and handed him a slip of paper. "This needs to be taken care of tonight."

"Tonight? What happened to next week?" He held the paper close to his face, straining to read it in the dim light. An Iowa City address was written in Virgil's shaky script. Closer to downtown than he would have preferred. Downtown meant students and that meant dealing with marks who were either too drunk or too stupid to be intimidated for their own good. It also meant more cops.

"They made the buy earlier than expected." Virgil shrugged. "What can I say? Who knew a bunch of college brats could come up with that kind of scratch on such short notice. All I know is that the pound that they got is getting lighter as we speak. Best to take it back while there's still something left to get."

Brenden stared at the address for a few minutes before saying anything. He shook his head from side to side and rubbed the stubble on his chin. "Nice if you let me know a little sooner, Virge." He pointed to the guys waiting impatiently in Todd's Corolla "I mean, goddamn. I got one guy who ain't completely spun over there and he don't know jack shit yet."

Virgil threw his hands up. "I just found out about this

right before you guys got here, Brenden. What do you want me to do?" He started for the door and called out without looking back. "Get it done tonight, Brenden. Call me tomorrow."

Brenden watched Virgil walk into his house and close the door behind him. The porch light went out and he was left in the darkness. Crickets chirped in the grass beneath his feet, keeping in time with the pulse that throbbed in his head. "Shit." he mumbled to no one but himself and the insects. Now he had to break the news to the guys.

CHAPTER 14

They made a quick stop to stash the money in Joe Woodson's shed. Splitting it would have to wait until this job was done and taking it with them was too risky. If anything went wrong, there was no point in losing twelve grand in the process. It was early and their father was still awake, presumably eating ice cream and watching reruns. Brenden hid the backpack safely behind a heaping pile of empty feed sacks.

"So let me get this straight. He sold these guys some drugs and now we are supposed to go steal them back?" Kori leaned forward to ask his brother, who rode in the front, leaving him sandwiched between the dueling body odors of the Campbell cousins.

"Man, why do you have to ask so many stupid questions?" Chris piped up. "And what was that shit back there at Virgil's, anyway? Fucking know-it-all bullshit."

Brenden switched the stereo off and turned around in his seat. "That know-it-all bullshit made us two grand more than we would have gotten. If you got a problem with that, get it out now before we get there."

Chris said nothing. He stared out the window with a dour look on his pimple scarred face. Brenden looked around the car, daring anyone else to chime in. Nothing.

"I didn't think so. So shut the fuck up and chill out." He settled back in his seat and turned the stereo back on. "We're pullin' double time tonight, boys."

Everyone maintained their silence as the highway hummed beneath the small car tires, lulling them into a comfortable stupor. They were not holding and the car was legally up to snuff. This allowed them to make the trek via the main roads. As long as Todd kept his eyes peeled for the occasional deer crossing the pavement they would be rolling back into Iowa City shortly.

Brenden studied Chris in the mirror. He could sense the frustration growing by the minute. They were all tired and irritable, but the little guy had it the worst. Kori's arrival had upset the dynamics of the crew and Chris was feeling it the most. He was already bottom of the pack and now he was afraid that the top had just gotten higher. It was something that they would have to deal with soon.

He knew that he would have to take special care to harness some of that angst and use it to their advantage. They were heading into unknown territory. A couple of college guys with access to enough capital to get their hands on a pound of cocaine. They may very well be a bunch of crunchy granola types like Virgil claimed, but they were twenty something college kids nonetheless. It was not going to be like rolling a kid or some drag queen. These marks would most likely not go down without a fight.

He yawned and stuck his arm out the window to let the late September air cool his flesh. Todd drove cautiously down the street, affording him an opportunity to take in the local scenery. The fall term had just begun at the university, but there were no students around. At least not in this part of town. They were still a good twenty blocks from the downtown scene. The only thing this part of town had to offer was the occasional gas station or store salted in amongst the lower income property rentals.

They passed a grocery store and a small group of black guys eyes them hostilely. They were young, probably in their late teens. One of them was pushing a shopping cart down the sidewalk. He yelled at Brenden for staring, who promptly responded by giving him the finger. The kid aimed the shopping cart in their direction and gave it a shove. Its wheels faltered on the uneven concrete and the cart toppled in the street, well short of its target. The teens whooped and danced around in unison, returning with gestures of their own.

"What the fuck? Pull over, man!" Soup shouted. "I'm

gonna shove that cart up that monkey's ass."

Todd gripped the wheel tightly and looked in the mirror. "I feel a hate crime coming on." He took his foot off of the accelerator and the car slowed down. The black kids interpreted that as a challenge and started toward them at a quick pace. Todd gripped the wheel tightly and looked in the mirror.

Chris giggled nervously.

"Don't even think about it." Brenden gave the order in a calm but authoritative tone. Soup, who already had a hand on the door latch, eased back in his seat like a dog ordered to heel. The black kids were getting closer and brasher with every step. Brenden slapped Todd on the arm with the back of his wrist. "Go!"

The front wheels gave a weak chirp and the car lunged forward, jarring all of them against their seats. Racial slurs were exchanged between Soup and the teens as a glass bottle arced through the air, exploding a few feet behind them. This inspired another fit of mindless dancing from the blacks accompanied by more obligatory name calling. They made the green light at the end of the block and left the small mob behind.

"I can't believe you, Bren!" Soup's face was beet red. "Those motherfuckers think they own this place. It's because everybody just stands back and lets them do whatever they want. " He looked through the back window and pounded on the seat. "Goddammit!"

“What do you care? You don't live here. Let 'em have it.”

“Whatever, man.” Soup replied throwing his hands up in disgust.

“Yeah, whatever,” Brenden said. He had better things to worry about than who was keeping the natives in line. He stared out of his window, trying to make out the numbers on the houses. It was comforting to know that at least one of his weary troops was finally getting into battle mode.

They approached the house after a heated debate on where to park. The finally agreed on a spot around the corner and two blocks down. Johnson Street was lined on both sides with apartments and teeming with students. Everyone was too busy partying to notice five guys wearing gloves and carrying ski masks. They were just another group of revelers out on the town.

Cars indiscriminately passed by them in every direction. Most of them were packed full of teenagers, violating the night air with overpowering bass rhythms. Raucous cheers poured from the windows along with an occasional empty beer can. Brenden was relieved by the absence of a police presence. It was still early by downtown standards and most of the uniformed cops were likely scouring the bars for underage drinkers. Good, he thought. Let's get this done and get out of Dodge.

It was not hard to find the house even though the porch light was not illuminated. They just followed the numbers down from the neighboring houses. It was a large two story Victorian with a porch that spanned the entire length of the front. Only a couple of windows showed light and Brenden considered the possibility that no one was home. The whole trip was starting to look like a waste of their time.

"Can I help you with something?" someone called out from the darkness. They jumped and fumbled with their masks, which they had not bothered to put on yet. The plan was for one of them to ring the bell and ask for Brad, the rich beatnik that Virgil's people had previously sold the quantity to. Then they would rush the greeter, control any other occupants and take back the dope. Of course the unseen source of the voice had thrown a slight wrench in that approach.

"Uh... yeah." Forced to ad lib, Brenden climbed the steps toward the voice. The others stayed down on the sidewalk. "Is Brad here? He told us we could stop by." He hoped to hell that this was not Brad he was talking to.

A lanky bearded guy was sprawled out on a threadbare couch next to the front door. He held his hands behind his head with his elbows propped up in the air. Between his legs rested a ridiculously large bong. The base of it was nestled in the crook of his crossed ankles. A neatly braided ponytail draped over his shoulder and across his bare chest.

"Brad's here, but he's not up for company right now. You need something, go down to the Deadwood and get it from Larry. You do know Larry, right?" There was a hint of dismissive arrogance in his voice that was beginning to piss Brenden off.

"Come on, dude. Isn't there anyway you could get Brad to help us out. Just a couple of grams. We were just heading out of town and we really don't want to fuck around trying to find a parking spot downtown. You know what I mean?" Brenden stepped a few feet closer.

The lanky guy shrugged his narrow shoulders and bent over the bong. He placed his mouth over the opening and mumbled, "Not my problem. Man." Water bubbled from the base of the monstrous apparatus and a flame danced over the tightly packed bowl.

"Wrong answer." Brenden responded with a straight gloved fist that caught the lanky guy's forehead. The force of the blow was enough to scoot the couch back a few inches. The legs of the outdated couch screeched against the wooden porch floor. The guy's head pivoted loosely on his neck and he let the bong slip from his hands. Brenden caught it before it landed and swung viciously at the guy's head. Bong water erupted from the opening, drenching them both. Embers from the bowl peppered the side of the lanky guy's face as he slumped over the arm of the couch. The rancid water extinguished most of the sparks on contact, except for a large red chunk that landed in the guy's ear. It smoked as it slowly died out, burning into the flesh.

"That's gonna leave a mark." Todd rushed the steps,

followed closely by the others.

They all donned masks except Kori, who stood wide eyed at the top step. He stared at the motionless man on the couch. He had never seen a dead body before, but was certain that he was looking at one now. A ringing started in his ears from way off in the distance. It grew steadily stronger with each beat of his pulse. He felt as if he was going to pass out.

Brenden slapped him on the back of the head, jolting him back to reality. He pulled the mask from Kori's back pocket and thrust it in his face. "Put this on and watch the door. Don't let anyone out." He motioned to body slumped on the couch as he followed the others inside. "And watch him."

Kori's legs trembled as he stood in the doorway and listened. The yelling started, followed by sounds of breaking glass and screaming from rooms beyond his view. Heavy footsteps pounded wooden floors and the unmistakable meaty smack of fists meeting skin. His eyes darted from the foyer to the couch and back. The lanky guy started to moan as he came to.

Kori panicked. He looked around and picked up the first thing that resembled a weapon, the bong. He tested the weight of it in his hands, shocked by how heavy it was at the base. It was a thousand wonders that the blow from it didn't kill the poor bastard. He held it over the couch and prepared to strike if the guy sat up, although he doubted that he could actually do it. Residual bong sledge flowed in a dirty brown stream down his forearm. He kept telling himself that this would be over soon.

Out of nowhere a hoarse cry erupted from the foyer, accompanied by the patter of bare feet on the wooden floor. Over his shoulder he saw a short husky man, with an uncanny resemblance to a hobbit, running straight for the doorway. His arms pumped like those of an Olympic sprinter. In one hand he carried a large briefcase by the handle. It swung heavily with each stride, alternately slapping against his arm and thigh.

Without thinking, Kori swung the bong in a deep lopping chop as the hobbit crossed the threshold. The base connected flush with the hobbit's jawbone, which was opened in mid scream. His stocky body dropped but momentum carried him several feet onto the porch. The briefcase was caught halfway underneath his belly with his hand stuck firmly in the handle. A wet mewling sound rose from his bloody mouth as his breathing was reduced to a series of faint gurgles.

The hobbit turned out to be the Brad they were looking for. By the time Brenden and Todd reached the foyer, the lanky guy had come to and was cradling Brad's limp body in his arms. "Brad? Oh, god. Oh, god. Oh, god." He was weeping either because he really liked Brad or the blows to his head had really taken a toll. Tears streamed down his bare chest, washing trails in the smears of blood coming from Brad's mouth. He looked up in time to see the laces of Todd's boot glide toward his own face. He was out once again, this time lying awkwardly across his friend's barrel chest.

Todd lifted him enough for Brenden to pry the briefcase out from under them. He opened it and studied the contents in the light of the hall. The sounds of punches landing continued in the background. Each one was accompanied by labored exhales, like someone hitting a heavy bag at the gym. Soup's voice echoed through the house, carrying with it a string of indiscernible profanities.

“Let's go, Ladies!” Brenden yelled through the doorway.

Soup and Chris appeared a few minutes later. Soup was completely out of breath and grinning wildly beneath his ski mask. His eyes were wide and his pupils dilated from adrenaline. Chris had created a makeshift sack out of a large white sweatshirt. The shirt was stuffed to the seams with various items, the spoils of war. Kori noticed right away that the shirt did not belong to Chris and that it was soaked with blood.

CHAPTER 15

Butch Tassler chewed on an unlit cigar and watched his partner pull out of the courthouse parking lot. He leaned against the patrol car and fumbled for a light. Dale always made it a big deal if he even considered lighting up inside the county vehicle. Damn kid was a stickler for the rules, just one item in a long list of reasons to despise him.

How Butch felt about Dale was no secret. He made it a point for it not to be. The other deputies all took a liking to the kid from day one. That was all fine, but they weren't the one riding with him. He lit up and pined for the good old days when he rode alone, before he was stuck with some camera happy newbie, whose primary goal in life was to bore him with policies and procedures.

It was pointless to complain to Whitey Baylor. That sorry excuse for a sheriff had his head stuck too far up the county attorney's rectum to give a shit about what went on in the field. Stu Fisher gets his ass handed to him by a couple of degenerates and everyone gets partnered up. Then Whitey, who should have retired two terms ago, had the gall to let the deputies pick who they wanted to be paired with? Of course nobody was going to pick Butch. No one wanted the only one on the force with a brain making them look bad.

So he found himself spending twelve miserable hours a shift babysitting the department mascot. The guy didn't hunt or fish and he hated smoking. The only thing that Dale showed any interest in was pointing that damned camera at everything. He wished someone would show him where in the holy handbook that said that was within policy. The kid probably never got laid either. Butch could not recall one time since wonderboy had made his illustrious appearance that he had seen him within twenty feet of a woman.

Damn snot nose probably thought he was too good for them. Like he forgot exactly where he had come from. Well, Butch never forgot. He remembered when Dale was just another lowlife piece of trailer trash from Cameron, living hand to mouth with that hot ass mother of his.

She was a real looker, that one. Seemed a little too good for everyone, just like her boy does now. Butch had entertained the idea of nailing her to the mattress once or twice, back in the day. He might have stood a chance if it wasn't for Stu Fisher always sniffing around after her old man died. Naturally, Butch was the only one with enough sense to notice. Everyone else had

Stu pegged as a saint.

One good thing about Dale was his choice of residence. For some reason he had it in his mind to move back to that dump where he had grown up. Trash always blew back to where it was first thrown out, Butch reckoned. Cop cars tended to get themselves vandalized when parked in shitholes like Creekside. At least Whitey had enough activity left in that pickled old brain of his to insist that Dale either move or let Butch take his turns driving the patrol car home. Damned if the idiot kid didn't choose living in the ghetto over free gas and use of a county vehicle.

It felt liberating to ride alone. Now he could do a few necessaries that could not be done under the watchful eye of Whitey's pet. First on the list was to cruise by his ex-wife's place on the way home. Technically the house in Cedar Ridge was still in his name, but a restraining order prevented him from actually entering it. Some spineless empathetic judge had the nerve to decide that he, a decorated officer of the law, could no longer set foot in his own home. A home that his own father had built. It was just par for the course, Butch knew. They always took up for the woman, didn't they?

Now his ex was shacked up with some punk ten years her junior. Some grease monkey from Tipton was running his dirty dick across bed sheets that Butch worked to pay for. It made his stomach churn just thinking about it. He promised himself that one day he would catch the little shit alone and break his jaw for him.

The first year of the separation, before the imminent divorce that followed, he found himself with his head in a bottle and his nose in a bible. These days he mostly just drank, leaving the god stuff to the true believers. One verse did stick with him, though. It rang in his head like a Balinese gong each time he drove near his former home. "If a man is found lying with a married woman, then both of them shall die. The man who lay with the woman, and the woman; thus you shall purge the evil from Israel." Well, he thought to himself, the Ridge was a far cry from Israel but he would see those two dead if it was the last thing he did.

He rounded the last corner and turned into the drive. The boyfriend was turning wrenches under the hood of a Chevy pickup when he looked to see who was pulling into the lane. The truck was parked in the middle of the lawn. It was beyond Butch's comprehension why the fool would junk up the yard with car parts when there was a perfectly good garage to work in. A garage that he had built himself just five summers ago.

As soon as he recognized the vehicle, the boyfriend wiped his hands on a greasy rag and hightailed it for the house. It gave Butch some satisfaction to see that he could still terrorize the man who had stolen his wife. It would have been more satisfying to step on the gas and mow him down with the deer guard on the patrol car's grill. One can only dream, he thought as he backed out to the road.

With that bit of business out of the way he dejectedly anticipated another two days of lonely binge drinking. It was too early to dust off the hunting gear and he had no desire to spend a depressing evening in a tavern. The locals that frequented Schroeder's Tap were not much for conversation. The majority of them avoided him like the clap anyhow. Even out of uniform, to a drunk, he was still a cop. When he bellied up to the bar half the patrons hit the door. The other half kept their faces down and drank in uncomfortable silence. He could feel Johnny Schroeder cringe every time he walked in, even if he was a heavy spender.

Even the idea of swinging by Virgil's and shaking him down for another gram of marching powder was out. The old pervert lived just a mile from his ex, but a short detour on the way out proved fruitless when he spotted Joe Woodson's piece of shit truck parked in the driveway. Now what the hell business would that old drunk have with Virgil? Oh well, not his business. With a sigh, he turned the patrol car in the direction of the main highway. It looked like it was going to be another Crown Royal night after all.

Just when things were at their bleakest, a shining ray of hope came along in the form of a silver Chevy Cobalt. He met the car at the crest of a hill as it sped by him in the opposite direction. His eyes met the driver's for a brief moment and the look of terror on that face made his heart swell. He glanced in the rear view long enough to see the brake lights flash. Too late, baby. He flipped on his lights and spun the cruiser around, hardly able to contain his delight.

Butch approached the driver's side with his thumb hooked over his holster. He drew his nightstick with a deliberately exaggerated slowness and tapped on the window. The glass retracted to reveal a blubbering teenage girl inside. She was sobbing so violently that her chest heaved with each tiny involuntary gasp. Tears streamed from her long lashed eyes and mingled with the snot that escaped her nose as she exhaled.

“What?” was all that she could manage to say. Her hands clutched the steering wheel as she stared ahead, refusing to look at him.

“Running a bit late from practice tonight aren't you, Carissa?” He placed his hands on the door and poked his head through the opening. His face was close enough that she could smell the odor of cigar on his breath. She nodded timidly and backed away. The strand of snotty tears slid back up her nose as she inhaled. How attractive, he thought to himself. “Why don't we step back to my car, huh?”

“Why?” Her sobbing escalated. She focused on the distant horizon, hoping for another motorist to pop over the hill. A potential witness to interrupt the encounter. Someone to make Tassler nervous enough to just send her on her way. She desperately prayed that her parents would come looking for her. After all, she was almost two hours late coming home. It was unlikely, though. They had never questioned her tardiness before.

Perhaps her boyfriend was feeling guilty about the argument that they had after practice. Could Jake feel so bad that he was compelled to follow her home and apologize for all the mean things that he had said? That was even more unlikely to happen than her folks showing up. No one was going to come to her rescue. She looked at him and tearfully repeated herself. "Why?"

"Because I fucking said so!" he snapped. He stepped back and his hand once again rested on his holster. His eyes narrowed and he nodded back to his patrol car. She complied, walking slowly back with him. He opened the front passenger door. She hesitated for a moment, looking at him with pleading watery eyes. He was not moved. He slammed the door behind her, locking her in as he walked back to her car.

Carissa Abbey watched helplessly as the policeman rifled through her vehicle in search of something she did not have. He dumped the contents of her purse on the seat and sifted through them. He opened the console and repeated the process. She shook her head and reminded herself to stay calm. Then he lifted her gym bag from the backseat and pulled all of her clothing out. He held up a pair of panties from the bag and flashed a devious grin in her direction. Her fear suddenly morphed into anger.

"You sonofabitch!" she screamed so loudly that it made her own ears hurt. She kicked madly at the floorboard and repeated herself. He threw the bag onto the seat and walked back to his car.

"Say something, sweetheart?" he asked as he climbed behind the wheel. His large body crowded hers as he shut the door. He tossed the panties on his dashboard. They were red satin with flowered lace trim, a gift from Jake for their six month anniversary.

"No." She stared at the panties and felt a wave of nausea run through her body.

"I didn't think so." He placed his hand on the back of her neck and squeezed hard enough to hurt just a little. He picked up the panties with his other hand and rubbed them on his cheek. He stuck them in her face and she tried to pull away. "Mind if I keep these?" She did not answer so he increased his grip, making her cry out in pain. "Huh?"

"No," she whimpered. Fear trumped anger once again. "You can have them."

"Thanks." He laughed and tossed the panties aside. His eyes grew dark enough to match his mood as he pulled her close. Carissa held her breath to block out the rank tobacco smell, but it was no use. He licked the drying tears from her cheek and whispered in her ear. "What else you got?"

"Butch, I don't want to do this. Please."

He reached in his breast pocket and produced a glass vial. Inside it was a small amount of white powder. He shoved it in her face. "Mommy and Daddy are gonna be hurt really bad when they find out their little princess got caught with this after practice. And what's that dyke coach of yours gonna say? You think they let felons keep basketball scholarships?"

The tiny amount in the vial did not come remotely close to felony criteria, but she did not know that. How would she? The girl had never touched so much as a cigarette in her life, let alone methamphetamine. To her that little bit of white dust might as well have weighed as much as the world itself. With it, he could ruin her life.

He unzipped his fly with one hand, still gripping her by the back of the neck. A weak moan escaped her throat as she steeled herself for the inevitable. She knew the routine. This was the third time that Butch had pulled her over that month. It was a cycle that had started in her junior year and played out like a bad reoccurring dream. As soon as word of her scholarship hit the newspapers, he was on her like a vulture ready to pick her bones clean.

One more semester, she thought to herself. That's all I have to get through. Then she would go off to college and forget that this had ever happened. Then she would never set foot in this rotten county ever again.

"Now quit stalling. I want to get home before dark!"

She closed her eyes let him push her head toward his lap. She tried to let her mind go and find that dark safe place in the far recesses of her subconscious. Before she fully separated her mind from her soon to be violated body, Carissa retracted all of the prayers that she had made earlier. She hoped to God that no one came over that hill and saw her.

CHAPTER 16

Kori felt that old familiar pang of fear churning in his gut as he parked his father's truck in Virgil's yard. Joe's truck was a beat up rust bucket with an exhaust riddled with holes. Virgil heard him coming from a mile away and was waiting for him on the porch. He was wearing the same ratty housecoat, leaving Kori to wonder if that was the only thing that he ever wore. He hoped that he would not have to spend enough time there to find out.

Virgil nervously looked around and held the front door open as Kori lifted the groceries from the truck bed. He made no attempt to help other than pointing the way to the kitchen. As soon as the last of the bags were inside Virgil locked the door behind them. He quickly put the perishables away and left the rest sitting on the linoleum floor. He offered Kori a seat in the living room.

Staying for small talk was the last thing Kori had in mind, but it seemed impolite to decline. He sat as far to one end of the couch as he could, hoping that Virgil would take the recliner. Virgil plopped down in the middle and crossed one leg over the other one. His bare foot came within inches of touching Kori's arm. Kori tried to hide his repulsion as he awkwardly repositioned himself. Virgil uncrossed his legs and his robe parted just below the belt line. A wrinkly testicle peeked out from the gap in the cloth and Kori quickly looked away. The smile never left Virgil's face.

"So," Virgil started. "First things first. Ready to give it up?"

"Huh?" Kori felt his lunch going into spin cycle. He wondered how fast he could manage the locks on the door.

"My EBT card. Little Chris did give it to you, I assume." Virgil stuck his palm out and waved his fingers in a come hither motion. Kori fished the card out with such a sense of relief that he felt like crying.

Virgil slipped the card in a pocket of the robe. He noticed his exposed nether region and sat up slowly. He showed no sign of embarrassment, just mild disinterest. He snatched a smoke from a pack on the table and lit it, never taking his eyes off of Kori. He took a drag and blew smoke from the side of his pursed lips. "Your brother tells me that you went to Iowa State. That how you know so much about those pills?"

Kori nodded. "I went for a couple of years."

"Why'd you quit?"

"Long story." Kori could tell by the look on his face that it was a rhetorical question. He wondered just how much Brenden had told him.

The smile on Virgil's face changed slightly, evolving in a way. "Know anything about agriculture. Growing things, I mean?"

"Not really."

"A couple of years at Moo U and you never took a botany class?"

"I was studying to be a veterinarian not a farmer." Kori was starting to become irritated. Despite his recent expulsion, he still harbored a sense of loyalty to his Alma mater. The misconception that ISU was a farmer school was a sore subject with him. He was not a damn farmer.

"Too bad." Virgil frowned and snuffed his cigarette out. He stood up and disappeared down the hallway, calling behind him as he went. "I've got something else that you might be able to help me with." Kori waited anxiously as the sounds of banging doors and boxes sliding across floorboards echoed from a distant room. He glanced at the cushion where Virgil had been sitting, wondering how many other parts of the couch his balls had touched. He forced the thought from his mind and hoped that it would all be over soon.

When the guys had delegated him to be the hermit's new grocery getter, they never mentioned that he would be expected to entertain the nasty bastard all night. He silently cursed his brother for getting him into this mess. He cursed Chris for pulling his so called rank and pawning his duties onto the new guy. Most of all he cursed his mother for abandoning him like some unwanted mutt, while she and Clayton were chumming it up with the locals in some other backwoods inbred part of the country. He could not wait until this nightmarish three months was over.

"Here we go," Virgil said, breaking the turbulent monologue playing out in Kori's head. He poured the contents of a paper grocery sack onto the table. Drugs of all kinds and forms covered the glass top. "You were dead on with that Diazatram stuff. I've got a couple pain clinic managers from the South drooling over the whole lot. Gonna come out real good, thanks to you."

"Diazepam," Kori corrected him, watching with wonder as practically every square inch of the table was covered with pharmaceuticals.

Virgil stopped and shot him an annoyed look. "Yeah, whatever. Can you tell me what any of this other shit is? Or better yet, where I can unload it? I'll make it worth your while, kid."

Kori did the math and pondered the possibilities, dollar signs flashing in his head. His entire year of tuition would have been locked up tight if he had his hands on that much inventory when he still lived in Des Moines. By the time Clayton and his mother came to rescue him in three months, he could have enough money to enroll for classes again. No more peddling feel good pills to bored housewives. No more juicers calling him up at three in the morning, looking to compensate for their tiny penises and fragile egos.

After this deal he was done. He could focus on school without worrying about paying for it. That was if the university would have him back. No sense in stressing over that though. He would leave that up to Clayton and Dr. Ross. It would take a lot of ass kissing on his part, but never again would he have to worry about tuition.

"Just how much of this stuff do you have?"

Virgil picked up a random vial and squinted to read the fine print. He shrugged and let the vial roll from his palm and back onto the table. "I don't know. Five, maybe six more bags like this."

Kori stared at him in disbelief. He did not see that one coming. Hell, he was going to make it all the way to grad school without sweating tuition. "Virgil, my friend, not only do I know what most of this stuff is, I know exactly where I can get rid of it for you."

"How soon?"

"As soon as I can get a way to Des Moines," he replied. "Can I borrow your van?"

"Not a chance," Virgil looked sternly over the top of his glasses. "And don't go asking your brother either. Best to keep this little arrangement to ourselves. Less ways to split the profits, the better. You know what I mean?"

"Yeah, sure. Whatever," Kori agreed, disappointed about the van. "Just between us then. By the way, what's in it for me? Fifty-fifty split?" It was a ballsy suggestion, but it never hurt to ask.

Virgil eyed him from over his glasses and scooped the motley assortment back into the paper bag. Kori cringed as the glass containers clacked roughly together. "Yeah, why not. I'm feeling generous. Besides, you're doing all of the legwork."

"Sweet. I'll stop back tomorrow after I figure out my ride." Kori could not believe his sudden stroke of good luck. He got up to leave before Virgil changed his mind, but when he reached for the deadbolt a hand slid over the top of his. The sweaty feel of it sent shivers down his back. Here we go, he thought. The old freak is gonna get all scoutmaster on me now.

"Just don't screw me over on this, okay? Because I will not hesitate to kill you if you do." Virgil's smile remained, but evolved once again. The look in his eyes told Kori that he had every intention of making good on that threat, if given a reason.

CHAPTER 17

It took less than five minutes to talk Todd into giving him a ride to Des Moines. It was not the promise of an easy thousand dollars, but an opportunity to break the monotony of another boring day in the Ridge that appealed to him. Todd had more money squirreled away than he knew what to do with. He had been rolling dealers for fun and profit for a long time. Getting him to agree to keep the plan hidden from the others took a little more convincing.

“It's not like we're going there to roll a bunch of drug dealers.” Kori said as he stuffed the bags into the Corolla's trunk. “Besides, everybody’s already been paid for the stuff we're taking up. We're not stepping on anybody's dick here, man. We do this and those guys benefit, too. They just don't know it yet.”

Todd raised his eyes and looked at him doubtfully.

“Think about it. If Virgil sees bank to be made from this run, he's going to be more willing to buy more of the same later on. Everybody wins."

"Alright. I'm down with that, but what do we tell Brenden? If he asks, I mean."

"I told him that I wanted to get some more of my stuff. Which I do, by the way. So you were gonna give me a ride home," Kori replied. It felt strange, referring to Des Moines as home. At one point in his life, the Ridge was the only home that he knew. Then the big city became his home. Now that seemingly simple word did not fit either location. A lonely sense of desperation came over him as he climbed into the passenger seat.

They left at noon, allowing them ample time for the two hour trip plus time to spare before their first stop. He had arranged three separate meetings by phone the night before. Most of the contacts he had during his short lived enterprise were excited to hear from him. Three of them agreed to meet with him, eager to fill the void that he had left after his sudden departure. Several wondered why he wasn't still in jail and got spooked when he called. One even threatened to "kill his narc ass" if he showed his face anywhere near them.

The reality of the situation put a damper on the prospect of earning some very fast cash. He was so nervous that he almost called the whole thing off. The idea of getting caught again, this time without Clayton or his mother to bail him out, terrified him. The pressure of the promises of big money that he made to Virgil also weighed heavily on his mind. But the thing that scared him the most was the thought of going back home.

It would all be waiting for him when he got there. The neighbors, not yet bored with regurgitated rumors of the preacher's wayward stepson. The busy bodies with their noses pressed to the window. Even some of his former customers would all be buzzing with new tales to tell after he rolled back into town. His biggest worry was with the handful of Trinity members that did not make the trip with Clayton. The last thing he needed was one of them getting on the phone and alerting his stepfather that he was back at the house. There would most likely be hell to pay, just for collecting a few of his own belongings.

Todd was uncharacteristically reserved at the beginning of the trip. At first Kori interpreted the quiet demeanor as nothing more than Todd being strung out from the crank. He had seen Little Chris get like that a lot. He quickly realized that Todd was just being himself for once. With no audience to entertain, the constant jokes were replaced with meaningful conversation. Before long they both let their loosened up and enjoyed the ride.

They passed the time by talking about things that neither of them would possibly be able to discuss with the others. They discovered that they shared similar taste in books and music. Kori never imagined that he would meet another person who held both Chuck Palahniuk and Vonnegut in the same regard. As the miles behind them accumulated, the conversation digressed to the years before Kori moved away.

"Remember that time on the I-80 Bridge?" Todd asked. He spoke of it as though he were remembering one of the fondest moments of his life.

Kori laughed and said he did. He remembered it well.

He was about twelve when it happened. Todd, who was almost a year older but in the same grade in school, would have been thirteen. It was toward the end of the summer before their first year in junior high. The unincorporated berg of Cedar Ridge had little to offer two adolescent boys in the way of entertainment. Every other diversion from the mundane had been exhausted weeks ago. That day they had only their bicycles, an empty ice cream bucket and the entire day to waste.

For some unexplainable reason Todd picked up a stick and poked it into a pile of dog crap in the grass behind the Woodson's garage. It was something only an immature and extremely bored thirteen year old boy would be compelled to do. He proceeded to chase Kori around the yard, threatening to brand him with his smellier version of the mark of Zorro. Another stick was drawn and another dog pile was disturbed. Fortunately for the both of them a truce was declared before either of them landed a direct hit.

They spent the better part of the next hour, also for reasons unbeknownst to them, filling the bucket from the unlimited supply of dog waste in the neighborhood. Then with half a bucket of dog shit and the rest of the afternoon to kill, the two boys peddled their bikes toward the interstate.

It was a good three mile ride to I-80. They regularly made the trip, sans bucket-o-poop, whenever they had a few dollars to spare and a lapse in parental supervision. The latter came more frequently than the former in those days. The KOA motor camp behind the truck stop was just the thing to feed a bored young soul. A few dollars lasted quite a while in the beat up arcade games that lined the back wall of the camp office.

They never made it to the game room that day. It was a blistering afternoon and even young men have their limitations. As they reached the bridge Todd pulled over and carefully leaned his bike on the guardrail, minding not to spill the rancid cargo that they reluctantly took turns balancing on their handlebars for nearly three miles.

"I can't do it anymore," Todd declared, breathing heavily. He licked the beads of sweat from his upper lip and leaned over the rail. "Too hot for me."

Kori joined him and watched the semis and cars as they appeared from under the bridge. Looking straight down, the vehicles seemed to come out of nowhere. One after the other they came from beneath the bridge, sometimes in bursts of three or four, sometimes nonstop for minutes. The smell of diesel exhaust and road dirt blew up in their faces. The soles of their shoes vibrated as the massive big rigs rumbled through.

"We're almost there," Kori declared, nodding to the other end of the bridge. The truck stop sat just a few hundred feet beyond the off ramp. "Let's at least get a pop or something for the ride back."

"Nah. Let's just rest here for a while," Todd replied. "I ain't got any money anyways."

"You made me come all the way up here for nothing?" Kori was in disbelief. "Goddammit, Todd! Why didn't you say something? I only brought like three bucks. I could have gone home to get a couple more for you." He picked up his bike and started across the bridge.

"Where you going?"

"I'm gonna go get a damn pop. I'm thirsty as hell and I'm not riding home without getting something to drink first." Kori rode toward the truck stop, peddling halfheartedly.

"Hold on a second and I'll go with you."

Kori looked back and saw that Todd had his pants halfway down and his back arched. He stopped the bike and stared. "What the hell are you doing?"

"I'm taking a piss. What's it look like?" Todd stood with his back to him, alternating the stream of pee between the vehicles below and the bucket. Flies that had found their way to the growing stench buzzed away from the bucket momentarily with each spray. When the stream was redirected the flies reclaimed a stronghold on their new bounty. "Hold on. I'm almost done."

"How does so much juice come out of such a tiny pickle?"

"Ha ha. You're a funny one, Woodson," He zipped up and flipped Kori the bird. "Now what were you saying about buying me a pop?"

Kori giggled at his own joke. It wasn't really his joke, though. He had overheard it from one of the high school guys, razzing his buddy in the bathroom at the Pizza Hut in Cameron. He'd been waiting a month for the right opportunity to repeat it. "Why should I buy you anything, Hillyer?"

Todd ran to the opposite side of the bridge and looked out. There was a rare lull in the oncoming traffic. Only a lone car could be seen in the distance. A slow one from the looks of it, chugging along as if it were the only one on the road. In a sense it was. He watched intently as the car approached and then walked back to the other side. He picked up the bucket and grinned. "Because I'm gonna blow your mind."

"What the hell are you doing?" Kori screamed as Todd dangled the bucket over the rail and took aim.

Todd dismissed him with a wave and shushed him. The car vanished beneath the overpass. The hum of the slow moving car tires altered as the sound echoed off the supports below. A hollow whooshing as it glided through and then the screeching of tires as the brakes locked up.

"Holy shit! I nailed it!" Todd yelled. He mounted his bike and started peddling. "Kori, come on!"

Kori stood frozen in horror as the vehicle came to a stop. The occupant of the car slowly climbed out and he thought to himself, we are so dead. Todd peddled back to him and tried to get him moving by pulling on his shirt. Kori let himself be turned in the direction of home but never took his eyes from the car or the giant that stepped out of it.

"Man! That's gotta be the fattest guy I've ever seen." Todd's voice must have carried because the fat giant looked in their direction. He pointed at them and screamed something that they could not quite make out. A fist as big as a catcher's mitt pumped in the air. "Man, we are so dead."

"What do you mean, we? You did it!"

Before Todd could respond, the man walked half the distance between his car and the overpass. By the time he reached a stopping point his face was flushed and his breath came out in a raspy wheeze that the boys could almost hear. The man eventually regained enough of his composure to walk until he was directly below them. He threw his hands up in the air and looked up at them. He yelled, "What the fuck was that?"

"Uh... sorry about that, mister. Was an accident." Todd yelled back.

"Accident, my ass. I'm gonna accidentally clean that windshield with your dead fucking bodies." Even though it was close to a hundred degrees that day, the fat man was wearing a long sleeved flannel shirt. He rolled up his sleeves and walked to the base of the grassy embankment. To their horror, he began to climb up.

Todd leaned over and whispered in Kori's ear, “Wait until he gets about halfway up, then we bolt. His fat ass will be so winded, he'll never catch us. By the time he makes it back to his car, we'll be gone.”

Kori looked at his friend, wondering exactly when he had suddenly become retarded. “Are you serious? It's three miles to home. Even if he drives to the Cameron exit and back we're dead. He'll catch up to us before we make it halfway.”

“You gotta better plan?” Todd inched his bike to the end of the bridge so that he was looking directly down at the struggling man. He shook his head and smiled. “Maybe we don't need a plan. This guy's gonna have a heart attack before he gets to the top.”

Kori sidled up between Todd and the guardrail. He peered over the edge and saw the fat giant had made no progress in his attempt to climb the embankment. He was on all fours, wheezing as he grasped at tufts of foxtail and vetch for support. He would make it five feet up before his feet would slip on the weeds that he had torn from the hillside. Then he would slide, belly down, back to where he started. Occasionally he looked up at them and cursed, muttering threats to body parts they did not even know they had. The threats possessed less and less conviction with each failed attempt to ascend the hill.

"Come on, fat ass! We ain't got all day. My mom says I have to be home before supper," Todd yelled over the edge. He kicked at the shoulder with his toe, sending a scoop of gravel raining down on the guy's head.

"Dude, are you crazy?"

The man gave up on the climb and waddled back to his car. The spot where he had made his attempt looked as though a weed eater had been through it. Kori started to pedal away. When he realized that Todd was not behind him he stopped and circled back.

"Todd. Come on, man. Let's get out of here," he said, almost begging.

Todd ignored him as the fat man squeezed back into his car. He slammed the door shut and started the motor. By this time the shit water that covered the entire front of the vehicle had started to dry. He turned on his wipers which only succeeded in smearing the mess into an even layer across the glass. He climbed back out of the car and grumbled as he unrolled the right sleeve of his shirt.

"Oh, man. What's he doing?" Kori whispered. It had not occurred to them that the man had no idea what the brown sludge was that covered his windshield. They watched in amazement as the guy reached over the hood to wipe the glass with his sleeve.

“Time to fly,” Todd yelled, laughing wildly. Kori furiously pumped at his bike pedals, trying desperately to keep in pace with his friend.

As they peddled away they could hear the fat giant screaming at the top of his lungs. His voice was hoarse and full of disgusted anger. “Shit! Fucking dog shit!”

They laughed about the memory for miles until both of their faces were streaming with tears. It did Kori's heart good to reminisce of some of the better times of his childhood for a change. They exchanged a few other less remarkable stories of their misspent youth before the conversation took a more serious turn.

“Does it scare you? What you guys do, I mean,” Kori asked.

“Hell yes it scares me. It scares the shit of me all the time,” Todd replied without hesitation. “Do you think I enjoy risking getting my head shot off every other day? I mean my head's not the prettiest thing to look at but I've kinda grown attached to it, you know.”

Kori ignored the weak attempt at humor and stared at a van loaded with school children in the other lane. For a moment he was lost in a fog of mild jealousy that adults reserve exclusively for the young and innocent. He wondered where the van was headed on such a beautiful afternoon. Probably returning from a class field trip to a farm or maybe the zoo.

Some of the children waved as they passed them by.

"Then why do it?" he finally asked.

"You do know that we get paid, right?" Todd looked at him as if he were and idiot. "I mean, why are we doing what we are doing today? Driving across half the state with a trunk full of drugs, just asking to get shot or thrown in jail. Come on man, you already know the answer to that. We're all just slaves to the mighty dollar."

"But how much is enough? When does it end before somebody finally gets killed?"

"Oh, I've got an endgame," Todd said, waving back at the school children. "So does your brother. He's got his farm to pay off, and then he'll walk. You've got your schooling, so you can be a dog doctor or whatever. We all have something to live for after we get out. Just gotta risk dying for it first."

"What do you have that's worth dying for?" He immediately realized how callous that may have sounded. "I mean what's your endgame?"

"Oh I've got myself set up just fine. Don't you worry about me," Todd replied, smiling. "I'll tell you about it sometime. Just not today."

"What about Chris and Soup?"

The smile faded from Todd's lips as he settled in behind a semi pulling a trailer full of new cars. He shook his head and looked over at Kori. "Those two got nothing. I'm gonna tell you something right now, just between the two of us. Watch yourself around those two. They would stab their own mothers in the back without a second thought if there was something in it for them. When that endgame does come they are gonna fight it hard. They piss away every dime they earn on dope and god knows what else. Without me and Brenden they got jackshit and they know it."

"Then why mess with them?"

Todd shrugged and signaled to pull around the semi. "Can't run a crew with only two guys. Four was hard enough. Besides Virgil pretty well pushed the idea of pulling them in. I think they have some weird side thing going on with the Perv."

"Side thing?" Kori raised his eyebrows.

"Virgil's got some underground porn thing going on in his basement or something. Twisted shit from what I hear. I don't know much about it, don't really want to. I think those two dipshits have their hands dirty in it somehow." Todd drove a minute, debating how much to tell. "You know they had some sort of sex charges filed against them about ten years ago?"

"What?"

"Yeah, they supposedly went down to Amish country and tricked some girl into leaning into their car to give them directions. Those Amish kids are so sheltered that even Soup's pile of junk must of seemed like something special. Word has it that they rolled her head up in the window and took turns tagging her from behind. Her brother heard her screaming and showed up in his horse and buggy. They beat him half to death. Hurt him pretty bad, I guess. Now he does his chores from a wheelchair with wooden tires."

"No shit?" Kori asked. The fast food that they had stopped for before hitting the road suddenly did a double somersault in his stomach.

"The only reason the charges didn't stick was because none of the Amish would come forward to testify. They are a sick pair, man. Don't turn your back on 'em," Todd said. "Or stick your head in the car to give 'em directions, either."

Again Kori let the humor slide as he tried to digest the story he had just heard. He leaned back in his seat and stared through the window at the cars as Todd passed them by. He decided it was best not to ask any more questions for a while. He was truly afraid of what the answers might be.

As they approached the Martin Luther King expressway Kori began to see Des Moines in a different light. It was no longer the shining sanctuary from the dull existence of living in rural Iowa that it had once been to him. He could not put it into any clearer perspective than that. He had been gone less than a week, but the city seemed dirtier than he remembered.

The meetings with former buyers went as well or better than expected. By the end of the afternoon Kori was thousands of dollars richer, even after Virgil's half was figured in. The only errand left to tackle was to swing by the house and collect some of his belongings. His mother had packed only the bare essentials and he was in desperate need of some personal items.

They drove to the suburbs, leaving the grittier side of the city behind them. Todd drove slowly through the gated community and stared in wonder. Kori realized as he watched him that Todd had probably never been anywhere bigger than Iowa City in his life. He did not know whether to feel bad for him or envy him.

"This is where you lived?" Todd asked.

"Live," Kori corrected him. "This is where I live."

"How the fuck do you find your house here? They all look the same." Kori detected a hint of disdain in Todd's voice and found himself resenting it. Who the hell was he to look down on him for not living in some shit hole like the Ridge? As soon as he made the comparison a tinge of guilt crept in, leaving him feeling ugly and conceited.

"Right here. 604. That's me," Kori pointed to a large two story house on the left. For the first time he noticed that it did in fact look almost the same as 602 and 606. The only differences were the color of the blinds in the windows and the cars in the drive. That was when he saw the strange vehicles parked in front of the garage. "What the hell?"

"What is it?" Todd asked, slowing down.

"I don't know. Wait here."

He got out and approached the house quickly, anxious to get his things and get out before the god squad caught on. He could see that lights were on in the downstairs, but that did not concern him. It was probably just Maria, doing her Thursday cleaning. She probably didn't even realize the house was unoccupied. There was rarely ever anyone around when she cleaned on a normal day.

He punched in the code on the panel mounted beside the garage door. Nothing happened. He tried again two more times with the same result. Battery must be dead; he thought for a moment and then walked around to the back of the house. There was a key hidden under a flower pot on the patio. He shook his head, scolding himself for not thinking of it in the first place. Suddenly, the sliding glass door opened.

"Can I help you?" A middle aged man wearing a track suit stuck his head outside. The outfit was freshly pressed and matched the color of the sweatband that he wore on his head. Ear buds dangled from his neck playing what sounded to Kori like Wagner. He stepped out and flashed a smile that was as ridiculously flawless as his attire. He looked vaguely familiar.

"Uh, you can start by telling me what you're doing in my house," Kori replied.

"You must be Kori," the man said as he slid the glass door shut behind him. He extended a hand and introduced himself. "Robert Allen." He left his hand dangling in the air, waiting for Kori to take it. When he saw that the gesture was not going to be reciprocated, he began to fumble with the off switch on his iPod. "Reverend Allen, your stepfather's replacement."

"You're kidding me, right?" The fast food lunch did another somersault.

"No joke, son." the reverend waved his hand behind him. "Don't worry. I'll take good care of the place. You'll never even know that I was here when your folks get back in a year."

"A year?"

"That's right, maybe longer." The plastic smile reappeared, a preacher's calling card if there ever was one. "You never can put a time frame on God's work."

"Unfucking believable." Kori didn't know whether to laugh or cry. It was just like Clayton to pull something like this. Getting his mother to dump him off for a few months when he actually meant a year or more. It seemed awfully convenient that he just happened to get busted the day before the holy crusade. He wondered how much of this his mother knew ahead of time. "Can I at least get the rest of my things?"

"Your things?" The reverend looked puzzled. "The moving service packed all of your family's belongings days ago. If there's something you need, something I can help you with. We can sit down and talk. Maybe I can give your father a call."

"He's not my fucking father!" Kori screamed. He balled up a fist and stepped forward. The reverend backed away and squinted his eyes, the corner of his lips quivering in fear. As much as he hated Clayton, Kori at least gave him credit for not being a pussy like his replacement.

"I think you should leave," Reverend Robert Allen said with a tremble in his voice.

"I think you should blow me." Kori stormed away. Halfway back to the car his churning stomach betrayed him and he lost the lunch on the pavement. Fast food fries and gastric juices splattered the otherwise pristine sidewalk in front of 604 Ravencrest Drive. He climbed into the car and told Todd to drive.

"Didn't you get your shit?" Todd asked.

"Oh, I got a load of shit alright," Kori replied, staring at the house that was no longer his. "Let's just go home, man."

CHAPTER 18

Virgil Semler was a creature of habit. He firmly believed that a well structured routine was the foundation to a meaningful existence. Of course the dope heads, thieves and other questionable characters that he kept company with tested that philosophy on a daily basis. They were all unpredictable pains in the ass, but they also made him money.

He started his morning by holding a stubby finger under the tap until he deemed the water clear enough for his morning coffee. He lit a Winston with the same silver Zippo that he had used since his time in the navy, some forty years ago. The coffee brewed as he nursed the cigarette and gazed through the window above the sink. The lighter gave the first few drags a slight chemical taste. He grimaced and waited for the pot to finish.

He admired the bright autumn morning, at least what was left of it. It was almost ten o'clock and he was just waking up. Right on time as far as he was concerned. From his safe cozy kitchen he watched the world that was already stirring without him. Not one for the outdoors, he never left the sanctuary of the house without a damn good reason. Nature watching through the window was more his forte.

Songbirds battled for position at the bird feeders that were placed just beyond the porch, fattening themselves for their impending journey south. Sparrows and starlings picked over the crumbs below. He made a mental note to have the new kid pick up some seed on his next grocery run. He finished his smoke as his mind wandered.

The younger Woodson brother was due to show up any time. He hoped things would work out with the newest member of the dime bag thugs, though he had his doubts. The kid was not cut of the same cloth as his brother. Not even close. He certainly was nothing like those other three degenerates. For one, he was too clean cut. Too pretty. He was a smart one though. Hopefully smart enough not to get any funny ideas while hauling six bags of his merchandise halfway across the state.

If the kid screwed him over it would be the last thing he ever did. He would take it out on that sweet little ass for sure. The kid was too old to use in the internet photo scene, but maybe he would work well on film. A sick part of him almost hoped it would come to that. The very thought caused a stirring beneath Virgil's housecoat.

A knock came from the front door, startling him. The hot brew sloshed over the rim of the cup and he stepped back with his arm extended to avoid burning his feet. He damned his own frazzled nerves and rushed to the door.

"Hey Virgil, hope I didn't wake you up. Thought I'd get an early start."

Speak of the devil. Kori Woodson stood in the doorway with a sheepish look on his face. He wasn't alone. Todd fidgeted nervously behind him, combing his mess of long hair with his fingers. Virgil impatiently waved them in as he scanned the yard over their shoulders. The Hillyer kid's car idled quietly in the drive. Good, he thought. At least they did not plan to overstay their welcome. He looked them both up and down and scratched his head. "So much for keeping this just between the two of us."

"I had to get a ride from somewhere. I thought, since you know Todd..." Kori explained.

"Fine, fine," Virgil dismissed him with a wave. He motioned them both in and locked the door. He lugged the bags out of a nearby closet and placed them at their feet. "But it's coming out of your end, not mine."

"Not a problem," Kori replied. "Mind if I check these out real fast? It'll be nice to know what I'm working with. Know what I mean?"

"Yeah, well be quick about it." Virgil raised up a sleeve and glanced at his watch. "I'm expecting a little company and don't need you two tripping over your dicks when they show up. Comprende?"

"Sure," Kori said as he inventoried the stash, still trying to wrap his head around the size of it all. After each bag was assessed he handed them off to Todd, who quietly carried them to the car. "We should be back by ten if everything goes okay. Want me to swing by with your half?"

"No. That won't work. Just bring it by tomorrow. Say, noonish?"

Kori nodded, handing the last bag out the door. He dusted his hands off as he walked outside. Lacking anything better to say, he added, "Well, wish me luck."

"Luck?" Virgil scoffed. "Luck ain't got shit to do with nothing. Just remember whose money it is you're playing with, kiddo." He slammed the door before Kori had time to respond. He did not have all day to deal with small time pill pushers. He had bigger fish to fry.

He watched until they were beyond the end of the drive, glad to be rid of them. His heart rate increased as he systematically pulled all of the blinds on the first floor. After double checking the locks he went down into the basement. Time to mix business with pleasure, he thought as his bare feet padded down the cold gritty stairs.

He hurried across the cement floor, careful not to stub his toes. The south wall of the basement, the only one that was framed and finished, possessed a single door on the far right side. To the unsuspecting eye it appeared to be nothing more than a small closet. He removed a pair of bolts from the back, revealing a passage way into another room. This was his honey pot, where the real money was made.

He pushed the door open and then stopped, frozen in place. For a second he could have sworn that he heard something, a sound from somewhere upstairs. He held his breath and strained to listen, ready to reseal the secret room if necessary. He focused on the ceiling above; the only thing he heard was the whooshing of his own pulse running through his temples. He exhaled, disgusted with himself. It was good to be cautious, he told himself, but paranoia leads to coronaries.

He stepped inside his sanctuary. It smelled of latex and bodily fluids.

With less than an hour before his company was due to arrive, Virgil set to work getting the studio in order. A twin mattress, encased in a plastic covering, lay in the middle of the room. The light from the powerful tungsten bulbs in the corner reflected off of it, creating a blinding glow. Dark spots danced in the back of his eyes as he quickly threw a fitted sheet over the plastic. Sweat trickled from beneath his robe. He started up a pair of circulating fans, wondering why he hadn't done so in the first place.

Most of the camera equipment was still in place from the last time job. Except for checking the battery supplies on the auxiliary equipment, there was not much more to do until the performers arrived. He checked his watch again and determined that he had enough time to unwind before show time.

In the corner of the room was an antique trunk. Using a key that hung from his neck, he removed a single padlock and lifted the lid. A rush came over him as he stared inside, a feeling that he could not have matched if he were looking at the Holy Grail itself. Underneath a layer of blankets were stacks of photographs. Beneath them were hundreds of discs and cassette tapes. His personal copy of nearly every video that he had ever shot. Scrawled on each was a handwritten date, nothing more. He pulled a stack of photos from the trunk and sat on the mattress.

Few of the subjects in the photos looked even remotely close to being of age. That was the way he liked it. More importantly that was the way his business associates liked it. There were two things that kept his buyers coming in from all over the Midwest. Drugs and skin, both equaled the other in terms of quality. He served his product to customers with expensive taste, refined palates that required that their vices not be tainted from over handling. They wanted only the freshest and rawest.

He sat down on the mattress and thumbed through the photos. He slipped the cloth belt out of the loops of his robe and wrapped it around his neck. Slowly, he tightened the pressure to heighten his arousal. His pulse thumped in his ears like a rhythmic primal dance beat. Blood trapped above the belt swelled the skin on his face as he furiously worked his hands under his robe. He did not hear or feel the shot as it first entered his shoulder.

The belt loosened as the hand holding it lost the ability to grip. Muscle and tendon ceased to function as the slug tore its way through. The seductive trance of self-induced asphyxiation faded and pain seeped in. He regained enough of his senses to hear and feel the second shot. It nearly separated the arm beneath his robe at the elbow. The mattress that had seen its share of blood in the past steadily became saturated with his own.

His eyes welled up as he fought through the pain. He squinted to see the shooter that now stood in the doorway, but it was no use. His glasses had slipped from his face when the second shot hit him, rendering his vision to a watery blur. He tried to readjust them but neither damaged limb could manage the simple task. The blur moved closer, leaning down to place the glasses back on his face with enough force to crack both the frames and Virgil's nose.

"Remember me, asshole?" the intruder growled.

Virgil looked at the man towering over him and began to sob. He instinctively kicked at the legs of the man, but pain from his ruined upper limbs erupted as he moved. The beginning stages of shock were already setting in as he forced himself to look his attacker in the eyes. "Why?" he asked, almost pleading. "Why now?"

The only answer came in the form of another burst of gunfire. Rounds tore through the fabric of his robe and into the flesh surrounding his groin. He sank into unconsciousness, welcoming the reprieve from the searing agony. He was pulled back to reality for a moment by a splash of cold liquid that burned his open wounds. The smell of diesel fuel filled the room, robbing him of precious air as he struggled to breathe.

He watched the intruder emptying the contents of the trunk into a large bag. No matter the damage to his body, seeing his life's work being plundered hurt the most. He just hoped to stay alive long enough for the cavalry to arrive. He was not afraid to die. The only consolation he desired was to see the bastard who did this lying next to him, bleeding and dying.

He closed his eyes for what seemed like only a few seconds, but when he opened them he found himself alone in the room. He heard footsteps going up the stairs and into the living room above. He glanced over to the trunk, which lay turned on its side and completely empty. Hate filled his heart. That and the want for vengeance was the only thing keeping him alive.

He laid back and smiled, thinking about the hell that waited beyond the front door for the bastard who dared to hurt him. That smiled remained strong until he saw the smoke rising up from the crack under the door.

CHAPTER 19

The Lincoln Navigator pulled to the side of the road and let the emergency vehicles pass by. The driver watched carefully as the fire trucks and police cars congregated around the house, just a half mile away. The house was fully engulfed by the time the first hose was put into action. A crowd of curious onlookers formed at the end of the driveway, kept at a safe distance by two policemen. No sign of the contact was among them as far as he could tell. He turned the SUV around and drove away.

He pulled a throw away phone from his pocket and punched in a number. “Contact's gone. No, I mean gone as in gone. Okay. Yes, sir. See you tonight.” He dropped the phone on the seat next to him and sighed. He turned to the young girl riding in the backseat. She stared back at him with a distant foggy look in her eyes. “Looks like you just got the day off, sweetheart.”

He drove east for over an hour, as far in the opposite direction of home as time would allow. He crossed the

Mississippi river and into Illinois. A small waterside picnic area seemed as good as any place to do what had to be done. There were several boats in the distance, but no other vehicles in the parking lot. He got out of the Lincoln and walked around to the other side.

The girl looked up at him as he motioned her out of the back. The same dull expression remained on her face. It had not changed a bit since they had left Omaha that morning. It was as if she were seeing something a thousand miles away. He took her by the arm and pulled her to her feet. He looked down at her delicate bare feet and swallowed hard. He hated this part of the job.

He led the girl down a hiking trail that cut through the wooded area, running parallel to the river. She remained silent, even though he knew that the rough surface of the trail had to be biting into her soft feet. After about a hundred yards he stopped and turned her to face him. A faint glimmer of fear flashed through the drugged fog in her eyes as he studied her. His stomach knotted up and he quickly turned her around, unable to stand that look any longer.

He reached into the pocket of his jacket and pulled out another disposable phone. It was not unusual for him to go through three or four of them in any given week. He wiped the surface of the phone with his shirt and placed it in the girl's pants pocket. Then he pulled five twenties from his wallet and shoved them in behind the phone. "Stay here for a while before you come back out, sweetheart. Then call you folks and get your ass home, where you belong," he whispered in her ear.

The girl did not turn around as he made his way back to the Lincoln. He stopped and stared at the shimmering water for a moment, looking back to the woods. There was no sign of the girl as he climbed back into the vehicle and exited the park, knowing what he had just done was probably going to get him killed by his boss.

CHAPTER 20

Dale lingered close to the patrol car and watched as the firemen fought a losing battle to the flames. There was really nothing that he or Tassler could do until the Cameron fire chief gave them the all clear. Under normal circumstances the sheriff's department served little purpose in a house fire, except to control traffic. But this was no normal situation. Virgil Semler was a loner, practically a recluse. No one had any doubts that whatever burnt remains were left, would surely be found inside that house.

He nervously studied the other officers when the state crime lab van pulled in, wondering who would be the first to question why the DCI boys would be showing up to a fire call. It had only been an hour since the initial call had come in. Yet here they were, spit-shined and dressed to the nines. In a matter of minutes they would systematically pull rank on the local authorities. Most of the guys would take the intrusion as a blessing. No one wanted to dig through the ashes for roasted body parts.

By the look on Tassler and Sheriff Baylor's faces, Dale determined that they would rather keep the scene to themselves. Butch rushed the van with Whitey running behind, struggling to keep up. He looked on as his partner tried to incite a pissing match with the lead DCI man. The investigator stood his ground and calmly waited for the sheriff to wisely lead his enraged deputy away by the arm, leaving him alone with Dale.

"You partner seems to be taking this well, Deputy Scheck," he joked, extending his hand.

Dale shook his hand and nodded, hoping the display gave everyone the idea that the two had never met before. "Do you mean the fire or you state boys coming stealing his thunder?"

"Both."

"How you been, Bobby?" He felt eyes upon them as he and the investigator talked. The intensity of the stares rivaled that of the heat blazing behind them. "This isn't exactly what I had in mind when I told you I'd touch base with you soon."

"Yeah, I didn't see this one coming." Robert Hazelton shook his head and looked up as the firemen began to yell over the noise of the tanker engines. The roof began to collapse, putting everyone on edge until it slowly settled in on itself. Millions of sparks rose up as the glowing timbers cracked under their own weight. "We still have a lot to talk about, you and I. This doesn't end the investigation. Only changes it."

"Turns it upside down is what it does. Semler was ninety

percent of our case. Suddenly he's charcoal? And by who?" Dale absently dug the toe of his boot into the grass. "Where do we go from here, Bobby?"

"First of all, you can stop ripping up my crime scene. I already have twelve of Cameron's finest volunteers doing a bang up job of that. Secondly, we figure out who torched the pervert's house. Or maybe more importantly, who gets the most broken up about it." He nodded in the direction of Butch, Whitey and the fire chief. The three of them were huddled behind one of the fire trucks, engrossed in a tense discussion. "I'd start with them. Our conversation seems to be making them a bit nervous."

"Anything I can do to help here?" Dale asked, already knowing the answer.

"Go home and get some sleep. It's gonna be a busy next couple of days in Mayberry." He patted Dale on the back. "Keep an eye on that partner of yours. I'll see you here in the morning when the dust settles."

Dale left the investigator to do his job. He waited in the patrol car for Butch to drag his wounded ego away from the scene. Not a single word was spoken between them as they drove back to the office. Dale went home and spent a restless night, staring at the ceiling of his ancient trailer. At one point he crawled from his bed and showered himself off. The smell from the fire seemed to be trapped in his nostrils.

When sleep finally came, he dreamed that he had

inadvertently breathed in the smoky ghost of Virge the Perv. The ashes stayed in his throat and lungs, eating him from the inside out. That was all that he remembered from the dream in the morning. The rest dissolved into his subconscious when he awoke. A nauseous ache in his chest lingered until the next afternoon.

Back at the scene, he and Butch found themselves demoted to the menial role of gatekeepers. The state boys had stretched a line of yellow tape across the driveway during the night. Another run of tape encompassed the smoldering ruins of the house and yard. Two DCI men and the state fire inspectors milled about, taking photographs and processing evidence. Dale sensed the growing frustration building up in his partner as they stood on the outside, looking in.

He decided to play along and play up the scorned local yokel routine. "What the hell are we doing here, Butch? If these state guys are running the show now, why is Baylor wasting our time standing on the sidelines?"

"Why don't you ask your new friend over there?" Butch grunted, nodding toward Hazelton. He tossed the remains of his cigar on the ground and stepped on it. "He seemed to take a liking to you last night."

"Ask him yourself," Dale replied. "Here he comes."

Hazelton stepped over the yellow tape and walked down the drive to greet them. In his hand he held a leather bound notebook. He continued jotting down notes as he went, stopping occasionally to finish a thought. It was obvious to Dale that the investigator was purposely taking his time to get under Tassler's skin. He snapped the notebook shut and slipped it inside his jacket as he neared them.

"Gentlemen," Hazelton called out. He smiled and offered a hand to Butch. "Deputy Tassler, I don't believe that we've been formally introduced."

Tassler stared at the hand, disdainfully. He ignored the gesture and spat close to where his discarded cigar butt littered the ground. The muscles in his jaw became rigid as he stared the investigator down. "What are we doing here, Hazelton?"

"Besides contaminating my crime scene, you mean?" Hazelton looked down at the scattered tobacco crumbs and shook his head, disapprovingly. He waved a hand toward the entrance of the drive and to the road beyond it. "Why, you're here to fend of the throngs of looker-loos and reporters. Doing a fine job if I do say so, myself."

"Since when does a house fire suddenly become a crime scene?" Tassler asked.

"When the fire Marshall finds indisputable evidence of arson, deputy Tassler. That's when it becomes a crime scene." He studied Butch before continuing, gauging his reaction carefully. "And when we find the burnt remains of the homeowner in the basement."

Butch did not take the bait easily. His face showed little reaction as he stared at what was left of the smoldering house.

"Actually I have a few things that I wanted to bounce off of you local guys. I have no qualms admitting that you fellas know more about this area than we ever will. The home field advantage, if you will." He walked back toward the house before stopping and calling back to them, "That is, if you don't mind abandoning your post for a few minutes."

They skirted the foundation, stepping around the debris and puddles left from the firemen. At the back of the house Hazelton pulled a flashlight from his pocket and shined it down on the lower level. "The body was recovered there. Official identification won't be completed until tomorrow, but surprisingly there was not much damage done. One fire was started in the same room as the victim, but it was only a flash fire. Quick to start, quick to die out. No adjuvant was used here."

"Adjuvant?" Tassler asked.

"Something to make the flames stick," Dale answered. He found it curious that Tassler was suddenly hanging on every word Bobby had to offer. He may have just been warming up to the idea of being involved in the investigation, but he doubted it. Butch was more than likely collecting as much info as possible to cover his own ass.

"Very good, deputy. They told me you were a sharp one."

Butch rolled his eyes before pressing for more

information. "You said one fire was started here. What does that mean? There was more than one?"

"That's right. Trace analysis will need to be done, but it looks like the fire on the main level, the one that caused most of the damage, did use an adjuvant. Most likely oil or liquid detergent. Kept the accelerant on the surface longer."

"Interesting," Dale added.

"Yes it is," Hazelton agreed. "But I didn't bring you in here to conduct an arson seminar. There's something else I wanted to show you." He led them to the edge of the property, where the back yard gave way to a steep incline. He pointed down to a clearing at the bottom. "My guess is our firebug came in and out there. A single set of footprints going both directions lead right up to the house. Lucky for us it rained two nights ago. Makes for much more readable impressions."

"Anything you can tell from the tracks?" Butch was becoming a regular teacher's pet.

"Actually there is. The right impression of each print indicates that our arson had a significant injury to the leg. Possibly a limp," Hazelton pulled out his notebook and looked at both deputies. "Know anyone that fits that bill?"

"No." Both deputies answered simultaneously. The curious look they shared and the speed at which they had responded gave Hazelton the feeling that he was being lied to. He decided to let it go for the time being. He trusted Dale and if he felt it necessary to withhold information then there had to be a good reason. He would eventually corner him alone and get the truth.

CHAPTER 21

Brenden stared at the bundle of cash in silence. He had made no mention of it since the night before when Kori reluctantly handed it over. His gaze shifted from the money and then back to Kori and Todd. The beginnings of dark circles were forming beneath his eyes. The lack of sleep from working both day and night was finally taking its toll. Not to mention the newly added stress caused by Virgil's untimely end.

It was too soon to know if anything in the burnt house could lead the authorities back to them. The pervert was meticulous about covering up loose ends, but that did not help lesson his worries. He looked out the living room window and frowned as the Campbell cousins rolled into the driveway in Soup's Impala. Quickly, he stuffed the money back into the paper bag and slid it across the table. "How much?" he finally asked.

"Six thousand," Kori replied. "There's still another three to collect next week. Probably see at least half of that without begging for it."

"Who else knows about this?"

"Nobody but us and now you," Kori answered.

"And Mr. Crispy down the road, but he's not gonna be talking anytime soon," Todd added, jokingly. Brenden shot him a cold glance that wiped the smirk right off his face. He put his head down and stared at his socks. "Sorry."

"Good. Now go stash it before Beavis and Butthead get in here," Brenden said. "And let's keep this between the three of us for now. Less ways to split it up that way."

The similarity between his brother's and Virgil's approach to partnership was not lost on Kori. It made the money in his hand seem even more tainted than before. After stuffing the bag under his mattress he stopped to scrub his hands in the bathroom on the way back out.

The others had all congregated on the porch by the time he was done. When he stepped past the screen door he could feel the tension in the air. Todd and Chris had gravitated to a bench on the far end for a smoke, leaving Brenden and Soup to a heated discussion. Kori sidestepped around them and joined the smokers.

"And you just want to walk away now?" Soup asked, throwing his hands in the air. "Five years and one little setback. You just want to hump up like a bitch and quit. Goddamn, Woodson! I thought you had more balls than that."

Brenden stepped close enough to Soup to almost touch

noses with him. He arched his shoulders back and held out his arms as if daring Soup to take a swing at him. The others shared a nervous glance before resuming their attention back to the ground below them. Todd lit another cigarette from the previous one even though it was still only half gone.

"Balls, Soup? It ain't got anything to do with balls," Brenden snapped. "In case you didn't hear, the guy we run all of our shit through is a chunk of charcoal in the basement of his own house now. Whatever deal we had up there just went up in flames with him." He waved a hand in the general direction of Virgil's property, from which faint plumes of smoke were still visible over the tree line. "That's not a little setback. That's a fucking sign to walk away while we're still in one piece. You're just too stupid to see it."

Soup scoffed and glanced across the porch to make sure the others were listening. "You think that Virgil was the end of the trail for us?" He reached into his pocket and pulled out a scrap of paper and held it up. "I got a phone number right here for the next stop on the pipeline. I make the call and we are back up and running by nightfall."

"What are you talking about?" Brenden eyed him suspiciously.

"What? You thought you were the only one with your hooks into the old pervert? He knew you weren't in it for the long haul. He knew you'd eventually run out of sack and close up shop, pay off your little farm and play green acres with the Jew doctor. So he gave me this little insurance policy in case anything ever happened to him." Soup waved the paper scrap under Brenden's nose before pocketing it.

Brenden shook his head slowly. "You have no idea what you're getting into, Soup. Those guys will chew you up and spit you out. Besides, how do we know it wasn't them who torched the pervert's house? Maybe just tying up loose ends or something. We could be part of those loose ends, too. That thought ever cross your mind?"

"How do I know you didn't torch it yourself?" Soup countered, but with less conviction than before. Possession of the phone number insured the security of his livelihood, but in no way did it prevent Brenden from beating him to a pulp.

"I'm going to forget you even said that," Brenden said through clenched teeth as he backed Soup up against the front door. "But if you ever so much as breathe that stupid idea again, so help me God, I will cut out your tongue."

Soup did not have to respond to let Brenden know that his short lived power play was all but over. He did his best to make eye contact and look tough, but he was afraid and they both knew it. For all he knew Brenden was right. Making a call to the phone number that Virgil had given him over two years ago could very well get them all in over their heads with the big boys. Or worse yet, he could be leading them like lambs to the slaughter. He had no idea who snuffed the old pervert. It could have been Brenden but he doubted it. There was no gain and too much to lose for any of them to make a play like that, especially Brenden.

"Yeah, I got it," Soup said softly. He became painfully aware that the others were listening closely, hanging on every word. He puffed out his chest for their benefit and added, "Now get out of my face."

A vehicle pulled in behind his Impala. Brenden had his back to the driveway and Soup was not about to concede his position in the stare down, so neither of them paid it much attention. They also failed to notice the nervous shuffling from the others as two car doors slammed in succession. It was Chris who ended the standoff with a tremble in his voice. "Uh, guys, we have company."

"Well, boys. What do we have here? A domestic disturbance or a lover's spat?" Tassler said as he walked across the yard with a swagger that only a cop could possess. He had one hand resting on the butt of his service revolver and the other wrapped around the cord of his radio mike.

"What do you want, Tassler?" Brenden asked with an irritated tone in his voice. He expected a visit sooner or later, considering the events that happened the day before. The fact that they were coming so soon meant that they probably found nothing in Virgil's house to connect them to him. They were simply here to break his balls for a while.

“I'm here to talk to your old man. He around?” Butch stepped onto the porch and peered through the screen door. He reeked like he had spent the morning huddled around a campfire. Another odor, one slightly less evident, came from him as well. Brenden was pretty sure that it was not the smell of roasted marshmallows.

“He's out back. Why? What do you want with my Dad?” Brenden asked, stealing a worried look in Kori's direction. Kori stood up from his seat and moved closer to the conversation. Six years of not giving a shit one way or the other about his father dissolved at the mere thought of this psycho cop questioning his old man.

“I'll ask the questions, dipshit. Not you,” Butch snarled. “Now go get him!”

Dale stepped in between the two before things got out of hand. He did it less out of civic duty and more just because he knew Tassler wanted it to end badly. His partner had been in a foul mood ever since they had arrived the on scene at the fire the previous night. He knew Butch was itching to take out his frustrations on the first person that crossed him. He was not about to let it happen here. “Your Dad's truck was spotted at the Semler place a couple of days ago. We just need to ask him a few questions, Bren. That's all.”

“I was in our Dad's truck at Virgil's the other day. If

anyone should be answering your questions, it should be me," Kori interrupted. He surprised even himself by speaking up. Did he really just offer himself up to the police? After all the crap that he had done in the last few weeks, the word *GUILTY* might as well have been tattooed on his forehead. He didn't crack under questioning back in Des Moines, but that was just after getting caught skimming pet meds from his boss. Would he be able to bottle up the guilt of strong armed robbery, felony possession and possibly attempted murder with a bong under pressure?

And did that cop just call his brother, Bren?

"Oh yeah?" Tassler turned to him and sneered. He eyed Kori up and down the way Virgil did when he had first met him. Only it was not so much a homosexual lust thing like Virgil. It was more of an intimidating prison sex, *I could rape you if I wanted to,* sort of way. "Was it business or pleasure, mama's boy?"

Kori did not know if the term was meant as a personal attack or just redneck ignorance. God knows that Soup and Chris had repeated the same thing with the most derogatory of intentions. Normally it would have gotten under his skin, but he forced himself to maintain his composure. "Business. Virgil paid me to shop for his groceries. Paid me forty bucks for my trouble. See?" He pulled two twenties from his front pocket and showed them. It was the change he received from a hundred for filling up Todd's tank and buying dinner on the way back from Des

Moines.

Dale told him to put his money away and asked him a few questions. None of them were very pointed and revealed nothing incriminating. He asked Butch if he was satisfied and was answered with a grunt and a dismissing gesture. After watching Butch stalk back to the patrol car in a huff, he could not help but to crack a smile. He looked at Brenden and stuck out his hand. “Long time no see, Woodson. How have you been?”

Brenden shook his hand with the fervor one reserved for long lost friends. It was not until Kori read the nameplate pinned above the deputy’s breast pocket that he recognized him. Dale Scheck and Brenden were teammates and best friends in high school, at least during the years that Kori spent in Cedar Ridge. They were both state champion wrestlers in their senior year, the first and last time that Cameron High had produced champions in two weight classes in a single season.

“Doing good, Scheck. How about yourself?” Brenden asked. He held onto the deputy’s hand and sized him up, a habit that he had developed over the past few years. Earning a living through means of violent acts had a funny way of changing a guy's perception of other men.

“Oh, I can't complain. The job's not bad, but my partner is a bit of a prick,” Dale replied.

This got a chuckle from everyone. Even Little Chris, who hated cops more than personal hygiene, let out a nervous giggle. He glanced at the cruiser out of the corner of his eye and was met with a look of hate laden disgust coming from Tassler. He quickly looked down, suddenly finding his shoes very interesting.

"You don't have to tell us," Brenden concurred.

"How's the leg?" Dale asked, hoping to disguise the question as concern rather than direct questioning from an officer of the law. "I never heard how that turned out after I left for St. Ambrose. Better, I hope."

"The leg?" Brenden appeared a little perplexed by the question for a second. "Oh that. I'm not running any marathons but it's okay. I never had to have the surgery. I don't know if you were here when they decided that or not."

"No, I never knew." Part of Dale regretted bringing the painful subject up. The injury had cost Brenden a full ride to Iowa and a chance to wrestle under some of the most elite coaches in the country. He considered himself a good wrestler but Brenden was phenomenal, a natural technician on the mat. He nodded back to the patrol car and made his excuse to leave. "Nice seeing you again, man. We'll have to have a beer some time."

"Yeah, a beer. We'll do that."

They let out a collective sigh of relief as the police car faded down the road and out of sight. The unexpected visit was somewhat unnerving and left them all a bit uneasy. Poor Chris was left especially rattled by the confrontation and proceeded to chain smoke from Todd's pack of cigarettes. “Fucking tinfoil badges,” he muttered.

“No doubt,” Brenden agreed. “That's exactly the kind of shit I don't need right now.” He pointed in the direction that the deputies went and looked directly at Soup as he spoke. “Cops showing up at my doorstep, ready to shake down my old man. Fuck that. I don't care what the rest of you assholes do, but I'm out.”

He stormed inside the house before any of them had a chance to respond. The hinges on the screen door growled their rusty cry as he stepped over the threshold. The wood smacked wood as the door slammed shut, announcing yet another angry departure.

“Go ahead,” Soup muttered, careful not to speak loud enough to actually be heard. “We don't need your uppity ass anyhow.” He looked across the porch at the other three. They all stared back with a shell shocked look on their faces. “Ain't that right, Cuz?”

Chris perked up like a faithful yard mutt and puffed up his chest, contemplating his place in the apparent shift in the hierarchy. With Brenden out of the picture and Soup leading the way, he stood a good chance of finally shaking his low man status. He liked that idea a lot. “That's right, Cuz. Screw him.”

“What about you college boy? Feel like starting up your

own pharmacy?" Soup asked, with his eyebrows raised.

Kori looked at Todd and tried to get a sense of how he should respond. Mental images of some young Amish girl played in his head, flailing hers arms with her head rolled up tight in the window of Soup's Impala and struggling in a futile effort to keep her purity intact. If Todd had an endgame, he thought to himself. It had better be a damn good one to stick with these two.

"Just the four of us?" Todd chimed in. "I don't see it."

"I can get some more help if that makes you feel better," Soup replied. He already had someone in mind as a matter of fact.

Todd looked to Kori, shrugged and then he gave him a reassuring nod before answering for the both of them. He knew that by saying yes he was risking his friendship with Brenden, but having friends did not put cash in his pocket. The greatest risk that he foresaw was being blamed for facilitating Kori's decision to get involved. If anything happened to his brother, Brenden would never forgive him.

CHAPTER 22

Dale slept like a baby that night for the first time in weeks. Just the idea of not having to look at Butch Tassler's ugly mug for two straight days had a calming effect on him. He woke up refreshed and ready to tackle some much needed projects around the trailer. It was a long overdue feeling, especially after the previous day's events.

He hated holding back information from Bobby Hazelton, but he needed to clear up a few things before sharing any theories on the Semler arson with him. He hoped to hell that he was wrong about the gut feeling he got when he saw the drag marks in the tracks behind the hermit's house. Tassler had his own ideas about who might have torched the place. He did not bother to share them with Dale, but then again he really didn't need to. Dale hoped to hell that Tassler was right and he was wrong.

Not only did his partner hold out on him, he barely spoke two words after the stop at the Woodson place. Dale had a feeling that there was going to be even more tension between them than usual for a while. He hoped that Butch at least had some good luck hunting during his days off. Early bow season had started that morning and killing something always seemed to brighten him up a bit.

He stepped out of the shower and was toweling off when a knock came from the front door. He slipped on his favorite pair of sweats and hurried to answer it with a sinking feeling in his chest. There was an urgency in the knock that gave him a sneaking suspicion that his plans were about to change.

Detective Hazelton stood next to his white sedan, resting one elbow on an opened door. He slowly drummed his fingers on the hard metal top with the other hand. The solemn look on his face confirmed Dale's suspicions. He slapped the top twice and said, "Get dressed. There's something you ought to see before the press and the local brass go ape shit with it." He didn't wait for Dale to respond before climbing back behind the wheel and slamming the door shut.

"Oh, man. This does not sound good," Dale said to himself as he hastily threw on a pair of jeans and a jacket. As an afterthought, he pulled his personal revolver from a drawer beside his bed and clipped the holster to his waistband.

As soon as they arrived at the scene, Dale was certain that another body had been found. At least twice as many DCI agents were trolling around in the freshly harvested field than at the Semler property. They slowly walked between the rows of soybean stubble, systematically scanning the ground as they went. Although they stood only a few yards apart from one another, the line of men covered at least half an acre.

An agent that Dale remembered seeing at the arson scene stepped out of his own vehicle and greeted them at the gate. He was slightly on the husky side and looked completely miserable as the brisk morning wind rippled the fabric of his tailored suit. He stuffed his bare hands into his pockets and gave Dale a lingering once over that left no doubt about his feelings on sharing notes with the local authorities. Hazelton tried to break the tension with introductions, but it did little to loosen the agent up. Mathers, as Hazelton had called him, simply pushed his hands deeper into his pockets and led them into the field.

It wasn't until they had rounded the tree line that flanked the field on the south that it dawned on Dale where they were. The field abutted the acreage that Tassler and his ex-wife once shared. In fact, he could almost make out the rooftop of the house that Butch sometimes insisted on driving by during their shifts. An ominous feeling welled up inside him as they walked deeper into the field.

They crested a small hill close to the tree line. At the bottom were two investigators, dressed in clothing much more appropriate for the weather than agent Mathers. They stood on either side of a tarp that was weighted down by clods of dirt, apparently procured from the recently plowed ground. A massive lump rested beneath it, giving the illusion of movement as the wind blew across the loose covering.

"The coroner's only done the prelims, so we figured it was best to keep him covered up," Mathers told Hazelton. He tapped his muddied dress shoes on the edge of the tarp to illustrate his point. Then he turned his attention to Dale and added, "Don't want the natives getting all restless, do we?"

"That's fine agent Mathers. I think we can handle it from here," Hazelton said. Mathers briefly protested but Hazelton quelled it with a dismissing hand. "Go on and get back to your unit before you freeze to death. And next time watch the weather channel before you leave your hotel room for Christ's sake."

Dale watched the Mathers walk back to the entrance with his hands once again buried in his pockets. He allowed himself a bit of guilty pleasure as the agent momentarily lost his footing and was forced to pull his hands free to regain his balance. It was difficult to say, with the wind blowing so hard, but he thought that he heard him cursing as he trudged on. He turned back to Hazelton and the two guarding the tarp in time to catch them smiling as well.

"Kinda reminds me of my own pain in the ass partner, you know," he remarked. Immediately the smiles vanished from the agents faces. They shared an awkward glance amongst themselves before regaining their stoic expressions.

“Ooh,” one of the agents muttered.

Hazelton shot the agent a stern look before placing a hand on Dale's shoulder. Even though they were roughly the same build, Dale suddenly felt very small in comparison. He stared down at the lump beneath the tarp and back to the investigator, dumbfounded. He opened his mouth to speak and quickly closed it as his saliva glands went into overdrive. For a second he felt as if he would pass out. Finally he forced out a single word. “How?”

Hazelton nodded to the agents. They lifted two corners of the tarp and carefully folded them over, revealing what lay hidden underneath. Dale let out a startled gasp. He looked first to the two agents and then to their superior, waiting for the punch line. It had to be some sort of joke, albeit a horribly sick one.

Tassler's body rested almost in a fetal position, only his knees were not pulled up to his chest nearly far enough to call it that. He laid on his side with one hand stuffed down the front of his unbuttoned pants. The other was stiffened in the early stages of rigor mortis, hovering close to his face. It would have appeared that Butch had been sucking his thumb, except for the fact that it was nearly bitten in two. What Dale believed to be an arrow was buried halfway down the shaft into his throat. Another pinned the hand in his pants firmly to his pelvic region. It too was sunken in almost to the fletching.

And that was not the shocking part.

Nestled firmly behind Tassler was the body of a freshly killed doe. The front legs of the deer were positioned on either side of his shoulders. The lower legs were fixed in the same manner, one under him and the other lay over his Butch's hip. It was almost if the animal and he were in an intimate spooning position.

“What the hell?” Dale exclaimed. “What sick bastard stages something like that? And why?” He wanted to stop staring at the pair of bodies but could not pull his eyes from them.

Hazelton sighed before answering. “Hate to tell you this, but I don't think this was staged. All prelim forensics indicate that your partner there...,” He stared down at Butch's body with a look of mild disgust. “He was in that very position when he took one to the throat.” He motioned with the flat of his hand to the space between Butch and the doe. “Angle is right and the shaft went straight through him and into the deer. So did the one in the happy hand.”

“You mean to tell me that he was...,” Dale did not know how to articulate what he was thinking. He could not bring himself to say it out loud, wouldn't know what to call it even if he could. “With a goddamn deer?”

“No, I think that came first. No pun intended,” Hazelton replied. He kept a straight face and glanced over to his men, daring them to even think of doing otherwise. “Can't be for certain until the labs come back, but we found quite a bit of what appears to be semen on the deer and the coroner did a test on the animal to see if..."

"Oh, Jesus Christ! Don't tell me anymore!" Dale put his hands to his ears and walked in a looping circle. He was thankful that he had not had time to have breakfast before Hazelton had showed up at his door. If he had he almost certainly would have lost it then and there. He stopped and looked up with watering eyes. "What the hell is going on here, Bobby?"

Hazelton did not answer right away. First, he ordered the two agents to give them some privacy. The agents looked grateful to be relieved of their duty and hurried to join the rest of the crew, policing the area for evidence. When they were out of earshot Hazelton turned to face him, his face twisted into an angry scowl.

"Why don't you tell me, Deputy Scheck," he said. He spoke each syllable of the word deputy as if he were spitting. It came out, *dep-you-tee*. "I've got two bodies in as many days in this godforsaken place and both happen to have been key persons of interest in a very important case. If I might remind you, a case that has taken two years for me to build. A case that you are supposed to be part of. So why don't you tell me what in the hell is going on."

"I have no idea." Dale stared at the bodies, wishing that the agents would have thrown the tarp back over them before they made their headlong retreat. His hands started to shake and his watery mouth suddenly went dry, making his response sound even more like a lie than it already was.

"Bullshit!" Hazelton snapped. He rushed in to close the distance between them. Dale blinked in surprise and backpedaled until he was pinned against the thicket of trees behind them. "You were both holding back on me the other night. Don't blow smoke up my ass by denying it, either. I expected that from this scumbag," He pointed back at the nestling bodies, who both stared off in the distance with the same dull glaze in their eyes. "It was in his best interest to lie to me, but you on the other hand..."

"Bobby," Dale interrupted him, pleading.

"No," Hazelton's palm shot up in the air. "Let me finish, goddammit! You on the other hand are my only inside shot at this case. I put my neck on the line by sending you in this alone. Put all of my trust in you. You start holding back on me and shit like this happens, guess who's gonna end up looking like the idiot." He eased back some, giving Dale just a little bit of breathing room before answering his own question. "Me, that's who."

Dale measured his words very carefully. He let out a breath and admitted that he had made a mistake. He explained his hunch that the arson with a limp may have possibly been Brenden Woodson. It seemed plausible, given the fact that Woodson had deep ties to Semler. He spun a story beginning with Brenden's knee injury in high school and ended with a file filled with photos of Brenden and his band of misfits frequenting the hermit's property. It was at least partially the truth, although Brenden was not the first one that popped into his head when he saw the drag marks in the tracks.

"I just wanted to be certain before I reported anything to you," Dale explained, taking care not to break eye contact. He could not tell if Hazelton was buying his half-truth or just giving him enough rope to hang himself. He was not really telling him anything that he didn't already know. He put the finishing touch on the lie by adding, "I'm damn glad I did, because I'm having serious doubts about it now."

"How so?" Hazelton raised an eyebrow. He seemed genuinely curious, not suspicious.

"Well. I got to thinking after Butch and I questioned him yesterday," He looked down at the bodies as if he expected Butch to corroborate his story. It occurred to him that his partner most likely wouldn't have vouched for him even if he wasn't laying there in a post-coital embrace with a deer. "Woodson has too much to lose and nothing to gain by killing Virgil Semler. Besides, he has an alibi for the time frame. Says he was in Cameron buying supplies at the Farm Supply. Then he had lunch with his boss at Mable's. He's got at least half a dozen witnesses at each place. Maybe more."

"And you verified these alibis yourself?"

“Not yet, but I will,” Dale admitted. “I have no doubt that they'll all check out.” He was feeling more confident that he had successfully covered his butt, so he decided to shift the focus back to the investigation. “What about the ex-wife and her boyfriend?”

Hazelton shook his head and waved a hand in the direction of the house. “They've been out of town for days. It was his nephew that called it in. Says that his uncle and the ex-wife left for a car show in Springfield two days ago. Won't be back until Monday. Lucky for us that the dispatch got routed to the state patrol and not your guys. Otherwise every Barney Fife in Catalpa County would be here right now, mucking up my crime scene.” A cruel grin formed on his face. “No offense to you, by the way.”

“None taken,” Dale responded, forcing a smile. He liked Bobby Hazelton, but he had the sudden urge to slap that grin from his face.

“It won't stay quiet for long, though. The nephew and a couple of his buddies were hunting when they found the deer whisperer and his companion here. For all we know, there are already a dozen photos floating around on the internet by now. Fucking Facebook.” He pulled off a glove and clamped it between his teeth as he punched a series of keys on his phone. Dale grimaced at the sight, wondering just what that glove had come into contact with before it ended up in Bobby's mouth. The investigator barked orders to someone on the other end, presumably agent Mathers, to "get this freak show out here before the spectators showed up."

A DCI van approached in the distance, its wheels bouncing and swaying violently against the uneven terrain. Half a dozen agents on foot kept pace with the slow moving vehicle, all thankful to be walking in the cold instead of having their guts battered inside the warm cab. Dale hoped like hell to be on his way out of there before anyone got any funny ideas about asking him to help load the dead. He doubted that he had the stomach for it.

Hazelton took in the gruesome sight one last time and then threw the edge of the tarp back over the bodies. He walked over to the fence line, where he had recently unleashed his fury on the deputy, and bent down to retrieve Tassler's hunting gear. A compound bow and quiver lay in the fallen leaves along with a small backpack. Hazelton slipped his glove back on and picked up the bow. He tested the weight of the drawstring with a few quick pulls and nodded in approval.

"Is that such a good idea?" Dale asked. He could not believe how carelessly someone as by the book as Hazelton was handling the most likely murder weapon on the scene.

Recognizing his concern, Hazelton shook his head and smiled. "This bow didn't kill anyone, deputy. Except for maybe Bambi here." He walked over and peeled back the tarp once again, making Dale wish he had just kept his mouth shut. He pointed to the fletching on the shaft protruding from the side of the doe. It had the same orange coloring as the ones in quiver. “That is an arrow.” Then he pointed to the ones in Tassler's body. “Those are not.”

“I think I'm missing something here.”

“That's because you don't hunt,” Hazelton explained. Even though the contemptuous tone was not there, Dale still thought of someone else who made it a point to remind him of that fact almost daily. The detective removed one of the arrows from the quiver attached to the side of the bow. He held it in approximately the same angle as the one sticking out of Tassler's neck. It was more than twice as long as the one that killed the man. He repeated the comparison with the crotch shot and explained, “These are crossbow bolts. From an entirely different weapon that, unless I'm missing something, is no longer at the scene of this crime.”

“Crossbow?”

“Yep,” Hazelton confirmed. “With a scope it's basically a rifle that shoots arrows. Somebody could have sat for hours with it cocked and ready to go. From the looks of it they got a hell of a show for their efforts. Only problem is, crossbows are not rifles. No messy paperwork to buy one. If it was bought with cash, no records at all. Looks like we're back to square one. I don't suppose you have any idea which of your local good ol' boys favors a crossbow, do you?"

Dale shook his head and bent down to study the fletching on the bolt protruding from Butch's hand. It made him sick but it was still better than looking at his face. The feathery vanes were a dull black. They were unlike the bright orange of Tassler's gear, which could easily be spotted from a distance in case of a missed shot. Whoever selected these was not concerned about finding them after they were fired. He shrugged his shoulders and put on his best hell if I know look.

"Tell you what," Hazelton said. He sighed and rubbed the side of his head through his gloves. "I know these are your people. You want what's best for them, but holding anything back from me is not going to help anyone." Dale opened his mouth but met the palm once again. "Find me something, Deputy Scheck." This time it was just plain old deputy, nothing venomous about it. "Soon, before I run out of patience."

CHAPTER 23

Kori stood with his back pressed against the back of the chute and slapped the stubborn cow in the ass. His hand stung despite the thick leather chore gloves as he continued to coax the animal forward, sending plumes of dust in the air with each blow. There was nothing between him and the thousand pound cow except for a shit crusted two by six, held precariously in place through slots on either side of the chute. The other end of the chute led into a stock trailer that apparently presented no appeal for a mother cow being separated from her calf.

"Twist her tail a little, she'll go," Todd suggested from outside the chute. He held a firm grip on the board that separated Kori from the unruly cow, keeping well out of the animal's line of vision. Moving cattle was dangerous work and the last thing he wanted was to spook her. Todd had assisted in the yearly weaning of the calves before. He was by no means farmer material, but he knew enough of the more important do's and don'ts.

"Seriously? Does that work?" Kori strained to peer over the high boards and nearly slipped. He carefully readjusted his footing on the side of the chute and focused his attention to the cow's tail. He seized it with both hands and gave it a gentle twist. The tail flexed in his hands and rose up, but the cow did not budge. He was about to increase the torque when a stream of loose crap erupted from underneath it, covering both the backside of the cow and his arms.

Kori gagged and yelled at the top of his lungs. He divided his verbal assault equally between the cow and Todd, who unsuccessfully tried to hold back his laughter. The tail was now greased in its own slippery mess, but he twisted with one hand and punched the cow in the back with the other. He closed his eyes to avoid the splatter. Finally the animal lurched forward and stepped into the trailer.

Todd let loose of the board and hurried to close the gates on the front end of the chute. The sounds of heavy clanging metal startled the cow and she shifted around inside the confines of the trailer. The rig shifted under her weight until she settled down.

"Told you she'd go," he said, chuckling as he climbed the first two boards of the chute to look in on Kori. The look of disgust on his friend's face only made it that much harder not to laugh.

"You are a complete idiot," Kori snapped. "You knew

that was going to happen." He climbed out of the chute and ripped his gloves off as he headed for the water hydrant. His vocabulary expanded as he stalked off.

"Careful there," Todd warned, jokingly. "I'm the one holding the board. Remember? Talk like that is what got your brother's knee all busted up in there. I'm just saying'."

Kori stopped scrubbing his hands and looked up. A coldness washed over him that had nothing to do with the water running down the length of his bare arms. He pushed down on the handle and let the hose fall to his feet, ignoring the weak residual trickle that soaked his boot as the water drained out. He glanced at the stock trailer as it rocked from the force of the bellowing cow, mourning the loss of her calf. "What are you talking about?"

"You didn't know, did you?" Todd shifted uncomfortably as Kori approached him.

"Didn't know what?" Kori asked, trying to make Todd look him in the eyes. He wiped the water from his arms with the front of his shirt. Todd had retrieved his jacket from a nail on the fence and offered it to him. Kori ignored the gesture and pressed the subject further. "Tell me, Todd."

"Hey. I thought you already knew, man. I think it's best if you ask your brother."

"No, go on and tell it." Brenden appeared from the side door of the barn, where he and Jens had been busy corralling the next cow in line to be moved out to pasture, away from their offspring. He put his arm around Todd, who was at a rare loss for words. Brenden mussed the top of Todd's long hair as if to tell him it was okay. He gently nudged him in the arm and said, "You started the story, might as well finish it. He deserves that much."

Todd reluctantly told the true story of Brenden's knee and how it was injured, just months before Faye Woodson shocked the entire family by pulling up stakes and moving out. An injury that nagged him for years, even though he would never admit it. The one that cost him his full ride to Iowa and pretty much his entire future outside of Cedar Ridge.

By the time Todd finished, Kori came to learn that no wrestling practice mishap ruined his brother's knee. Instead it was the result of an accident that culminated from a long standing rift between Brenden and his stepfather. Clayton, who had heard one too many pointed comments muttered under the breath of his hired hand during the daily chores. Clayton, who carelessly forgot to lock the front door one afternoon when Brenden showed up early for work, wondering why his mother's car was parked in his boss's driveway.

Clayton began to despise everything about his mistress's eldest son, especially after Brenden saw the truth about them firsthand. Faye insisted that he keep a close watch on the boy by keeping him on the payroll. He was strong and very useful around the farm, but that just made Clayton despise him that much more. The fact that he kept their dirty secret to himself should have made him appreciative, but that only furthered his contempt. Soon Brenden would go to college, become something better than a chore hand and create distance from the rest of them. Clayton saw Brenden as a threat and men like Clayton only know one way of dealing with people that they feel threatened by. That was to destroy them.

Late one fall after one of the first practices of the season, they were transferring a load of cattle onto the trailer. Clayton had rented a patch of pasture just down the road and told Brenden he wanted to get them moved before dark that night. Brenden was inside the chute pushing the animals through while Clayton held the board in place and Todd, who had tagged along after practice, manned the gates. A particularly stubborn steer put up a fight as they hurried to get done. It was late October and soon it would be too dark to continue.

"Your brother made some smart ass comment to Clayton. I don't remember what it was exactly. About starting so late, I think," Todd said. He looked to Brenden for verification only to realize that he and Kori had been left alone to finish the story. "Anyways. That's when the board came loose and the steer slammed Bren against the back of the gate."

"Shit," Kori whispered.

"Shit's right!" Todd exclaimed. "I've never heard anyone

scream like that before. And Clayton just stood there with this goddamned grin on his face, watching him. I thought he was gonna try and stop me when I went in there to get him out. He didn't try, but he didn't help me either."

"He just stood there?"

"With that stupid grin," Todd reiterated. "I could have sworn he was laughing, too. I just couldn't tell for sure with Brenden screaming in my ear." He ran his hand over his hair, brushing his long bangs out of his face. "I know this is gonna sound bad, but I still think Clayton let go of that board on purpose."

Kori said nothing for a few minutes. He let the idea of Clayton purposely hurting his brother sink in. As absurd as it sounded, it made total sense the more he thought about it. He had seen that hateful grin plastered on his stepfather's face many times before. It was always when he thought he had the upper hand or when he knew that he had caused great hurt to someone. The more he thought about it the angrier he became. There was only one thing that he did not understand.

"Why didn't he tell mom what really happened? Why lie about it?"

"I don't know," Todd replied. "What do you think?"

"Maybe he didn't want to upset her. That Clayton would do something like that."

They walked over to the chute as the next cow clamored

out of the barn. She immediately began to fight against the narrow boards that constricted her. The cow attempted to back out the same way she had come in but the gate was already closed behind her. Already her orphaned calf cried desperately in the distance, but she was too caught up in her own state of panic and self-preservation to notice.

"Yeah, maybe," Todd said. "Or maybe he was afraid that she wouldn't believe him."

CHAPTER 24

Dale collapsed on the carpeted floor of his tiny living room seconds after walking in the door. His chest thumped so rapidly beneath his jacket that he wondered if he were having a heart attack. For a brief weak moment he welcomed the idea. It would have been the easiest plan of escape from the overwhelming stress that he was now under. A surefire way to wipe away the sights, the smells and the sounds of the depravity that he had been subjected to.

After melting into the plush rug for what seemed liked hours, he suddenly felt the need to throw up. His empty stomach had been threatening to betray him all day. Now he was in the comfort of his own home, where the embarrassment of losing complete control was no longer an issue. He steadied himself on weary legs and started down the hall toward the bathroom. His foot snagged something on the floor, breaking his stride just enough to make the short run to the toilet an impossibility. He dry-heaved over the sink as spots danced in his vision.

He held a cold washcloth against his face as he stepped back into the hallway. There he saw the thing that had nearly caused him to fall flat on his face with a mouthful of puke. It was the heavy canvas bag that he brought with him from Stu's. The strap was broken free of the hook, where his boot had pulled it half the length of the hall. He stared at the bag and sighed. Whatever possessed him to agree to take the damned thing anyway and what the hell was he supposed to do with it now?

He had not been home five minutes after Hazelton had dropped him off before his phone started ringing. Not his cell, but the house phone that he had almost forgotten he owned. He only had it because the local phone company would not provide him with internet service without it. Half expecting a telemarketer on the other end, Dale waited until the fourth ring and hit the send button without speaking.

"Dale, are you there?" He recognized the voice on the other end immediately, even before she continued. "Dale, if you're there pick up. I didn't hear a message so I don't know if this is working or not, but if you..."

"I'm here, Margaret," he interrupted. Her voice sounded desperate and panicked.

"Oh, thank god you're there." She definitely sounded out of sorts. "Dale, it's Stu. He hasn't acted right all day and I'm really beginning to worry about him. He hasn't come out of his workshop since he came home this morning and now he won't even let me in there to bring him his lunch."

"Where did he go this morning, Margaret?" Dale asked, even though he thought he already knew the answer. "Did he tell you?"

"He hasn't told me anything. The only time he's spoken all day was to scream at me to leave him be. You know that's not like him, Dale. There has to be something terribly wrong and his blood sugar has been so irregular lately. He needs to eat." Her voice cracked as she spoke, on the verge of breaking. Margaret Fisher was one of the sweetest women that he had ever met and it broke his heart to hear that degree of worry in her voice. If his suspicions were true, her problems were about to get one hell of a lot worse.

"I'll be there in twenty minutes," Dale assured her and hung up the phone. He got there in fewer than fifteen.

Armed with the plate of food that Margaret insisted that he take with him, Dale cautiously tested the knob on the workshop door. It was not locked as she had previously told him, which was less than comforting as he called out Stu's name. He was glad that Margaret could not see him from the house as he drew his Glock. Retired or not, Stu was a lawman and Dale knew better than entering a cop's castle without expecting a fight. Even from an old man with a leg full of bone fragments.

The lights were not on and the early fall dusk offered

little to help his eyes adjust to the interior of the building. Smells of freshly worked lumber filled his nostrils and brought with it the nostalgia of better times. He fumbled against the wall until his hands found the light switch. The shed lit up but revealed no signs of Stu. His heart sank as he scanned the room, stopping on a workbench along the far wall. A compound crossbow sat on the bench top, contrasting with the otherwise neatly arranged collection of tools.

To the right of the workbench was the door to Stu's office. A light flickered from the crack beneath it, an inconsistent dancing blue glow of a television set. Dale sat the plate of food down and gripped his weapon with both hands. Slowly, he approached the door and called Stu's name once again. He held his breath and prepared himself for the inevitable. He was about to push the door open with his foot when Stu answered back.

“It's not locked,” Stu called out. His speech was slurred and muffled.

“Stu, I'm coming in,” Dale answered back. He glanced to his left at the crossbow, the one that he was sure had ended his partner's life earlier that day. From there he could also see a dozen short black arrows scattered beside it. Bolts, Hazelton had called them. “Is that gonna be a problem?”

“Not as long as you're alone, son,” Stu mumbled. “Got no bone to pick with you.”

Against his better judgment, Dale holstered his gun and

pushed the door open. He knew in his heart that Stu would never cause him any more harm than he would his own son, if he had one. Hearing the old man refer to him as such only solidified that belief. Stu may have possibly committed two murders in the past few days, but he was still like a father to him. Besides, if he really wanted to hurt him; Dale knew that he would not have answered him first.

The tiny room reeked of scotch and cigarettes. It surprised Dale because he had only seen Stu drink on a few rare occasions and never knew him to smoke. Like the shop, the lights in the office were all off. A television filled the center of Stu's desk, providing the only illumination. Stu slouched in his chair, his right hand alternating between a remote control and a nearly empty bottle of Johnny Walker. The flickering set created an aura like glow around his body, adding to Dale's increasing sense of disquietude. Half a dozen wires connected it to both a DVD player and a VCR. Hundreds of tapes and discs were stacked on every remaining available inch of the desk's surface. It was not until Dale entered the room that he fully comprehended the images playing on the screen.

"What the fuck?" Dale managed to choke out, staring at the television in disgusted horror. Over Stu's shoulder a scene from a pornographic movie played out at an accelerated speed. Even with the actors racing through the motions of coitus at a blurring pace, Dale could clearly see that they were extremely young. The scene ended and another set of equally underage actors flashed across the television screen.

“She's on there, Dale. I haven't found her yet,” he slurred, motioning to the stacks of media on the desk. “But I know if I keep looking...” He started to cry as the disc ended. He impatiently waited for the player to eject the disc, tossed it aside and inserted another.

“What in the hell are you talking about?” Dale asked, his anger building up. To think that the man that he had respected like a father his entire life was sitting alone in the dark watching kiddie porn while his sweet wife worried herself sick about whether or not he was getting enough to eat for lunch. He resisted the urge to brain him with the butt of his gun.

“Gabby,” Stu replied, crying even harder as the name left his lips.

“Your daughter?”

“Those bastards took my little girl for this filth! Stole her from her mother and me for filth.” He looked to Dale with pleading eyes. “Help me find her, Dale. Please help me get her back.”

Dale averted his gaze from the obscene images and reached across Stu to turn off the television. The maddening display ceased, allowing his mind to stop reeling for a moment. He had tried to digest about as much insanity as a person could take in one day. First it was Tassler with the spooning deer and the yet to be identified bodily fluids splattered on its hide. Now Stu, shit-faced and crying with his video library of abysmal hedonism. Any respite was a welcomed blessing. That was when he noticed the gun in Stu's left hand.

It was a small snub-nose revolver, the kind many cops kept strapped to their ankles as a backup piece. It was impossible to tell whether or not Stu saw him notice the gun. The old man never took his eyes from the screen even after it went blank. The gun vibrated against the arm of the chair, creating a shadowy blur against the light shining in from the other room. Dale kept his eyes trained on the Stu's left hand as he carefully weighed his next words.

"Stu, whatever you have done. Whatever this is all about." He picked up a cassette tape from the desk and waved it in front of Stu's face. Immediately he threw it back down as if it were toxic. "This will not bring Gabby back. I can call someone to help you through this. Someone that can make all of this right."

"No!" Stu screamed. "I won't just turn myself in. Not like this." The gun in his hand became still as his finger slid inside the trigger guard. He pointed it in Dale's direction. His sobbing continued, evolving into something between garbled laughter and howling. It reminded Dale of coyotes in the summertime.

"Okay!" Dale extended both hands forward, palms out. All of his law enforcement training seemed to escape him at the moment. He was riding on pure instinct and of course fear. "Take it easy, Stu. Tell me what you want then."

"I can't let Margaret see this... this filth," he replied. Pushing his chair away from the desk, he gave himself enough room to open a large desk drawer at his feet with his right hand. The remote control dropped to the floor as he pulled out a heavy canvas bag. He turned his swollen red eyes to Dale and said, "You take it and burn it."

"Stu, I..."

"Do as I say, boy!" Stu ordered. He opened the bag and began sweeping discs and tapes into it with the hand holding the gun. Dale cringed as he saw that the finger never left the trigger guard. Stu worked frantically as if he were putting out a fire instead of filling a bag. He looked at Dale and slurred, "She's a good woman, my Margaret."

"Yes she is," Dale agreed. "But I can't just take these and not report them. You know me better than that."

"Please, boy," Stu begged. "I can't have her seeing this. It would break her heart for good." The look on Dale's face told him that pleading was not going to work. The boy was just too by-the-book for his own damn good. He placed the gun on the desk and changed his tactic to one of bargaining. "The only thing these tapes will do is hurt her and the families of the others. The bastards who made them don't give a damn about that. If you let this filth get out it will rip open old wounds that have taken so long to heal. Don't let them destroy her all over again. I swear on my life that I will let you drive me to the station if you just take these filthy things away and promise to burn them."

Dale thought about it for a minute, accessing the situation. At least the gun was out of his hand and on the desktop. He would have liked it better if Stu had gone the whole nine by handing it over, but it was a start. He watched as Stu finished filling the bag and zipped it shut. "You want to at least eat before we go? Margaret sent a plate in with me."

"Does that mean you'll do it?"

Dale sighed. He could only imagine the grief he was going to get from both Hazelton and Sheriff Baylor for breaking the chain of custody with evidence. Seeing no other way to coax the distraught man out of his office, he put on his best fake smile and said, "Okay. I'll do it."

"Promise me, no one will ever see these," Stu begged as he handed over the bag.

"Okay, I promise."

Stu settled back in his seat and let out a deep breath. He looked as if a thousand pounds had just been lifted from his chest. He thanked Dale repeatedly and cried some more. This time the crying was not accompanied by the desperate sobbing. Dale took the bag from him and started out the door, shocked by the sheer weight of the contents.

"Bring that plate back in with you, will ya?"

Dale smiled and walked out to his truck. He hoped that Margaret was not watching him from the house. The thought of her made him consider keeping his word to Stu. Maybe the old man was right. There would definitely be an investigation, but what would really become of it? The bodies of the perpetrators were already growing cold. That was assuming that Stu had killed the only ones involved. Somehow he doubted that was the case. Even so, what did it matter?

With no experience in cases like this, he could only guess how many resources would actually be utilized to identify the victims in the videos. Sadly, he thought to himself, more than likely very little. Like runaways, child victims in cases like this were unfortunately labeled as victims of their own devise. The only certainty was that Margaret Fisher's life was about to become undone. Exposing her to Stu's suspicions about her daughter's disappearance would devastate her.

He walked back to the workshop, already devising several plans on how to dispose of the bagful of smut. He was reaching for the plate of food when a muffled gunshot echoed throughout the building. Stunned, he let go of the plate and strained to listen. He wished desperately for Stu to call out a "sorry" or "oops" or anything that someone who didn't just put a round into their own skull might say. The only sound his mind registered was his own pulse whooshing through it. A watery gasp rose up in his throat as he silently bid farewell to a lifelong friend. Unable to tolerate any more bloodshed in one day, Dale cursed his own cowardice and stepped back outside to call 911.

After weathering the barrage of questions from the first responders and escorting a devastated Margaret Fisher to the home of a family friend, Dale found himself alone in his trailer once again. His throat stung from stomach acid and his head throbbed. Too weary to lift the bag, he dragged it into his dark room and shut the door behind it. I'll deal with that tomorrow, he thought to himself, but right now I need sleep. He knew that he should eat first, but his stomach threatened to erupt again at the mere thought. So he turned off the living room lamp and collapsed on the couch.

Sleep came almost at once but not without a price. His mind played out recent events, mixing them into a potpourri of chronologically out of order scenes. He was jolted awake several times by some of the more disturbing ones, especially those that defied logic. A spooning deer pawed at a plate of leftovers, while Tassler and Margaret Fisher played euchre against Stu and a smoldering Virgil Semler. They played hand after hand, sitting Indian-style around a deerskin rug. Semler coughed up smoke from holes in his body that should not have existed, chanting the words “Highdrugs” over and over as he dealt. Dale knew on some conscious level that euchre was not a betting game, but he was also aware that stacks of pornographic DVD's were being wagered like poker chips. Tassler and Margaret were winning by a considerable margin.

No matter how hard he tried, Dale could not escape the bizarre purging of mind clutter as he dozed. The harder he tried to let much needed sleep take hold, the faster the dreams came. They flashed behind his eyelids in fast forward like scenes from Stu's television set. Suddenly his heart skipped a beat and he sat upright. The DVD, the one in the player. There was still a disc in the machine when he had shut Stu's TV off. He had to get that disc, assuming no one on the scene had already discovered it.

He grabbed his keys and rushed out the door in such haste that he never bothered to lock it behind him. He looked at the clock on his dashboard. It was nearly midnight. Surely, enough time had passed that he would have the Fisher residence all to himself. The cover of the night was his best hope of saving his dead friend's wife a lot of heartache.

CHAPTER 25

Kyle Collins watched from his front step as the cop dashed out of his trailer. Hoping to remain unnoticed, he cupped a hand over the tip of his smoke and sat still. The cop climbed into his truck and spun his rear tires as he exited the trailer park. His attention appeared to be anywhere but on the spying neighbor across the lane. That suited Kyle just fine. He and his cousin had spent the better part of the evening matching each other, beer for beer. The last thing he wanted was to wind up in the county drunk tank.

He waited until the sound of the cop's truck faded in the distance before standing up. He considered waking his cousin, but quickly scratched the idea. Delbert had snorted up the last of his oxys days ago, long before his prescription was due for a refill. With the perv gone, there was nobody left to fix him up right when the well ran dry. Delbert was in a bad way and waking him after a drunk would be asking for a fight.

He looked around to make sure none of the neighborhood

brats were outside. Then he ran across the lane as fast as his drunken legs could take him. With the bottom of his shirt covering his fingers, he tested the knob on Dale's front door. He was so shocked that the knob turned and the door swung inward that he stood there for a moment, staring at the room beyond it. He took one last look behind him and then he went inside.

By comparison, the cop's trailer was so much nicer than his own shabby dump. The carpet looked new and it did not have that propane fart smell that old trailers all seemed to possess. Hell, no wonder everyone in town thought the guy was queer. Nobody's place should look that neat and clean. Rage rose up from his insides as studied the room, fueled by alcohol and his deep hatred for the police. It surfaced in the form of a hawked up ball of phlegm, which he spat all over a mirror on the wall.

He did not bother to steal anything of value as he went through the rooms other than a few handfuls of loose change. The real purpose of his visit was to somehow defile the smug cop's perfect little castle, to remind him of who he really was and where he lived. He thought about lifting the back of the toilet, climbing up and taking a nice dump in the tank. The pain pills Delbert had, the ones he shared before running close to being out, always tended to stop him up. So that was out.

He could piss though. Drinking an eighteen pack of Old-Style saw to that, he thought as he proceeded to spray the walls of the trailer like a dog marking his territory. When his bladder was emptied he commenced to kicking holes in doors and walls, which proved quite difficult given his state of drunkenness and the trailer's tight quarters. He kicked the last of the doors in the hallway and found something that piqued his curiosity.

He first poked at the large bag with his foot. Whatever was inside was heavy and solid against his touch. The shape and color of the bag looked army issue, leading him to believe that he had just scored the cop's personal arsenal. He had a job lined up for the next night and some firepower would come in real handy. To think, he thought, a pig's guns being used in a dope grab. How priceless was that? He hoisted the bag onto his shoulders and made a mad dash back to his own trailer. He couldn't wait to tell Delbert.

Unaware that the remainder of Stu's final secret was out of his possession, Dale Scheck sat in the cab of his truck and laid his head back. He had parked along a quiet stretch of River Road and closed his eyes. The disc that was still in the player, where his dead friend had left it, was now at the bottom of the Cedar. For a moment he regretted not bringing the entire lot with him. He gladly would have tossed them one by one into the deep water and been done with them.

As soon as the thought passed through his mind, he realized how foolish that would have been. What if, by some freak chance, a fisherman happened to snag one of them? One disc in the water made that outcome a near impossibility. But hundreds of them? No, the only true way to erase them from existence was to burn each and every one of them. That was exactly what he intended to do, first thing in the morning.

He sank further into his seat and let the running water lull him into a deep slumber.

CHAPTER 26

They waited for the others to arrive at the campground, just down the road from the burned out remains of Virgil's property. Kori figured that it was for the best to meet at a neutral location, considering how Brenden felt about the two of them going out without him. It was not that his brother was angry that he and Todd were going along with Soup's plan to do a score, especially so far from home. He had never seen Brenden so at peace with himself since the day he had broken all ties with the Campbell's. The only time he had voiced any concern was after learning who Soup had brought into the fold in his absence.

Kori knew very little about Kyle or Delbert Collins, except that they came from a rough family, even more dysfunctional than the Campbell clan. He had heard stories about how Delbert had either shot or had been shot by a cop a few years back. He and his brother had beaten the cop and left him for dead after the altercation. Delbert had just been released from a surprisingly brief stay in jail and was chomping at the bit to make up for lost time. According to Todd, he was actually the less psychotic one of the bunch.

Kori was uncertain but he thought the cop was the same one who had supposedly killed himself the night before. It had been plastered all over the front page of his father's morning newspaper, along with the story about a deer hunting accident that happened a few miles from their house. They had watched the fire department pass back and forth by their place several times the day before. So far, the names on that one still hadn't made the paper.

A thought occurred to him as they waited in the fading sunlight. Since his return to Cedar Ridge, two people had died. Maybe more if the hunting accident turned out to be serious. That was pretty extraordinary for an area that claimed roughly two hundred residents if you didn't include the population of nearby Cameron. He considered the notion that maybe he had brought some kind of bad mojo back to the place. He tried to share his theory with Todd, but was brushed off immediately.

“Man, don't talk like that before a job. You're giving me the creeps,” Todd said, not really paying attention. He was hunched over a glass tray, manipulating a pile of white powder into neat lines with the edge of a plastic card. When he was satisfied with his handiwork he banged the card on the glass before licking it clean. Kori saw that it was a library card that he was using.

"That's what's giving you the creeps, dude," Kori countered, pointing to the tray. Todd lowered a rolled up bill to it and made one of the lines vanish. He offered the tray across the seat and Kori shook his head. "No thanks. I'm nervous enough the way it is."

"You sure? This will settle you down." Todd continued to hold the tray in the air. Kori stared at the tray and back to him, doubtful. "I'm serious. A little bump won't hurt you." He leaned over and snorted another line, rubbing his nose vigorously as he sat back up. He handed Kori the rolled bill. "Give you legs, bro."

"How do I do it?" He took the bill and stared at it, wondering just how sanitary it was to touch something that had just been in another man's nostril. He steadied the tray with one hand as Todd held it in front of him, bent forward and inhaled. Instantly, the inner lining of his nostril felt as if he had just snorted fire. The pain subsided after a few seconds, but not before his eyes brimmed over with tears. He rubbed the side of his face and grimaced. He tried to speak but the drainage in the back of his throat stopped him. He swallowed hard and nearly gagged from the bitter chemical aftertaste.

"There," Todd grinned, pulling the tray away. "Better?"

"No."

Todd laughed, "You will be."

He was right about that. By the time Soup's Impala came to a stop beside them, Kori felt a warm sensation of well-being wash over him. His scalp tingled and the hairs on the top of his head felt as if they were moving involuntarily. His nostril no longer burned, but the flesh around the sides of his face felt stiff and wet. His throat was raw and his tongue became very dry, making him regret not bringing along something to drink. Electricity ran through his muscles and he suddenly felt as though he could take on the world.

Kyle Collins exited the Impala, bringing with him a large canvas bag. He wrestled the bag into the back of Todd's vehicle and climbed in beside it. Todd handed him the glass tray and he greedily snatched it up. He deftly snorted up the remaining lines from the tray as Todd followed closely behind the Impala. The tray was passed back to the front but the rolled bill mysteriously did not make the return trip. Todd either didn't notice or at least did not let on like he did.

Kori became extremely verbal as the hour long trip progressed, so it was only a matter of time before the obvious question was asked. Leaning his head between the headrests, he ogled the bag with an enthusiasm that put Kyle Collins on edge. He poked a hand through the seats and pointed. “What's in that thing anyway?”

Kyle placed a forearm over the nylon straps, pulling the bag closer. He leaned forward and snarled, “How's about you mind your own business, fuckhead.” His lips curled back, exposing what was left of his drug ruined teeth. His eyes were wide and glassy, like an animal just starting to feel the effects of the tranquilizer dart sticking in its hide. The pendulum of Kori's high took a sharp downward swing as he quickly retreated back to the safety of the front seat. Kyle sniggered through his nose and continued to stare at him.

"How about you mind who you're talking to in my car," Todd said. His eyes blazed as he stared at his backseat passenger's reflection in the rear view. He gave Kyle a few seconds to respond before adding, "Fuckhead."

Kyle laughed nervously and leaned back in his seat. He pulled the bag onto his lap so its weighted mass draped over him like a shield. He held it tightly against himself, despite the jagged corners of plastic that poked through the canvas and into his thighs. As with most bullies, it made him uncomfortable being outnumbered and not in control. He stared out the window into the darkening sky and scowled. "You and your girlfriend just stay the hell out of my way when we get there, maybe you'll both make it home tonight."

"Yeah, maybe," Todd replied, unmoved by the veiled threat. "Until then, shut the hell up and enjoy the ride."

Kori was touched by the way Todd had defended him, but the confrontation had left him with a nervous buzzing in his head as the effects of the drug intensified. He still felt as though he could take on the world, but at the same time got the uneasy feeling that he was actually going to have to. Thoughts passed through his brain at such a high rate that they canceled each other out before fully registering. He felt paranoid, responsible for the tension inside the car and obligated to fix it. "I just wanted to know what was in the bag."

Todd shot him an irritated glance. "I know, man. Now shut up."

He wasn't sure if he could, but was willing to try. An endless ribbon of lines in the road zipped toward them, and then disappeared beneath the car. Each glowed brighter than the last as the headlights reflected from their surface. Kori focused on them, willing them to soothe him into a calming trance. He could feel his pulse on the side of his neck without even touching it. It was both fascinating and frightening to him. He wanted out of the car badly. He wanted a drink even more. Most of all he wanted to do another line.

Brake lights flashed from the back of the Impala and Todd pulled off to the side of the dirt road. The sudden change in momentum jolted Kori from his stupor. He looked up and wondered how long ago they had left the highway. He had lost all track of time while concentrating on keeping the effects of the crank under control. With the car stopped, the speedy sensation crept back in. The overwhelming need to empty his bladder came without warning. He stepped out of the car and let loose a stream onto the hard packed dirt without bothering to shut the door.

Held captive by the marathon pissing session, Kori

surveyed his surroundings. He could barely make out a faint light in the distance. It was several miles further down the road, which was not much more than a cow path surrounded by fields. He assumed that the source of the light was the place that they were headed. Seeing it gave him an uneasy feeling. He felt like running, but where would he go? Through some dark field in the middle of nowhere, fifty miles from home? His heart threatened to leap out of his chest just from pissing. He could only imagine how far he could get before keeling over, dead.

"I always wondered if you did that standing up, college boy." Soup was leaning over the hood with his elbows propped under his chin, watching him. His lips formed a devilish grin through the mouth hole of his mask. He let out an impatient sigh and asked, "Are you done yet?"

"Uh, yeah," Kori replied, zipping his fly. He felt his face become flush with embarrassment. "Sorry."

"Then load up. I don't want to spend all night here." Soup turned away and walked back to the Impala, where the others busied themselves with last minute preparations. Todd pulled a pair of gloves and a mask from the trunk, warning him to shake them out first. Short aluminum ball bats were doled out next. Kori reluctantly accepted one and tested its weight in his hands.

The feeling was surreal. The wheels were set into motion and there was no turning back.

The moon was nonexistent and navigating the road

without headlights proved more difficult than Soup had planned. The entire job hinged on the element of surprise, so it was decided that they would abandon both vehicles much sooner than they would have liked to. This meant nearly a half mile hike separated the crew from the house at the end of the road. Kori and Todd took up rear and purposely lagged behind.

"This would have never happened if Brenden was here. This is all bullshit, Kori. Something ain't right about this," Todd complained. He lifted his mask and sniffed the air. "Smell that?"

"What?" Kori sniffed, smelling nothing but his own stale breath beneath the fabric.

"Fucking anhydrous." He pulled his mask back down and cursed.

Kori had no clue what that meant but it didn't sound good, whatever it was. "What do you want to do?" He glanced over his shoulder at their vehicles, guessing the time it would take to run back if necessary. The paranoid sketchiness eased its way back into his psyche. He started to wonder if the effects of the drug were going to linger forever. He promised himself that he would never touch hard drugs again.

"I don't know. Just stay close and keep your head down."

They caught up to the others as they crouched behind a row of low shrubs at the edge of the property. An exterior light was mounted on a pole between the house and a garage. It hummed as it cast a yellowish glow over the sparse lawn between the two buildings. Its range fell just shy of their hiding place. Every window in the house was dark. The only activity came from the garage in the form of music, heavy with bass and guttural vocals.

While the others discussed the plan of attack, Kori killed time by watching Chris. He had first noticed the little guy's peculiar behavior before they had set off on foot. Chris was extremely fidgety under normal circumstances, but even more so that night. He was down on all fours, combing through the grass and carrying on a conversation with no one but himself. Every so often he would press an ear to the earth, listen for a moment and then smile widely. Several times he abruptly sat up and glanced around with an expression of bewilderment on his face. Kori made the decision right then to steer clear of him if at all possible.

As Soup did his best to lay out a workable game plan, Todd sidled up and shoved him hard enough to knock him over. Soup fell face first into the bushes, snagging his mask on the lower branches. It sat slightly askew on his head, revealing a look of astonishment. Todd hovered over his prone body, seething. “Did you know this was a goddamn cookhouse, you idiot?”

Soup grunted as he got back to his feet, using the bat for support. His hands choked up on the handle and he lifted it in the air, glaring at Todd with fire in his eyes. He held it there for a moment before lowering it back down. Leaning close to Todd, he pointed at the house and answered in a low voice, “This is the address they gave me, man. I don't give a rat's ass what goes on here. Not my business. All I know is that we're all gonna get fat off this job. But if you ever...”

“How fat?” Todd interrupted.

“What?” Soup straightened the mask, his eyes darting nervously around at the rest of the group. They all watched the two of them intently.

“You heard me. How fat?” Todd kept his tone low, but made sure that everyone else could hear him as he put Soup on the spot for an answer. He waved a gloved hand around the group. “How much are we getting paid?”

“Really?” Soup threw his arms up and rolled his head back. “Do you really want to discuss this now?”

Todd shook his own head in frustration. “Never mind. Let's just get this over with.”

“That's what I thought,” Soup said. He reached over and slapped Chris on the back of the head. The blow seemed to bring his dazed cousin back to land of the living. “Let's do this.”

They turned their attention back to the garage and quietly stepped out of the darkness, slowly creeping across the yard. The others went directly to the walk-in door of the garage and positioned themselves on either side. Todd tugged Kori's arm, leading him to the backside of the building and motioned for him to stay down. Kori was more than willing to sit in the dark and wait out the ensuing shit storm. He was fearful that Todd intended to leave him there and join the others, but Todd stayed put beside him.

A stack of firewood provided cover from the light, but did little to muffle the heavy bass thumps coming from inside the garage. Kori was not exactly sure what genre of music it was, but it sounded to him like someone being tortured. The chemical smell that Todd had recognized right away was much stronger behind the garage. He was thankful that the mask provided at least some protection from the stench. Regardless, he held his breath as much as possible and took shallow breaths when he could not.

Suspicious of their whereabouts, Little Chris stepped around the corner and whispered their names. His own level of paranoia was in overdrive and the argument between his cousin and Todd had only made it worse. They crouched lower as Chris's footsteps crunched across the gravel, stopping right above them. He peered over the top and called out loudly, “What the hell are you two doing back there?”

It was no surprise that he spotted them so easily. There was barely enough room for them both to fit behind the small stack of unevenly cut logs, let alone hide there. What did shock them was the violent reaction that ensued after they were discovered. They watched with horrified fascination as Chris burst into a tantrum, fueled by speed and days of sleep deprivation. Spittle flew from his mouth, along with a flurry of insults as he kicked at the pile of wood. Kori blinked as pieces of bark sprayed his face.

"Jesus. He's gonna get us all killed," Todd said. He whispered the words but it was futile. Chris's voice carried across the yard, loud enough that windows in the house began to light up. Somewhere close, a dog started to bark.

Chris continued his attack on the logs to the point of nearly tipping the stack on top of them. He rambled incoherently at the top of his lungs, "Are you gonna flake on us now, you pussies? You think you can hide behind your fucking tinfoil badges!"

"What the hell is he talking about?" Kori yelled, doing his best to avoid the falling pieces.

"He's spun bad," Todd replied, no longer bothering to keep his voice down. "We gotta bail before he gets us all killed." He stood up, pulling Kori to his feet as he went. Immediately, the barrel of a gun was shoved in his face.

Chris held the pistol in one outstretched hand, while the rest of his body turned sideways. He kept the barrel pointed at Todd, while he slowly sidestepped in the other direction. His other hand waved back in a come hither motion to something or someone that only he seemed to be able to see. He kept the hand outstretched as if holding the apparitions at bay. Satisfied that his hallucinatory reinforcements had his back, he lowered the gun down. He giggled and said, “Somebody's gonna get killed alright, but it ain't going to be nobody from my team.”

Kori blinked and tried to comprehend what happened next. One minute he and his friend were in a standoff with a deluded speed freak and his imaginary army; the next thing he knew Chris was on the ground writhing in pain. The dog had lunged from out of the darkness and latched onto the outstretched hand with such ferocity that the sounds of bones cracking were audible, even over the screaming. Every time Chris attempted to free himself from the bite, the dog shook his head and dug deeper into the hand.

Kori and Todd stood, frozen as the chaos unfolded. Self-preservation eventually trumped panic and Chris remembered the gun in his free hand. He raised it to the dog's muzzle and fired twice. Jaws ruined from the blasts, the dog relaxed its grip and dropped dead on the ground. Chris fell backwards and landed sharply on his back. He giggled uncontrollably and raised his hand to access the damage. The laughter quickly ceased as he saw the stump where his hand used to be, the hand that he had just shot off.

Kyle Collins rounded the corner of the garage to see what the commotion was about. The precious element of surprise was completely gone and he figured there had better be a damned good reason for it. If there wasn't, someone was going to bleed.

He emerged from the shadows of the building and saw Chris laying on the ground, studying something mangled and bloody in the light. Startled by the sudden movement, Chris drew the pistol with his one good hand and shot Kyle in the face. Kyle fell backwards, dead before his body touched the gravel.

Chris stumbled to his feet and cried out in triumph. A woman stepped out of the house and onto the front stoop, screaming the dog's name as she went. She was little more than a silhouette in the foreground of the lamplight, but Kori clearly saw the shotgun in her hands. She raised the weapon to her shoulder and fired a shot in their direction. The buckshot missed Chris by mere inches. It sailed past him and slammed into the woodpile, where Kori and Todd ducked for cover.

The steady thumping of music ceased from inside the garage, replaced by a barrage of gunfire. The woman screamed in pain and discharged her shotgun again. Todd pulled Kori up by the arm and the two of them fled in the opposite direction. They ran aimlessly across the unlit fringes of the property as fast as their legs would take them back to the dirt road. Behind them, the crescendo of firepower and angry voices intensified. Something exploded with enough force to vibrate the ground beneath their feet, but neither of them dared to look back.

Kori's shoes slapped the dirt surface as he furiously pumped his arms. He had no problem outrunning Todd, whose smoker's lungs wheezed in protest with every step. Adrenaline prodded him beyond his limits as the distance between himself and the chaos widened. Only when the Corolla was nearly close enough to touch did he stop to let his pounding heart relax. He doubled over and sucked in much needed oxygen as Todd caught up and did the same. They walked the rest of the way to the car, still panting as they climbed inside.

From the path that they had just traveled, a figure emerged out of the darkness. They both gasped as they watched Chris sprinting straight toward them. He held the remains of his left arm in front of him, high in the air like an Olympic torch bearer. Blood spurted from the stump with every beat of his weakening pulse. They watched helplessly as his knees collided with the front bumper. Momentum pushed him forward as his torso and face slammed down on the center of the hood, leaving a shallow dent. The arm that was a hand longer than the other hit the windshield first. The stump connected a split second later. A wide swath of blood smeared across the glass as his body came to a halt.

"Where the hell did he come from?" Kori yelled.

"Same way we did, I guess," Todd replied. He cautiously stepped out of the car and felt the side of Chris's neck for a pulse, keeping the open door between them in case he miraculously sprang back into action. He personally hoped not to feel any sign of life from the little bastard that had nearly gotten them killed, but saw right away that he was still breathing. He sighed and looked to Kori. "What do you want to do with him?"

As much as they would have rather pulled him free of the hood and left him lying in the road to die, neither had the heart to do so. They quickly lifted him up and shoved him in the backseat next to the canvas bag that the newly deceased Kyle Collins had left behind. Looking at it as they sped away, Kori could not help but to wonder once again, just what was in that bag?

CHAPTER 27

Detective Hazelton watched the young deputy frantically search through the rooms of his disheveled trailer, growing more frustrated with each passing minute. This behavior had been going on since he had arrived. He could not help but to feel at least partly responsible for the current mental state of the man he had come to think of as his friend. Sure, he had exploited the obvious history Dale had with the county when he had recruited him for the assignment, but he also assumed that he had the natural fortitude to handle it. Doubt about that assessment was starting to creep in.

"It was right here, Bobby. I swear it." Dale pointed to the spot on the carpet, just inside the doorway to a spare bedroom. It was one of the few areas of the trailer that was not sopping wet and reeking of stale piss.

Hazelton poked his head beyond the door frame and studied the room. He had heard about the darkroom that Dale had assembled, but was still taken back by the number of photographs that covered the walls. The absence of light prevented him from making out any of the subject matter, but he had a good idea of what the general theme was. He nodded to the broken latch and asked, “Other than the door getting busted in, does it look like anything else in the room has been disturbed?”

“Nothing except for the missing bag of, er...” Dale paused for a moment. “Except for the evidence.”

Evidence that you failed to inform me about until it grew legs and walked away. Hazelton kept the thought to himself, not wanting to further Dale's agitated state. He pointed to the part of the door where it had been kicked open. “Well, there's no chance that whoever did this used the knob to get in, so that means no prints. I don't know what else has been touched since you got home, but I'm going to ask you to stop now. I'll get a couple of techs in here to dust the place down. Okay?”

“Okay.” Dale had a hand gripped around the outer frame of the door. He quickly pulled it away and stared at it sheepishly. “Sorry.”

“Don't sweat it,” Hazelton said, offering him a comforting smile. He hoped that Dale had not inadvertently destroyed any possible prints that his crew could lift from the place during his brief meltdown. It was understandable, given the recent events. Watching a good friend eat his own gun was enough to put the zap on anyone's head. He took out his phone to call in the lab techs, asking Dale a few questions as he waited for dispatch to pick up on the other end. "Any idea who did this? Any pissed off exes, anybody you've dealt with on the job, neighbors with a beef?"

Dale's eyes narrowed at the last suggestion. "I know exactly who did this."

"Care to share?" He relayed the address to the operator and snapped the phone shut.

"That piece of shit across the street, Collins."

"Collins?" The name rang a bell for some reason. Hazelton racked his brain to find the connection. He raised his eyebrows and looked at Dale, quizzically. "Not one of the same Collins that had the run in with your pal, Fisher?"

Hearing Stu's name spoken stung like a slap, especially when used in the same sentence as one of the Collins scumbags. Images of the last few minutes of Stu's life flashed through Dale's mind. A renewed anger surfaced in his heavy heart. Without being aware of what he was doing he pulled at the straps of his shoulder holster, cinching them painfully tight against his torso. He started for the door as he answered, "Not the same one, but might as well be."

Hazelton grabbed his arm and spun him around as he passed by. Dale stiffened against his grip but did not try to pull away. Dark circles under the deputy's eyes accentuated the wrath that they harbored within. Underlying sadness flickered beneath the angry stare like a wavering flame, desperately trying not to shine through. Bobby found himself staring into a face that had aged decades in the past few days. He wrapped an arm over his shoulder. "And where do you think you're going?"

"To find the fucker who pissed on my walls!" he hissed.

"And do what? Arrest him, kill him, beat him to a pulp? Without a shred of proof?" Hazelton pulled him closer and pressed a finger into his chest. "You are a good cop, Dale. Start acting like it. Okay?"

"They came into *my* home, Bobby." Tears streamed over the stubble on his cheeks. His lips quivered as he wiped at the waterworks with the back of his hand. The tough guy persona crumbled and he leaned his head against Hazelton's shoulder, sobbing. "My goddamn home."

"I know, buddy." Hazelton nodded his head and pulled him back toward the darkroom. "All the more reason to wait until we have solid evidence. If there are prints, my guys will find them. Collins is in the system. If he was here, we'll know it. Then, and only then, you and I will go get him. Until then, why don't you come back in here with me? I think you have some pictures to show me, huh?"

CHAPTER 28

For Kori, sleeping was an impossibility. They had beaten the sun home by only an hour before he had a chance to lay his head down. The speed had left his muscles drained and gelatinous, but his brain continued to race a mile a minute around the inside of his skull. In a way he was thankful for the inability to let his mind drift away, because that meant no dreaming. He wanted no part of dreams after the night he had experienced.

Sprawled out in the backseat of the Corolla, he finally felt the soothing warmth of fatigue settle in. The only thing keeping him from giving in was the unmistakable smell of blood in the car. Todd had done his best to clean up most of the mess, but it seemed as though Chris had bled on every square inch of the interior. Several quilts covered the stains that were too stubborn to scrub out. Even so, the unpleasant coppery stink lingered in the air.

They had made the frantic trip back home in record time,

only stopping long enough to pick up Brenden on the way to the hospital. There they had parked a block from the emergency room entrance and carried a barely conscious Chris the rest of the way. Stripped of his mask and gloves, along with several other incriminating items in his pockets, Chris was roughly shoved into the empty lobby as soon as the automatic doors slid open. They did not wait for the body to hit the linoleum before running for the sanctuary of Todd's little red car for the second time that night.

In all of the commotion they had forgotten about the canvas bag until Brenden questioned them about it as Todd pulled in behind their Joe Woodson's truck. He pulled at the straps and wrinkled his nose at the tacky residue left on his fingers. The top half of the canvas was now stained dark, saturated with blood from Chris's weeping stump. They carried it inside the shed to examine the contents under better lighting. Kori watched with anticipation as his brother worked the zipper open, expecting nothing short of a treasure trove of wealth to be unveiled. He was both disappointed and confused by what was inside.

Brenden thumbed through the discs on the surface, his expression turned grave as he looked at Todd and slowly shook his head. He examined one of the copies, instantly recognizing the sloppy scrawl of Virgil's handwriting. He tossed the disc to Todd and said, “This is not good.”

"Oh shit." The color drained from Todd's face.

"What?" Kori asked, still confused. "What are they?"

"Our death warrant," Todd replied.

Brenden randomly pulled several stacks out of the bag and transferred them into his backpack. He closed the zipper back shut and buried both bags beneath the pile of rubble that covered the floor of their father's shed. He offered no explanation other than to say that the smaller bag was their little insurance policy. Todd nodded in agreement while Kori remained confused.

They mutually agreed to keep a low profile for the day, given the fact that they had no way of knowing what had transpired at the cookhouse after their untimely departure. Kyle Collins was dead, that much was certain. What had become of his cousin and Soup was anyone's guess. Except for the woman with the shotgun, neither of them had actually seen any of the people that they had intended to rob. By the sound of the gunfire, it was a safe bet that the home team outnumbered the visitors.

Best case scenario was that after half of his crew had bailed on him, Soup's chances of making it out whole were slim to none. If he didn't, there would be nothing to connect Kori or Todd to the cookhouse, except Chris. It was highly unlikely that he would talk, assuming that he even survived the night. Todd's backseat was proof that the little junkie lost an exorbitant amount of bodily fluid during the two hours he had laid there.

Worst case scenario was that Soup did make it out. He was going to be livid that they had left him hanging. It wasn't their fault that Chris had lost his mind and blew everyone's cover, but Soup would not see it that way though. His first shot at leading the charge had left at least one man dead and another severely maimed. What was promised to be a big payday netted nothing but pain and empty pockets. He was going to feel the sting of betrayal and would need somebody to blame.

It was Brenden's idea to make the road trip to Des Moines and collect on the debts owed to Kori for the pills Kori had unloaded earlier in the week. It was far enough away from home to lay low and let the dust settle. Besides, he had only been to the big city once before on an elementary school field trip. Touring the Capitol Building and lunch at Marc's Big Boy was pretty much the extent of that adventure. He was curious to see the rest of it, the place where half of his family had faded from existence for so many years. Kori suspected that he also missed the undeniable rush that went along with the drug trade.

The bag, the one that Kyle Collins never had a chance to reclaim before he died, was now safely stashed in the hayloft of Jens's barn. That was also Brenden's idea. Although he did not seem too pleased with the idea of possibly getting an innocent old man caught up in their mess, it was the least likely place anyone would think to look. He promised himself that it was only temporary, just until they figured out what to do with the contents.

By the time they had reached the city limits, Todd helped to bring Kori up to speed on the situation. Never one to sugarcoat things, he wove a disturbing back story that left Kori feeling repulsed and afraid for his life. The contents of that bag contained enough damning evidence to put a lot of people behind bars. Todd had alluded to his suspicions that the Campbell Cousins involvement with Virgil went far beyond the dope trade. It was a sure bet that somewhere on those discs was proof of that. It was also pretty safe to assume that they would stop at nothing to get that bag back. That ruthless sense of self-preservation was not just limited to Cedar Ridge either. Virgil was a sick freak, but he was also an entrepreneur. Somebody was paying him for the garbage that was in that bag. That someone would no doubt be willing to kill to regain possession of it.

"That endgame I was telling you about," Todd explained. "Well it's here, buddy. Now we have to decide who loses and who loses worse. 'Cause there ain't no winners here." He saw the look Brenden was giving him and shrugged. "What? You don't think so?"

"About the endgame part maybe, but I'm not about to lose to these psychos," Brenden replied. "I slung some dope and cracked a few heads for that pervert, but that other shit ain't on my hands. I have no problem dropping that bag on Baylor's doorstep tonight. Let him sort out who goes down for what."

“Baylor?” Todd scoffed. “You think that old drunk will do anything for us? Maybe he's just as much a part of this as they are. Ever thought of that? How else has this shit gone on for so long without anyone getting busted? Even if he isn't in on it, do you think he's gonna stop them from putting a slug in all of our heads?”

Brenden ruminated for a while before giving his answer. Conspiracy theories involving the Sheriff and god knew who else had never once crossed his mind. It was obvious that Todd had given it a lot more thought than he had given him credit for. He deserved at least a decent response. “What about Dale?”

“Dale Scheck, as in Tassler's partner?” Todd waved his hands, dismissing the suggestion and then realizing that Brenden was being serious. “Think we can trust him?”

“Yeah.” Brenden stared out at the busy noon hour traffic before looking back at Todd. He waited for his friend to look him in the eyes before he confidently added, “I do.”

They rolled into the big city, each quietly mulling over the possible options to themselves.

They let Kori do the majority of the talking as they scoured the suburbs in search of the outstanding debtors. They blended quietly into the background while the cash exchanged hands. In only one location did they find it necessary to make their presence known, to persuade some tightfisted loudmouth to reluctantly honor his financial obligations. He was a scrawny desk jockey at a franchise type gym in a strip mall. When he suggested calling a few of his beefy clients to decide whether or not he should pay up, Brenden grabbed him by the neck and asked him how hard dialing his phone would be after it was jammed up his ass. Miraculously the cash appeared on the counter in a matter of seconds.

All in all, it was a profitable afternoon. They had collected almost three thousand in less than two hours. They spent the rest of the day driving around the city, taking in the sights. Brenden said very little while he hung on every word of his brother's narrative description of each point of interest. Never once did he ask about the house where Kori and their mother had spent the last six years. Kori was grateful for that. The last visit to the neighborhood had left a bad taste in his mouth. Todd had been kind enough not to make him feel ashamed of living in such an affluent area. He did not have to. It was written all over his face. The difference between Ravencrest and Cedar Ridge was beyond comparison. He did not want to relive that with his brother.

They stopped for dinner at Der Frauen Haus, a German restaurant that had always been their mother's favorite place to eat. Kori was not particularly fond of the food, but felt compelled to eat there for some reason. For the most part, the speed had run its course and he found the food easy to put away. He was ready for a nap by the time he paid the bill and walked back to the car.

As he approached he saw his brother and Todd leaning on the trunk in a deep discussion. He purposely slowed his pace to give them time to finish it. Oddly, they concluded with a handshake and then a lingering hug.

"What?" Kori said as he closed in. "I pay for the date and you two get to first base?"

The two of them burst into laughter, maintaining their embrace. As he got closer Kori could see that Todd had been crying and Brenden was close to doing the same. It was so out of character for both of them that it was hard to watch. Kori immediately felt like an idiot for making a joke during what was obviously a serious moment.

"Don't be jealous." Todd stretched out an arm and grabbed Kori by the shirt, pulling him into the huddle. Passersby stole curious glances as Kori struggled to break free, sandwiched between the chests of the two larger men. They held him tightly and rubbed their knuckles over the top of his head. The louder he squealed in protest, the harder they laughed.

"Get the hell off of me you freaks," he yelled as he finally wiggled loose. His scalp tingled as he combed a hand through the tangled mess of his hair. He scowled at the pair and slapped away Todd's hand when he reached out to help. "What the hell's the matter with you two, anyway?"

"Come on, little man. Don't be like that." Todd patted him on the butt. "Better get the love while you can. Won't be much of that where I'm going."

"Going? What, where are you going?" Kori stared dumbly, wondering what he had missed. Todd looked back at him, grinned and moved in to hug him again. Kori stiff-armed him in the chest to thwart the advance. He looked at Brenden and asked, "What's he talking about?"

"Rehab," Brenden replied. "Big dufus here is finally pulling his head out of his ass and getting his shit together. I'm checking him in on the way back. He set it all up before we left this morning. Wanted to surprise us." Brenden threw his hands up in mock astonishment. "Surprise."

"Now?"

"No time like the present, right?" Todd said shamefully, looking down at the sidewalk. "This has been a long time coming. Thought I could do this on my own, but it ain't working." He stuffed his hands into his pockets and turned his chin up to face Kori. "Besides, almost getting your face shot off has a way of changing the way you look at things. Kinda makes you want to look in the mirror and like what you see every once in a while."

"I understand you wanting to get clean and all. I get that, but what about the crap going on at home?" He motioned to Brenden, who was quietly stretching his back across the hood of the car. The back of his head sunk into the fresh dent in the center. "Are we supposed to just go back and face all that by ourselves while you sit around in beanbags, spilling your guts to a bunch of twelve-step bleeding hearts?"

"Don't be a dick, bro," Brenden chimed in. He sat upright and folded his arms, staring coldly at him. "It is what it is, so lighten up."

"I'm not trying to be a dick about it, Brenden. I'm just saying that we need all the help we can get right now and he picks today to go to rehab? What am I supposed to say to that? Good luck, buddy? We'll take care of this while you're off fixing yourself?"

Brenden pushed himself away from the car and lunged forward, getting right in his brother's face. "Yeah, that's exactly what you should say. You know why?" He turned to look at Todd, who shifted uncomfortably from one foot to the other behind them. He stepped even closer and backed Kori against the building. "Because that's what friends do. They cover each other's asses when things get all fucked up, even if it means putting your own ass out there to do it."

With his back pressed into the cold brickwork, it suddenly occurred to Kori that he had never actually developed any kind of genuine friendship in the past six years. No one in his life could be considered a real friend in the true sense of the word. Sure he hung out with some of the TEFL crowd, but they were just people thrust upon him by either Clayton or his mother. Just casual acquaintances with shallow personalities, impossible to relate to when conversation strayed beyond the realm of the church. He had his customers, but that was based on the concept of instant gratification on both ends. Dope on theirs, cash on his.

The revelation left him with a sinking feeling that settled in his chest like a weight. For the first time in his life he had friends. The burden that came along with it was something that he was not prepared for. Up to that point he had been functioning solely on his own selfish needs. He had no idea how to act when facing a friend in need.

"Sorry, man." He offered his hand to Todd, feeling like the dick that Brenden had accused him of being. Todd took his hand and pulled close. This time Kori made no effort to resist the impending hug that followed.

They arrived at the rehabilitation center an hour after they had left the city. Kori sat in the car while Brenden helped carry in the suitcase that Todd had secreted in the trunk before they had left. He studied the building that looked more like a school campus than a rehab center. The only difference was that there were no bars on the windows of this place. He wondered if they pushed faith as a method of getting people clean from drugs and alcohol there. He hoped not. Todd would make a lousy bible beater.

Brenden walked back to the car alone. Instead of approaching the empty driver's side he walked up to the passenger window. Kori's heart palpitated. He had seen the television show where family and friends lured unsuspecting loved ones into hotel rooms, only to reveal some cunning ruse that left them in tears as they checked into rehab clinics. Had Todd told him about the methamphetamine that he had done the night before? His mouth went dry as Brenden knocked on the glass.

"I only did one line, I swear," he said, rolling the window. He left it halfway up, just enough to make it impossible for his brother to pull him through the opening if it came to that. "I didn't even like it."

"Okay, good for you." Brenden gave him a puzzled look and twirled his hand, motioning for him to roll the glass down further. "He's about a grand short. Apparently they didn't add the taxes and meals into the quote they gave him on the phone. Go figure, huh? How's about floating me some of that cash until we get home?"

"A grand?" Kori stared at him with an expression of relief that Brenden mistook for hesitation. He had no way of knowing how close Kori had come to locking all of the doors and peeling out of the parking lot to avoid being committed against his will.

"I'll pay you back when we get home for Christ's sake," Brenden snapped.

"Oh, Yeah. No problem," Kori mumbled, digging the roll of cash from his pocket. He counted out a thousand and handed it through the opening. “I thought that you wanted to... well, never mind.”

Brenden took the money and counted it. He stared at his brother for a long time, shaking his head in dismay. He pointed his thumb to the clinic behind him and said, “Man, I don't know about you sometimes. And I thought I was leaving the goofy one in there, but now I'm not so sure. We've got to work on that when we get you home.”

CHAPTER 29

Life in Cedar Ridge slowly reverted back to the dull existence that it had been before the killings took place. It was surprisingly easy for a town that had not seen a murder in over four decades. At first the residents coped by regurgitating varied accounts of the crimes through the social grapevine, over morning coffee or across neighboring fences. Each day the facts became more skewed until the truth was no longer relevant. The blinding reality of a tragedy is always much easier to stomach when the finer details remain hazy.

Satisfied that the dragon had slain itself, most of the State investigators pulled up stakes and rode off into the sunset. Detective Hazelton remained behind to tie up the loose ends, namely Dale Scheck and his lost bag of key evidence. He still had faith in the young deputy. He was not about to sit back and watch him piss away his career over one mistake, no matter how foolish it was. He had invested far too much of his own efforts in the man to do that.

Two funerals took place over the course of the following week. One fallen officer was given a traditional police service, complete with a full escort and a twenty-one gun salute. The other was unceremoniously interred at the same cemetery two days later. No visitation preceded the discrete service and only a handful of family members came to pay their respects. Dale quietly stood behind Margaret as his dead friend was lowered into the earth, less than one hundred feet from where the man he murdered was buried.

The deer that was discovered with Tassler's body was processed by the state lab and then hauled away by a state rendering truck. No mention of it was made public, but several photos of the tender moment hit the internet before any of the bodies were cold.

Brenden and Kori spent the days working together on the farm, preparing for the winter months to come. No amount of bonding could make up the six long years that had separated them, but they did their best to fill in the cracks of lost time. They shared secrets and ambitions, the kind that only brothers would care to know. They reminisced with stories from the long ago past when they were once part of a happier family, oblivious to the fragile nature of strained marriages.

They pored over their father's newspapers every evening after work, hoping to glean any information about the disaster that took place at the cookhouse. Reports were sketchy at best, focusing primarily on the suspected methamphetamine lab that was discovered in the rubble. It was believed that the alleged lab had exploded in the garage and caused the fire that spread to the nearby house. An elderly woman and her two middle-aged sons were listed as residents of the home. No bodies had yet been located, except for that of the dog belonging to one of the owners.

Similar articles mentioned the incident as the weeks passed by. The new details added little to the original story other than to list the names of the owner and her two speed cooking offspring. Each follow up was buried deeper into the back pages as public interest faded. Never once was Soup Campbell or the other missing members of that night's crew mentioned.

It appeared as if they had dropped off the face of the planet, but Brenden knew better than that. Not a single body was recovered from the scene, where at least nine people were known to have been. Even with a raging fire thrown into the equation, something should have turned up in the ashes. They may not have all made it out of there alive, but at least one of them did.

Word had it that Little Chris was slowly recovering from the loss of his left hand. The doctors were more concerned with the amount of blood that he had lost that night. Some of them even argued that the near-lethal levels of narcotics in his body had actually saved his life. He remained in critical condition, fading in and out of consciousness. Most of his waking hours were spent harassing the nursing staff and babbling incessantly about tinfoil badges.

Virgil's prized collection of tainted childhoods remained in the hayloft, stashed away between bales of musty clover. Bloodstains that had once saturated the canvas were now covered in a layer of fine dust. Bird shit spackled the exterior as mice padded their nests with gnawed off bits of the fabric. It literally loomed over their heads as they labored in the barn below. Although they never spoke of it, the mere act of possessing it weighed heavily on their minds. The idea was to wait until Todd returned from rehab. Together they would decide the fate of the miserable contents. A surprise visit from an old acquaintance abruptly changed that plan.

It was less than a week before Thanksgiving. Kori and Brenden had spent the morning in the doorway to the barn, mixing feed for the cattle lot. The process was simple enough, pouring grain and supplements into the hopper of the huge contraption until it was mixed into a coarse powder. The trick, Brenden explained, was to stuff in a few square bales of hay. The hay acted as a filler, cutting down the cost by making the feed last longer in the bunks. Kori did not question the practice. All he knew is that it was a dirty, noisy job.

Hundreds of hammer mill grinders whined at mind-numbing speeds as they stuffed layers of hay inside the hopper, filling the room with dust and dried plant matter. The debris floated thickly in the air before clinging to their sweaty arms and necks. The sound was so intense that Kori could not hear himself cough as his lungs rejected the dirty air. He stuffed the last of the hay into the hopper and watched as the grinders effortlessly pulled it in. Brenden climbed the ladder for another bale to add to the mix.

Beads of perspiration trickled down from his scalp and into his eyes. He pulled the front of his shirt over his face to wipe them dry. He had no idea that he was not alone until he felt the unmistakable sensation of a gun barrel pressing into his temple. He stood there, frozen, with the shirt still stretched over his head. His pulse drummed in his ears, nullifying all other sounds. He cringed and waited for the shot that he knew was coming at any moment, wondering if it would hurt or if he would even know it happened as the nothingness of death took hold.

"I believe that you may have something that belongs to me," a voiced shouted over the whirring of the machinery. It was a voice that he did not recognize. Slowly, he lowered his shirt and found himself face to face with a tiny man in a tailored gray suit. He was keenly dressed, as if he were standing in a five star restaurant and not a barn with cow shit on the floor. He was bookish and reminded Kori of a professor that he once had a class with. His smile was bright, but his eyes were narrow and cold. "Where is the bag, son?"

Out of his peripheral vision Kori could see that it was

Soup holding the gun. He barely looked like the same guy that he had seen a few weeks earlier. His face and forearms were splotched with partially healed burns, presumably from the cookhouse fire. Most of them were an angry red color, still weeping an amber liquid that was dried on the edges in sore looking scabs. His mouth was one solid blister, yet he managed to manipulate it into a passable grin. Two of his front teeth were broken off at the gum line.

Kori gulped nervously. The dusty air scratched at his throat as he spoke over the clamor, taking care not to turn his head as he did so. “Hey, man. You made it out, huh?”

“No thanks to you and your faggot friend,” Soup snarled. His deformed mouth and absent teeth rendered each consonant into a thhh sound. “Thanks for backing me up, douche bag.”

“It wasn't what you think, Soup. Todd and I, we were...”

“Shut up!” Soup hissed, pressing the barrel deeper into Kori's flesh.

The gun never wavered until a bale of hay crashed to the floor at the base of the ladder, followed by Brenden. Soup swung the gun in his direction and then returned it to the side of Kori's head. He wrapped a gauze covered arm around Kori's neck and pulled him backwards, through the doorway. The man in the suit stayed behind, smiling coldly at Brenden.

“If you have the bag here, then I suggest you get it quickly,” the tiny man shouted to Brenden. His voice was high-pitched and competed well against the noises. “Otherwise I cannot guarantee the safety of your brother for very long. Our mutual friend has had a rough go of it as of late. I find him very excitable these days.”

Brenden eyed the strange little man, reluctant to comply. “Who the hell are you?”

The little man laughed and spread his arms open, glancing around the interior of the barn. “I'm the one who helped you pay for this lovely place that we are standing in. The one that you have been working for all these years. A fine earner you have been from what I've heard, I might add. But sadly, it's time for us to end our previous arrangement. It's simple. You have something of mine and now I have something of yours.” His eyes narrowed as he nodded toward the doorway. “Now get me the fucking bag!”

“And if I say I don't have it?”

The little man pursed his delicately thin lips and whistled loudly. Soup reappeared with his arm wrapped tightly around Kori's neck. The barrel of the gun had migrated downward until it rested just below the jawline. A pleading expression of panic was on his Kori's face as he met his brother's eyes. The little man sensed this and was fully certain that now he had the upper hand. With a shrug of indifference he looked into the opening of the whirring hopper. “Then I guess the cattle will be getting a bit more protein in their diet this week.”

He nodded to Soup, who beamed with excitement. He carefully passed the gun to the little man and gripped Kori by the neck with both hands. Sparing a moment to glare at Brenden, he savored the look of anguish as he forced Kori's head into the opening of the hopper.

Kori instinctively planted both hands on either side of the metal lip as Soup pried down on the back of his neck. The rusty edges bit into his flesh as he stiffened his arms, resisting with all of his might. For a few minutes he maintained his distance from the spinning steel blades, but eventually his strength was no match for Soup's brute force. His face slowly lowered deeper inside the box until his head was past the top of the sides. The ceaseless whirring of the hammer mills blew against his hair and dried the sweat on his face. It was only a matter of time they made contact. He twisted his face to the side and screamed his brother's name.

“Okay, okay!” Brenden cried out. “I'll give you what you want. Just tell him to stop for Christ's sake.”

Soup released the pressure from Kori's neck. With what little strength he had left in his arms, he backed away from the grinder and crumpled to the ground. He drew his knees into his chest and panted uncontrollably. The little man stared at him unsympathetically, tapping the gun barrel on the top of his head and ordering him to stand. At first he was unsure if he could, but with a little unfriendly persuasion he was coaxed back to his feet.

Brenden climbed the ladder and quickly reappeared with the bag. He plopped it at the little man's feet. A month's worth of dust exhaled from the fabric, settling on the pair of ostrich skin shoes. The little man was unfazed.

"It had better all be there. I'll know if it isn't," he warned. He had no way of knowing how many copies were inside the filthy bag, but he was not about to let some smug little dirt farmer know that. After the fear that he had inflicted on them, he had no doubt that they would gladly surrender the entire lot.

"It's all there," Brenden responded. He stood back, rubbing his palms together as if to suggest he was washing his hands of it. "Just take it."

"Thanks, I think I will. Nice of you to offer," the little man sneered. He leveled the weapon and fired one round into Brenden's midsection. He promptly handed the gun back to Soup, who stood there in frozen astonishment.

The impact sent Brenden backwards and he landed on his butt in the sparse layer of hay beneath the foot of the ladder. A spray of red escaped his mouth and he doubled over in pain. He tried to speak but only managed a croaking sound that came out in pinkish bubbles. He pressed his hands against the wound to hold back the blood as it seeped through his fingers. His chin quivered, tilting downward until it rested on his chest.

Kori wriggled out of his shirt and fell to the ground beside him. He pressed it into the spot where the flow seemed to be the worst. Brenden fought him at first, screaming as the fabric grazed his torn flesh. Eventually he was too weak to fend off his brother's advances and let his own hands fall limply out of the way. Kori covered the hole and applied pressure, alarmed at how quickly the blood continued to flow. Within seconds the shirt was completely saturated.

"Hang on, Bren. It's gonna be okay." He knew that was a complete lie. Things were as far from okay as they could get. He stroked the side of his brother's face with his free hand and shuddered. Brenden's dirty neck was already growing clammy and cold. The rate of the blood seeping through the shirt was slowing down, but he knew it was only because there was less of it to lose. Panic filled him as he tried to think of something, anything to do. His brother was going to die if he didn't come up with something fast.

Shouting broke out over the sound of the machinery. Kori looked behind him to see a portly man squeezing past the feed grinder. A handgun was strapped to his huge rotund waist. The holster hung up on the door frame, forcing him to turn sideways to fit through. Beads of sweat formed on his bulbous nose and dripped onto his upper lip. His breathing came in labored gasps as he surveyed the room. "Aw shit!" he yelled at the sight of Brenden. His crimson jowls swayed back and forth in frustration as he approached the brothers. Towering over them, he pointed a fat finger and glared at the little man. "Goddammit, Sterling.

This was exactly what I did not want to happen."

"Oops." The little man, whose real name was Benson Sterling, grinned sheepishly and stared at the gun as if he had no idea how it had gotten in his hand. Slight creases in his tailored suit coat appeared as he shrugged his narrow shoulders. "I guess it's fortunate that you are here, Sheriff. Seeing as how we will soon have a corpse that needs disposed of. I hear you were quite proficient at that back in the day."

With surprisingly fluid grace for a man of his size, Baylor spun around and grabbed Sterling by the lapels of his coat. He lifted the smaller man until their foreheads almost touched. Sterling's feet dangled a foot from the ground, kicking frantically at the sheriff's shins. The urge to shake him like a rag doll until his frail little neck snapped was nearly impossible to resist. He twisted his grip until the stitching on the back of Sterling's suit began to rip apart. "What have you gotten me into?"

Anger flashed in Sterling's eyes. "You ignorant old drunk! You let it get to this point. All you had to do was shut Fisher up for good, but no. You said he wasn't going to be a problem for us. Look how well that decision has worked out for us." He nodded toward the canvas bag to emphasize his point. "If you had just done things my way in the first place, we wouldn't be having this conversation right now."

Baylor let loose his grip and let Sterling drop roughly to the ground. "How was I supposed to know he would break bad like he did?"

Sterling calmly smoothed the wrinkles from the front of his outfit the best he could do. He rolled his shoulders a few times to adjust the back. The coat was undoubtedly ruined, as well as the shoes. No amount of cleaning would ever remove the vile smell of animal dung out of the material. Still, there was no shame in at least making an attempt at a presentable appearance.

Without looking up he said, "Of course you wouldn't have known. Only someone with more than half a brain would stop to consider that the man's daughter had disappeared on your watch. You run a county the size of a football field for Christ's sake. People are bound to start talking. It was only a matter of time before he put two and two together."

Baylor's eyes narrowed. "What do you mean, on my watch?"

Sterling stopped picking unseen debris from his sleeve and looked up. "Weren't you the head swinging dick of this joke of a county then? As a father of three daughters myself, I'd like to think that I would have done the same thing if I were in his shoes. Only, I would have made you my first stop."

"You have children?"

"Does that surprise you, sheriff?"

"That repulses me," Baylor replied. "Anyway, don't you try to put this on me. I took care of my end just fine." He nudged the bag with his boot, shocked by the weight of it. "Besides, we got what we came here for. Let's get the hell out of here before the old Jew shows up. I don't want to have to add another body to the pile. Big enough the way it is."

"Speaking of which, we still have them to deal with." Sterling raised his eyebrows and glanced over to the brothers, one bleeding profusely and the other frantically trying to stop it. They were both in a world of their own, oblivious to the discussion transpiring around them.

"What about them?" Baylor eyed him suspiciously and then held his hands up in protest. "Whoa, hold on there! No way. If you think I'm cleaning this up, you're more out of your mind than I thought."

Wary of another outburst from the fat man, Sterling cautiously approached him and patted him on the back. "Mr. Campbell will assist you with whatever you need to get the job done. Don't worry about that, but the responsibility still falls on you to see it through."

Baylor shook his head. "I didn't sign up for this."

"Has it been so long since you've had to get rid of a body that you've forgotten how? Or is it that you're just not used to dealing with ones so grown up?"

"You're a real bastard, you know that," Baylor snapped. "And in case you haven't noticed, they're both still breathing. I'm not doing anything to change that fact."

Sterling nodded to Soup. "Care to do the honors, Mr.

Campbell?"

Soup stared at him blankly for a moment then looked down at the gun in his hand. He looked back at his boss as if to make sure that he was understanding what was expected of him. He slowly approached the Woodson brothers and lifted the gun to the back of Kori's head.

"Soup, please," Kori pleaded. He defensively covered his head with his free hand. The other stayed firmly planted over his brother's hemorrhaging wound. "You don't have to do this."

"Shut up," Soup hissed. His hand trembled, slightly at first and then so much that he had to lower it to his side. He took in several deep breaths and tilted his head back, steeling himself. He started to raise the weapon again when the shot rang out.

Baylor ducked with the same uncanny grace that he had displayed earlier. Instinctively, he reached for his own piece. Sterling, the natural coward that he was, ducked behind the sheriff's wide girth for cover. The gun tumbled from the fingers of Soup's hand which no longer functioned. The shot had torn through the back of his shoulder and punched out the other side, leaving a gaping hole. He danced on his feet in a diagonal direction until his legs finally betrayed him. Bewildered, he fell to the ground and writhed in pain.

Bobby Hazelton stepped into the doorway with his service revolver drawn. He fixed the sights on Baylor and inched forward, followed by three other agents. Dale Scheck brought up the rear. They systematically swarmed in and forced everyone to the ground. For the time being, everyone was considered a suspect. The details would sort themselves out later.

Baylor eyed Dale as he crouched over Soup Campbell with a pair of handcuffs. The deputy wrestled the Soup's hands behind his back, despite the shrill cries of pain. Infuriated that one of his own men had anything to do with the raid, Baylor slowly rolled to one side and eased his gun from under his round belly. If this was how he was going down, he'd be damned if that little Judas snot nose was going to walk away without seeing a fight.

"Just give me a reason to ventilate your fat ass, why don't you," Hazelton growled, pressing a foot on the top of Baylor's head. He pressed the muzzle of his service revolver into the fatty roll at the base of the sheriff's neck. "Let it go."

Baylor grunted and reluctantly complied. A curious sense of relief came over him as he relaxed his arm and let the weapon drop. Through squinted eyes he watched as Hazelton plucked it from the dirt immediately. Thirty years of constantly looking over his shoulder was finally over. He felt unafraid for the first time in a long while as the restraints were clamped down and he was rolled onto his back. He closed his eyes, smiled and felt his bladder let go.

Dale called out to him, "Sheriff. I hardly recognized you in civilian clothes. The look doesn't really work for you. Maybe orange will suit you better. Easier to hide the piss stains."

This got a chuckle from the other lawmen. Even Mathers, who considered a permanent scowl as part of his dress code, was nearly in tears over the remark. Baylor rested his head against the warm dirt and kicked his heels. The muddied crotch of his jeans clung to the skin of his thighs. He looked down, never wishing so badly that he could see past his gut.

Sterling took advantage of the short lapse in decorum to break free from his captor. He slipped from underneath the young agent on top of him and clawed his way to his feet. Before anyone could reach him, he latched onto the canvas bag and pulled it to his chest. With everyone else either laying or kneeling on the ground, he was able to make his way to the feed grinder untouched. He stuffed the bag into the hopper with so much force that he almost went in after it.

"Shut it off!" Hazelton screamed at the deputy closest to the door. He cringed at the sound of his evidence being rapidly chewed into useless fragments by the powerful machine. The agent stood stock still, unsure or unbelieving at what was happening. He was nearly knocked to the ground by Dale, who ran past him and leaped over the auger side of the grinder. He vanished through the doorway and was gone for what seemed to Hazelton like an eternity.

Finally the engine stopped. Seconds later the hammer mills ceased to spin. What was left of the bag once again became the inanimate object that it had been before the churning steel had vibrated it to life. Hazelton could hardly bear to watch as Mathers extracted it from hopper. Half of the canvas was still intact, but there was no telling how much of the contents had been lost. Please give me something, Hazelton prayed. Spare me one damn disc.

The look on Sterling's face was priceless.

At least two dozen discs crashed to the ground around Mather's feet, complete and undamaged. Only a few of the tapes had survived. Several more fell into pieces, ribbons of brown tape strewn across the dirt like shimmering guts. The remainder was pulverized to silver and black dust. Not the mother lode that Scheck had promised, but still enough to put them all behind bars three times over. They would bury the whole bunch of them under the jail with what lay at his lead investigator's overpriced shoes.

Sterling let out a weak sigh that was cut short by the two agents, who enthusiastically slammed him to the ground. A knee was planted at the base of his neck and another on the tender muscles above his knees. Handcuffs were clamped around his bony wrists, cinched so tightly that it would take until the arraignment for the bruises to fade away. The dapper little businessman from Lincoln gagged on the dusty remains of his own wares as the agents worked him over.

“Uh, Captain?” one of the agents interrupted. Hazelton

broke his gaze from the pile of evidence to see which of his men had addressed him. It was Ramirez, the rookie that had allowed Sterling to make the slip on him moments before. His youthful face was slick with perspiration and as pale as a sheet. He backed up a step and pointed his thumb to the brothers. “Think we have a situation over here, sir.”

Hazelton stepped over the pile of smut to take a closer look. He recognized the brothers from the collection of photographs taken by Deputy Scheck. The younger one was holding his brother's head in his lap. He was gently rocking him back and forth, the way a mother would hold a child while coaxing it to sleep. They held hands, fingers interlocked and caked with drying blood. Fresher pools coagulated beneath them.

Without looking back, Hazelton ordered the rookie to make the call for an ambulance. He crouched down and placed a hand on Kori's shoulder. For a second the gesture drew no response. Then, as if finally realizing that they were not alone, he looked up with tears streaming down his dirty cheeks. “I can't get it to stop.”

“Hang in there, kiddo. Help is on the way.” Hazelton replied. He stripped off his outer coat to remove the cotton parka underneath. He offered it to Kori in the hope that a fresh, drier compress would help to ebb the flow. Blood gushed from the wound when Kori lifted his drenched shirt to make the exchange. “Jesus,” he muttered, realizing that the situation was much more serious than he had first thought. “Deputy! A little help here.”

Dale hovered over them, unsure of what help he could possibly be. It was surreal to see his old high school buddy, bleeding out on the floor of some barn. The same barn that they used to sneak drinks of bourbon that they swiped from his mother's liquor cabinet. The very place that he and Brenden tried unsuccessfully to get past first base with the Dauber twins in ninth grade. The twins were two years older and way out of their league. In retrospect, bringing two uppity girls to a shit-stinking barn was a surefire way not to get laid. They had fun trying, though.

Brenden lifted his chin from his chest and stared at Dale sleepily. His mouth slowly opened and formed something between grimacing and a smile. Efforts to spit the blood out, rather than swallow it had stained his teeth pink. Still gripping his brother's hand in his, he extended a finger out to Dale. He tilted his head back and looked at Kori. “It's okay, bro. The guy with the tinfoil badge is here to save the day.” He mustered a weak laugh and coughed up a mouthful of red.

Kori looked down at him, confused. “What does that mean?”

Before Brenden could answer him he went limp and was gone.

CHAPTER 30

Kori sat with his elbows propped on the table and leaned over his untouched plate of food. The restaurant was electric with the chaos of the lunch crowd. Booths and tables around them were packed with diners, frantic to choke down enough sustenance to carry them through the rest of their busy day. He could not help but to notice a group of elderly women in the booth across from them. They watched with disgusted fascination as Todd devoured the meal in front of him.

He ate everything but the plate itself without taking so much as a full breath. He sopped the greasy plate with the last of his fries and popped them in his mouth. He immediately leaned back in his seat and released a slow drawn out belch. It was partially stifled by the back of his fist, but still within earshot of the gray quartet next door. Kori offered the ladies an apologetic smile to lighten the mood. He received nothing but cold stares of unforgiving contempt for his efforts.

"For four grand a month, they couldn't feed you in that

place?" he asked, shoving his own plate away.

"Oh, they fed me alright," Todd replied. He reached across the table, plucked an onion ring from Kori's plate and popped it into his mouth. He smacked his lips and nodded in approval before dragging the entire plate his way. "Everything tasted like baby food, though. Some kind of healthy new age hippy crap. Supposed to purge the toxins that built up from all the junk I ran through my body. All it did was give me the shits."

An exasperated murmur rose from the foursome across the aisle.

"Sounds delightful," Kori said. He tried to sink deeper into his seat to avoid the harsh stares. He unconsciously began to fold his napkin into tiny triangles. "Seriously, though. I'm glad to have you here. It means a lot to me and my dad that you took time away from your rehab to be here for us. I mean, five hours on a bus just to get back for your best friends... well, you know."

Todd stopped eating and looked at him thoughtfully. "I know, man. I know what you're trying to say, but I wouldn't have it any other way."

"Well you don't have to worry about the bus thing on the way back. I'll drive you back whenever you need to go, no problem."

Todd shook his head. "I'm not going back there. No way in hell."

"What about your...?

"My recovery?" Todd waved, dismissing the notion. "Man, I could have gotten the same results by locking myself in a room for a month with a couple cartons of smokes and a few skin magazines. I spent most of the time either listening to some sandal wearing freak preach about loving myself or watching the staff trying to bang all the female residents."

"Check, please!" one of the ladies cried out.

"The girls in there were all fat and ugly or exclusively into black guys, most of them both. Although, I did get a hand job during one of these stupid one on one role playing exercises that they always had us doing." He looked on either side of him and leaned across the table, but did not bother to lower his voice. "I was a little weirded out by the fact that I was supposed to be playing the role of the chic's uncle at the time."

"Now!" the ladies yelled in unison.

They stood up from the table and Todd placed a pair of twenty dollar bills under his empty glass. He nodded to the mortified group as he placed his hands on his hips and arched his back. He grunted a few times and then patted his gorged stomach. "Ladies," he said politely and walked toward the door.

Ashamed, Kori stared down at the floor and pulled out his wallet. He quickly fished out a hundred dollar bill and placed it on the edge of their table, barely looking up. The one who appeared to be the lead hen in the group snarled her nose and eyed it as if he had just defecated next to her Cobb salad.

"Sorry," he mumbled and hastily followed Todd outside.

Todd was asleep before they left the parking lot. He snored softly from the passenger's seat of his own car as they left Iowa City behind them. Kori followed the old highway that ran parallel to the interstate, taking in the scenic rolling hills as he went. Todd shifted uncomfortably in his seat and let out an airy fart. Kori just smiled and cracked the windows, happy to have his friend back home again.

It was not until they were five miles from the Ridge that Todd finally came to. He opened his eyes and squinted through the dirty window, trying to regain his bearings. They passed by Henson's fruit and vegetable market. The dilapidated shed had been there for as long as he could remember. It sat empty, abandoned for the winter. It was a sad sight to see, yet it still served as a welcoming landmark. He smacked his sleep-dried lips and yawned.

Kori noticed this and affectionately nudged him with his elbow. "Welcome home, man."

"Thanks." Todd lit a cigarette and stared at it thoughtfully. "So did you get ever get a hold of your mom?"

"No," Kori replied. He gripped the wheel tightly. The fine muscles in the back of his jaw flexed as he stared at the road. "I've tried for two days. Her cell comes up as deactivated and Clayton's just goes straight to voicemail. I even tried the church office, but they just gave me some bullshit runaround.

Told me they would try to relay the message, but the group was in the middle of some kind of isolation retreat. Whatever the fuck that means."

"Seriously?"

"Yeah, I mean her own son is dead and she can't be bothered long enough to take a fucking phone call? It's not like I'm asking her to fork out any of her precious prayer money to pay for it. I just thought she might like to show up and for the..." He stopped, searching for the right words. "To see him off."

"Damn, that's cold." Sensing the growing frustration in Kori's voice, Todd immediately regretted bringing the subject up. The kid had been through enough over the past week. The last thing he needed was to be reminded of how sorry his mother was. He thought of his own family and how worthless they had always seemed to him, always drunk or busy trying to kill each other. At least they would probably bother to show up for his funeral, for the free food if nothing else. "You need help paying for the cremation? I hear that shit's pretty spendy."

"No." Kori shook his head slowly. "Well I don't think so. I've still got some money left from the pill run. Jens wants to pay for the whole thing, but I don't want to put it on him. He's done enough already." He looked to Todd, eyes wet and on the verge of tears. "Thanks for the offer, though. Really, I'll be okay."

"Damn right you will." Todd studied him for a moment before saying anything more. He wanted to gauge whether the kid was holding anything back from him, how much Brenden had actually told him before he died. The blank stare on Kori's sad face said it all. "You don't know do you? No idea at all."

"Know what?"

Instead of explaining himself, Todd instructed Kori to keep driving past the turnoff to Cedar Ridge and head to the farm. Kori followed him to the calving shed, a converted fifties era chicken house that Brenden sometimes spent long nights waiting to deliver the newborn calves. Nestled between the machine shed and Jens's house, the building looked as if the only thing keeping it intact was the mass of overgrown vines that covered its exterior.

The door resisted at first, its hinges barely kept it from dragging across the rotting threshold. Todd pried up on the handle and rammed his shoulder hard against the wood. The stale air tickled the back of Kori's throat as they stepped inside. His eyes slowly adjusted to the darkness as he surveyed the tiny room. A roughly assembled bed frame was erected in one corner; the mattress stripped of any coverings appeared grungy and slightly stained. Aside from the bed there were only a few other furnishings. An equally primitive table and a pair of chairs summed up the décor. It was stocked with all the comforts of an efficiency apartment, complete with the musty paper stink of mouse farts.

Todd worked his way under the heavy bed frame until he

was in up to his waist. He cussed and muttered for several minutes before inching his way back out, lifting his butt in the air as he did so. He grunted as he dragged a long metal foot locker out into the middle of the room. A combination lock was built into the center of the lid, which Todd deftly worked to unlatch. He tilted the lid open and stood up to reveal the contents inside.

"There you go," he said, spreading his arms out. "The answer to your financial woes."

Two piles of neatly stacked bills filled the interior walls of the box, separated by the familiar blue backpack that Brenden often carried. On top of the backpack were two manila envelopes. Kori unsealed the one with his brother's name printed on it and examined the papers inside. His heart ached as he read through the will that his brother had drawn up less than a year earlier.

"He left me his share of the farm?" In disbelief, he looked up at Todd and then back to the document in his hands. "But this was done last April, before he knew I was coming back."

Todd shrugged. "I guess he knew you'd come back someday. He probably figured he'd get to tell you in person before you had a chance to cash in on it though. We both had wills made out last year when things started to get heavy. Wanted to make sure somebody got to benefit from our stupidity." He pointed to the other papers and said, "Keep reading. There's a life insurance policy, too. Split between you and your old man. Two hundred grand, same as mine."

"And the cash?"

Again Todd shrugged as if the piles of cash were nothing at all. "The pile on the left is mine. The other was his. Now it's yours. I don't know how much is in there, but I'll bet that it's enough to pay off the rest of the bank note and throw one hell of a wake."

Kori closed the lid and pushed the box back under the bed. "Yeah, we could do that. Except there's one problem with that idea."

"What's that?"

Kori grinned and punched him in the arm. "You, my friend, are in a fragile stage of recovery."

A devilish grin came over Todd's face. "Oh, yeah. Almost forgot."

CHAPTER 31

The following week Joe Woodson stood from a high bluff, overlooking the Cedar River. The bitter wind numbed his bare hands as he tightly clutched the ashes of his eldest son. He pried the top open and peered inside. When he had retrieved the remains from the funeral home, he was not really sure what he had expected to get. Whatever it was, a cardboard box that must have weighed close to five pounds was not it. He hugged the box against his chest so tightly that some of the grainy contents spilled over and onto his sleeve.

Kori watched from the edge of the clearing, allowing his father a few minutes alone. When he saw the old man begin to choke up, ashes pouring down around his feet, he rushed to his side. Together, they leaned precariously over the wooden rail and held out the upturned container. The powdered remains spilled out and drifted in the wind. They watched tearfully as the last of Brenden Woodson floated out of view, falling to the churning waters below. Then, for the first time in years, his father wrapped his arms around him and hugged him tightly.

Jens and Todd joined them at the railing to pay their respects. The four of them seesawed between jags of tears and laughter, sharing memorable stories. Kori mostly just sat back and listened. Other than his childhood memories and the past few months, he barely knew anything about his brother. As fascinating as the tales were to him, he found his attention wandering elsewhere.

Some small part of him still held out hope that his mother would pop up over the hill at any time, tearful and grieving. Maybe he wanted her to show up just to let him know she actually cared. Maybe he just wanted her to feel some of the same pain that had weighed so heavily on his own heart for the past week. Either way, he did not care as long as she came.

The bitter sting of reality gnawed at him as he stared off in the distance. Deep down inside, he knew she would never come back to Cedar Ridge. Not even for a dead child.

He left the others to reminisce amongst themselves and walked the path back to the road. Cresting the hill, he saw Dale Scheck's truck parked behind the Corolla. Dale leaned against tailgate and patiently waited for him to approach. He pulled a hand from his jacket pocket and waved meekly. Without the uniform he looked different, out of place.

“Tell me you're not here to write us a ticket for littering,”

Kori said.

Dale looked down at his civilian clothes and laughed. “I'm not exactly on duty right now, so I think I can turn a blind eye.” He cautiously stuck out his hand, almost fearful that the gesture would not be returned. They shook hands spent a moment sizing each other up. After a brief uncomfortable pause Dale added, “Sorry about your brother, Kori. I mean that.”

“Thanks,” Kori replied, numbly. “So, what do you want?”

Dale tucked the hand back into the warmth of his jacket and sighed. He gazed out at the treetops as if the answer was dangling somewhere among the leafless limbs. His eyes were watery and swollen. It could have been from the sharp wind, but Kori suspected that he may have been crying. “I just came to pay my respects. If that's okay by you, that is.”

Kori stared at him for a moment before answering. For some reason he could not help but to feel some sense of pity for the guy. There was an undeniable air of weariness about him. Even though Dale and Brenden were the same age, the man who stood before him looked decades older. He looked as if he were on the verge of a serious meltdown. “Yeah, sure. Everybody's still down there by the eagle lookout, telling stories,” Kori said, pointing in the direction of the path. “Dad will appreciate that a lot.”

“I appreciate that, too.” Dale shifted nervously as if he

had more to say, but could not muster the nerve to get it out. Then he turned and started for the path.

Kori let him get just a few yards before calling out to him. “Can I ask you something?”

Dale stopped and turned slowly as if expecting something horrible to happen next. “Sure.”

“What does tinfoil badge mean?”

Dale gave him a peculiar look. What little color that was left in his complexion had drained away. “Come again?”

“You heard me. What does it mean?” Kori approached him. “I've heard that saying quite a few times in the past month. The last time it was directed at you.”

Dale reached in his back pocket and pulled out his wallet. His trembling fingers sorted through the credit cards and other documents until he found what he was looking for. He stared at it for a moment and sighed, shaking his head. Reluctantly, he pulled out a laminated card and handed it to Kori.

“Internal affairs?” Kori asked, turning the card in his hand. At a glance it really did look as if it were constructed of tinfoil. The hologram background that surrounded the photo of Dale glimmered in the sun, even in the weak lighting of the overcast sky. The picture didn't even look like the same person that was standing in front of him. It was more like the younger version that still had no idea how fast the job would eat him from the inside out, starting with his soul. He handed the card back to

Dale. “You’re a cop narc?”

“I guess that's one way of putting it,” Dale replied, flinching slightly at the term. To him it meant, traitor. Rat. He slipped the card back into his pocket without bothering to return it to his wallet first. “I was supposed to be flying under the sheriff department's radar, but somehow my recently deceased partner caught wind of it. I don't think too many others have caught on yet and I'd prefer to keep it that way for now. So let's just keep this between you and me, okay? I'd like to hold the bounties on my head to a minimum, at least until after the trials get under way.”

“Trials, as in plural?” Kori felt a lump rise up in his throat.

Dale picked up on his apprehensiveness and immediately went into damage control mode. The last thing he wanted to do was to scare his star witness into doing something stupid like skipping town before the trial even started. He put his hands in the air, motioning for Kori to stay calm. “Don’t worry. You're only going to be testifying against Sterling. There's no getting around that. You were the only one there who's not under indictment now.”

“Or dead,” Kori added. He glanced beyond the clearing where his brother's ashes had been cast into the wind. He could not help but to blame Dale for Brenden's death. He did not pull the trigger, but he sure as hell didn't make any effort to stop it from happening either.

"Um, yeah," Dale replied, for a lack of anything better to say. "The rest of the charges don't involve you, at least not as far as the state is concerned."

"Really?" Kori looked at him doubtfully. "And no one's asking how the hell that bag full of crap landed at our feet in the first place? How we ended up with eighty pounds of kiddie porn that belonged to the same guy that killed my brother?"

"Nobody has so far. They don't care how it landed as long as it can be tied to the whole lot of them," Dale replied. "I wouldn't count out the possibility of Sterling's lawyers bringing it up though. You have to expect that, you know. I mean, he owns like half of the newspapers in Nebraska. He's not just going to check out without a fight."

Kori frowned. "He's probably got a shit ton of high dollar lawyers in his back pocket."

Dale smiled weakly and shook his head. "Don't worry about him. You've got an entire team of state attorneys on your side." He gently nudged Kori's arm. "And you have me. You and me, we're not like them. We gotta stick together and take care of our own. Right?"

Kori looked down at his arm, the place where Dale touched him. He felt the sudden urge to punch the guy in the mouth and walk away. Instead he asked, "How long did you know that Sterling was in town before you showed up that day?"

"What do you mean?" The guilty look on Dale's face said it all, even more than the long pause before his response.

Kori moved closer, forcing Dale backwards until he was pinned against the door of his truck. Their faces came so close that Dale could feel the heat radiate from his skin, the hatred burning from his eyes. "I mean could you have stopped him before he got there or did you let my brother die just so you could make your fucking case?"

"Kori," Dale started, measuring his words carefully. He knew that at any moment he might have a fight on his hands. "It wasn't my call to make." He broke away from Kori's harsh gaze and stared at the ground. "I know this is no consolation, but I was just doing my job."

"My brother and I, we were just collateral damage?" Kori hissed.

"Kori, I'm so sorry. You have to believe me. If there was any way to change what happened I would."

Kori backed off a little, but the burning hate in his eyes remained constant. The look of fear on the deputy's face was somewhat satisfying. He liked the feeling and suddenly understood the rush that his brother and the rest of the guys felt while working a job. It was a feeling that he could see himself getting used to. "What about the others? What's gonna happen to them?"

A gust of bitter wind kicked up and left them both

shrinking deeper into their jackets for warmth. Dale nodded toward his truck and said, "Come on, heater's not been off that long. Let's jump in before we both catch pneumonia. This could take a while."

Despite the welcomed reprieve from the elements, Kori had a difficult time getting comfortable in the close confines of Dale's truck. It wasn't that he didn't trust him, or even that he was a cop. He just did not like him. It was something that he could not quite put his finger on, other than that he exuded some sort of nervous desperation. Dale was trying just a bit too hard to cover his uber cop image by playing the 'good old boy from the same neck of the woods as you' routine. It was not working for him.

He reminded Kori of Eddie Rupert, a kid he once went to grade school with. Eddie came from a really fucked up home and had transferred in during the middle of the year under some sordidly peculiar circumstances. He was just aching to get in everyone's good graces from the second his feet hit the linoleum. Then, after everyone finally started to get used to him, he started dumping his heavy dark secrets on them at the most inopportune times.

Nobody wants to hear about how some kid's old man wakes him up in the middle of the night with a hard on every time he comes home a little too drunk to see straight. Especially not while they are busy choosing teams for kickball. That kid will always get picked dead last every time, guaranteed. If he keeps talking long enough, he will eventually find himself becoming the kickball. Eddie became rather intimately familiar with the business end of most everyone's gym shoes until one day he quit coming to school.

Kori had to concentrate to differentiate between the pathetic little boy from his childhood and the spineless cop in the seat next to him. The cop who may or may not have been able to prevent his brother's death. He would have rather stepped out of the truck and not looked back, but he needed to know the fate of the others involved. It was for his own piece of mind as well as his safety. He needed to know which faces to look for every time he looked over his shoulder, every time he poked his head out the front door.

Dale told him the obvious first. Sterling was looking at a minimum of life between the manslaughter and the pornography. His trial was set to start in the next few months. Baylor would have a longer wait. Apparently he made a halfhearted effort to hang himself with the leg bottoms of his own pants while in county lockup. The weight of his own fat ass was too much for the threadbare jail issue fabric and he ended up with a concussion and a broken arm for his troubles. The last Dale heard, he was currently on suicide watch in a federal holding cell in Davenport.

“What about Soup and Chris?” Kori impatiently asked. They were the two that concerned him the most. Maybe Benson

Sterling had innumerable minions at his beck and call, but the Campbell cousins were just as easily capable of exacting revenge on anyone they believed to have betrayed them. The devils that he knew struck much more fear into him than the ones he did not.

Dale shifted nervously before he answered. He grew up with the cousins and apparently shared some of the same apprehensions about them as Kori did. “They're both still in the hospital, waiting for transfers to Davenport. Soup will probably go as soon as next week. He had second degree burns all over his body when they processed him. We think he had something to do with that meth lab fire over in Oxford Mills, but we can't prove it. As soon as he's cleared by the docs he's headed for federal lockup. Sooner the better if you ask me. I sat in on his arraignment the other day. It was done via closed circuit from his hospital room. The crazy bastard threatened me right there on camera.”

“No shit?” Kori asked, feigning concern.

“Yeah. I don't know how he even knew I was there. The judge is the only one in the courtroom that's on camera, but he called me out like I was sitting right in front of him. Said for me to just lie back down if I smelled smoke in the middle of the night, because it would already be too late. Can you believe the balls on that guy?”

Kori shook his head. He had seen the most sadistic side

of Soup over the past few months. He knew exactly how big his balls were, figuratively speaking at least. “Hmm. That's crazy. What about Little Chris?”

“Still in critical condition, last I heard. His infection got pretty bad and they had to amputate clear up to the elbow. Lucky for him that he made it to the ER as soon as he did.” Dale looked at him suspiciously. “You wouldn't have any idea how he might have ended up there that night, would you?”

“How much time are they looking at?” Kori asked, ignoring the question. Images of Chris lying across the windshield with his bloody stump in the air flashed though his mind. It came as a surprise that he lived longer than ten minutes after they had dumped him off at the emergency entrance. Even after everything that happened that night, he still felt a little guilty for leaving him like that.

“Not sure,” Dale replied. “Word has it that they are both singing like canaries, but it doesn't matter. There's so much video evidence on those tapes that the prosecutor wouldn't consider cutting them a deal, even if he wanted to. Pressure's coming from all sides to hang as many of these bastards as possible. Don't you worry about them. They are both going to be on the receiving end of prison justice for a very long time. Sex offenders always get it the worst in there, you know. Especially when kids are involved. I once heard about this pervert who got caught for...”

“Well, anyway.” Kori cut him off. He had gotten the

information that he wanted and had heard about all the white noise he could stomach from the tinfoil badge carrying cop. If he didn't get away soon he was going to end up punching him in the mouth. He opened the truck door to step out before turning back to Dale one more time. "You know, Dale. On second thought, maybe it's best that you don't go down there right now. I'm not sure how my dad is going to handle it."

"Handle what?" A hurt look spread across Dale's face.

"Seeing the guy who let his son die just so he could make a name for himself," Kori replied, coldly. "And do me a favor. Forget what you said about having my back. I've already seen what good that will do me. I'll see you in court, but until then stay the fuck away from me and what's left of my family."

He slammed the truck door shut and started back down the trail. The bitter wind bit at his ears and the back of his neck as he walked. The temperature must have fallen another five degrees in the short time that he sat in the cab. He could have pulled the hood of his jacket over his head, but he chose not to. He wanted to make sure that nothing muffled the sound of Dale's truck backing out of the parking spot and heading down the road.

It was the last time he ever saw Dale Scheck alive. Less than a week later a fire gutted his trailer in the middle of the night. The flames consumed the aging tinderbox so rapidly that Dale never stood a chance. When Kori heard the news he envisioned the cop lifting his weary head from the pillow and them just laying back down, waiting for the end to come. Despite his animosity toward the deputy, Kori hoped that the end was fast coming.

CHAPTER 32

Time seemed to grind to a halt during the months leading up to the trial. Benson Sterling's team of high dollar lawyers spared no expense when it came to jamming up the spokes on the wheels of justice. The last Kori had heard, the proceedings were not set to start until spring. The longer he was kept waiting, the more he dreaded testifying in court.

Todd made good on his promise to stick around until it was all over. By the middle of the winter they had settled into a mundane routine that consisted of little more than busy work around the farm. They were bored stiff. The only one who seemed to be enjoying himself was Jens. The old man had gone as far as to allow Todd to take up residency in a spare bedroom of his ancient farmhouse. It was a strange pairing, but both seemed to benefit from the company of the other.

At first Kori had his doubts about his ability to keep the business running without his brother to guide him. He soon found that the old man was a wealth of information and quickly those uncertainties began to vanish. Todd had spent a good many summers helping Brenden in the past and proved to be very helpful, even though he maintained that he was not farmer material. As the months passed, Kori began to get the feeling that his friend was never leaving, even after the trial. That was okay by him.

It was not until the first week of March that an unexpected visitor arrived, threatening to cast a dark cloud over the serene dynamic that they had developed. Jens was in the stockyard with Todd, sorting through the fattened herd for market ready prospects. They each waved long hickory sticks in the air above the confused animals, driving them this way and that. Kori waited behind the heavy gate, mindful not to spook the cattle as they pushed past him. They had just finished loading the trailer when the strange car pulled into the lane.

At first Kori thought that it was that state detective, Hazelton, again. He had stopped by several times since the trailer fire. At first he came asking a barrage of questions regarding the death of Deputy Scheck. He seemed genuinely broken up by the loss, but equally as pissed by the time lost in training someone who wound up getting roasted inside his own home. The other visits were thinly veiled as stops to check in on him, to see how Kori was holding up. It was obvious that he was just checking to make sure that his star witness had not blown town before his big day in court. Each visit ended with Todd telling him to get his ass off the property and leave them alone.

As the vehicle plowed closer through the slushy remains of the last snowfall, Kori noticed the absence of state issued license plates. The car was also far too extravagant to be driven by a cop, state investigator or otherwise. His heart skipped a beat and then sank when he finally recognized the face behind the wheel.

Walter Ross smiled smugly as he pulled the car to a stop. He got out and surveyed the property like a tax assessor picking apart a newly remodeled house. He produced a grossly oversized camera and began snapping frame after frame. He zeroed in on Jens's old farmhouse and pulled his face away from the eyepiece, snarling his nose in disgust. It was not until Kori approached him that he finally lowered the costly gadget.

"Kori!" he exclaimed. "Good to see you again, my boy. How have you been getting along?" He lifted a finely manicured hand from the camera strap and held it out. His eyes were already looking past Kori's shoulder to the barnyard.

Kori ignored the gesture. He looked over his shoulder to see what had caught the doctor's attention. In front of the main barn stood both Todd and Jens. They leaned against the stock trailer with their arms folded across their chests, a blend of confused suspicion on their dirty faces. Kori turned back to his former employer and asked, "What are you doing here?"

The doctor's lips parted to expose the starch white rows

of veneers beneath them. He placed a hand upon Kori's shoulder and stared at him, still smiling like a used car salesman. “Why I'm here to make you an offer that you'd be a fool to refuse, my boy. Then I'm going to invite you home.”

“Home?”

“Yes, home. To the city, where a gentleman can get himself a decent cup of coffee and not have to drink it in the company of men who reek of animal feces.” He leered in the direction of Todd and Jens, his face expressing the same contempt that he had held for the shabby farmhouse. He fumbled with the fancy camera for a moment and then placed it on the hood of his car.

“Where is my mother?” Kori felt the blood boil sensation of hate rising up from his chest. He had never wanted to hurt someone so badly. The urge to grab the good doctor by the collar, to shake him like a dishrag until that plastic smile fell off or disappeared, was almost impossible to resist.

“She and your stepfather are back in Des Moines for the time being,” Dr. Ross replied. “Their work is finished abroad and now it's time to focus on moving the church forward, closer to home. This location is ideal for that, Kori. Your stepfather has entrusted me with the task of making an offer to buy your share of the property. Although, if you ask me, I would think that the decent thing to do would be for you to sign over your share to the TEFL without compensation. Considering all that Reverend Cole and your mother have done for you over the years."

"For all that they've done for me?" Kori swallowed hard before continuing. "They didn't even show up for my brother's funeral service."

Walter Ross waved a hand, dismissing the statement. "The Lord died for our sins, my boy. To save our souls from damnation. Your brother, he died as a result of his own sinfulness. Do you really expect the reverend to take precious time away from the Lord to bother grieving over some heathen?"

Kori saw red and snapped. Before he realized what he was doing, his hands were wrapped in a death grip around the doctor's throat. The aging man's eyes bulged, threatening to burst from their sockets. His normally pallor complexion had turned a deep reddish purple. Through it all the smile never left his face. A trickle of drool escaped past his lower lip and spilled onto his trembling chin. Todd and Jens rushed forward, struggling to wrench his hands loose. Todd pulled him back and held him in a bear hug. The doctor dropped to his knees and gasped for air.

"Get the hell off my property you brainwashed fuckhead!" Kori screamed, fighting to break free from Todd's grasp. "You think you can come here, talk your shit and expect me to just hand you my brother's farm? Are you out of your fucking mind? You can tell Clayton and my mom that they can both go to hell. I'll die before this land ends up in their hands."

"Don't be so melodramatic, my boy. It won't have to

come to that." Walter Ross casually got back to his feet and dusted the dirt from the knees of his pants. He plucked the camera from where he had laid it down and pushed a button on the back. A recording of the last few minutes played loudly from unseen speakers. The audio was tinny, but the unmistakable sound of the threats Kori had spewed during his bout of rage were unmistakable. The doctor nodded his head in satisfaction as he watched the video play out on a small screen. He turned the camera around to share the last few moments with the others.

A painful knot manifested in the center of his gut as Kori suddenly understood what was happening. "You old bastard, you're setting me up?"

Dr. Ross shook his head. "No, my boy. You did this to yourself. Like every other foolish thing you have always managed to get yourself into. The supplies that you stole from me, your mother's car that you wrecked, the fire you started in the kitchen that nearly burned down your parent's home and now this. Your inability to evolve past your own genetic inadequacies always leads you to the same pathetic results, utter failure."

Kori watched as his former employer gingerly pressed the buttons on his camera and slipped it into his pocket. "What do you want?"

Walter Ross ignored the question. He spread his arms out, gesturing to the farm around them. "You will fail at this too. Eventually you will get bored with the idea and slip into financial ruin. Or you will find some way in your sinful heart to screw it all up like you always have before."

"What do you want?" Kori repeated. His words were barely audible.

The doctor's eyes narrowed for a moment and then he pulled a slip of paper from his breast pocket. He handed the paper, not to Kori but to Jens. "It's all in there. An offer of fair market value. My number and address as well as the Reverend's. I'll give you a week to respond." He patted the lump in his pocket where the camera rested. "After that, this attack on my life will be made available to the authorities. Does assault and battery sound about right?"

"Attack on your life?" Kori scoffed. "Are you serious? That's bullshit and you know it. Either way, what's the worst that could happen to me? A couple days in jail? A fine?"

"Oh, believe me, your problems go far beyond today's little temper tantrum." The smile vanished as he opened the door to his car. "I'm not sure that even you are aware of the amount of pharmaceuticals that you absconded from my practice, but rest assured that the Polk County prosecutor will know if you do not agree to our generous offer. He's a member of the church if you didn't already know that."

Walter Ross shut the car door without another word and drove away, leaving the three of them watching after him in total disbelief. Jens tried to remain stoic as he pored over the paper, but Kori saw the look of worry on his face. He gently reached over and pulled it from his hand. The old man quietly walked back to the stockyard and continued his work.

"You think he's just blowing smoke?" Todd asked. "Just trying to scare you into selling out?"

"I don't think so, man."

"What are you gonna do?"

Kori glanced around the farm that his brother had loved so much. He quietly thought it over before folding the paper and stuffing it into his pocket. He looked toward the calving shed and sighed. "I need you to open the safe for me and then let me borrow your car."

"For what?"

"A little road trip," he replied, already walking to the shed.

"I mean, what do you need in the safe for?" Todd ran to catch up.

"Remember that insurance policy, the one that Brenden left in the blue backpack? I just figured out a use for it."

CHAPTER 33

They made a quick stop at the post office in Cameron and then headed west. The interstate was relatively quiet for a change. Kori hunched over in the front seat, scribbling addresses onto the prepaid mailers with his left hand. Between the rubber kitchen gloves and using his opposite hand, the task took nearly half an hour to finish. Todd's sketchy driving habits did not help. The penmanship was sloppy at best, barely legible and resembled nothing close to his own handwriting. That was the whole idea.

He divided the contents of the backpack into the four boxes, each package holding about a dozen discs. He closed them and carefully and studied his handiwork. One box was addressed to the Trinity church office, in care of his stepfather. Another was destined for the Trinity Ross clinic. The other two would go directly to the home addresses that Dr. Ross had left with him. It was a relief to finally seal them shut. Even through the gloves he felt dirty for having handled them. He placed the boxes on the floorboard, lit up a cigarette and stared out the window.

Todd never asked what the plan was. He didn't have to, because to him it did not matter. He just drove the car west, content to go wherever the flow carried them. That's what Kori loved so much about his friend. He was unconditionally loyal and willing to do whatever it took to stay that way.

Finding a public mailbox was harder than Kori had anticipated once they arrived in Des Moines. Locating a phone booth was even more difficult. It had not occurred to him how rarely people used things like that any longer. With e-mail and cellphones, they were rapidly becoming things of the past. It made him sad to think of how certain items that were once so easily taken for granted had become obsolete novelties. It was depressing how much he could relate to that, but not so much that he was foolish enough to consider using his own phone to make the call.

They drove around downtown until they discovered that the public library had several rows of each, lined up just inside the book return parking area. He prayed that there were no cameras directed on the mailboxes as he pulled back on the rusting handle with one gloved hand and stuffed the packages inside with the other. One by one they thumped against the bottom of the receptacle, sounding the fact that they were now out of his possession for good.

He pulled a slip of paper with a phone number from his pocket, one that he had Googled during the ride. The handset to the phone was slightly tacky and reeked of hair products and cheap wine. He held it away from his ear and listened as it rang for what seemed like forever. He was starting to worry that no one would pick up when a clicking sound came through the earpiece. A tired voice followed.

"First district, Jameson speaking." It sounded like the Federal agent was eating his lunch as he answered the phone. His breathing was heavy and intensified between each chew. There was something faintly disturbing about the sounds coming through the MadDog scented receiver. "Hello, can I help you?"

Kori kept the conversation brief. He pretended to be a disgruntled teenaged son that happened to stumble on his father's collection of kiddie porn. He told the agent on the other end that he suspected his father might be selling the stuff through the mail. He said he found mailers addressed to some doctor and a preacher in Des Moines. He rattled off the names of his stepfather and Dr. Ross. He made sure to repeat the names slowly so there would be no mistake when the agent ran a check on them. The strange information must have gotten the agent's attention because the obscene chewing and breathing stopped abruptly.

For a second Kori wondered whether he was still on the line. The shuffling of papers echoed through the earpiece. "It's a brave thing that you are doing, son. I know this must be difficult for you, but you are doing the right thing. Tell me, what is your name?"

Kori slammed the receiver down on its cradle and ran back to the car. Within ten minutes they were back on the road, headed for home. As he watched the city fade away in the side mirror, he made a promise to himself that he would never set foot in it again.

They drove east for nearly an hour without speaking a single word. Kori stared at the road ahead, reflecting on what he had just done. He knew he should feel at least somewhat sorry for the trouble that would surely follow. Guilty or not, a scandal like this was going to crush both Clayton and Dr. Ross. The court of public perception was the only one that mattered with the company they kept. They would become pariahs, socially and financially. No congregation or clientele would be caught dead associating with a couple of alleged sex offenders.

He felt no remorse, only an overwhelming sense of relief.

Todd shifted in his seat and rubbed his stomach in big exaggerated circles. He let up on the gas and turned his head to study a cluster of road signs. The next exit advertised gas, food and a college that he had never heard of in the town of Grinnell. He considered the idea of taking the off ramp for a moment before passing it by. "Man, we have got to grab a bite before too long. All this James Bond shit has got me famished."

"You should have pulled off then. They have a KFC and a Taco Bell together back there. We could eat burritos and mashed potatoes all in the same place," Kori joked. "Check out the hippy college chicks while we're at it. Maybe find you a nice girlfriend with longer armpit hair than you."

Todd laughed. He pulled his sleeve up to examine his armpit and grimaced. His eyebrows rose up and he said, "You know what else is back there? That hottie I met in rehab. You know. The one I was telling you about."

"The hand job chick?" Kori asked, excitedly. "No shit? She lives in Grinnell?"

"Yep, with her uncle. She moved in with him after her folks gave her the boot for mainlining in her grandmother's bathroom during Easter dinner. She said her uncle lost both of his hands in some kind of bizarre factory accident. Got them stuck in some metal press or something. I guess he raked in a sweet chunk of change from the company's insurance and now he spends all his time slamming piles of smack into what's left of his arms."

"That's messed up."

"No doubt." Todd shook his head in agreement. "The worst part is that he can't do it alone 'cause of his having no hands. So he shares part of his stash with her and her friends so they'll hang out with him and help him shoot it. He doesn't even sell it. Just uses it to get high and keep chicks around to do his housework and jerk him off and whatnot. You know, stuff that you need hands to do."

"Piles of smack, huh?" Kori replied after a few long moments of unsuccessfully trying to wipe the visual image out of his head. "That can't be cheap."

They continued down the interstate for a while in silence. The only sounds were the whirring of the tires and the constant flow of cold air from the partially cracked windows. Smoke rose up from their cigarettes and floated up in gray ribbons before bending toward the pull of the outside air. Hunger slowly crept up in their bellies as they passed the next few exits that offered nothing in the way of food.

Finally, with no need for further discussion they both looked at each other and Kori asked, "Are you thinking what I'm thinking?"

"Let's go talk to a no hand man about a horse," Todd replied. He took the next off ramp and they headed back west again.

ABOUT THE AUTHOR

Craig Furchtenicht lives in Iowa with his beautiful wife, Henrietta. His other works include The Blue Dress Paradigm and Night Speed Zero. He enjoys rock hunting, horticulture and spending time outdoors.

He is currently still searching for that angry giant in the old blue Mercury, to whom he owes a serious car washing.

Made in the USA
Middletown, DE
27 September 2018